M000306437

Virulent:

The Release

Shelbi Wescott

This is a work of fiction. Names, characters, places, and incidents are either the product of the author's imagination or are used fictitiously. Any resemblance to actual persons, living or dead, business establishments, events, or locales is unintentional.

This book is dedicated to:

Matthew:
My love, my support, my voice of reason and strength

and

Elliott and Isaac:
For you—everything is for you

PROLOGUE
365 days before The Release

Two thousand feet beneath the surface of the earth, two men stood on the edge of a dirt walkway. The generators around them hummed with vibrant energy, and the lights flickered in a syncopated beat. The rich smell of mineral-fresh dirt, mixed with the softer and foreign smells of clean plastic and cut lumber, filled their hearts with equal parts longing and anticipation. They exchanged a fleeting look before venturing further into their creation, stopping to peer over the handrails and the expanse of a white domed ceiling where sporadic 'sun'roofs let the men sneak a peek at the hard-hatted workers below.

"Our face-time conference is in five," the younger man said to the older man, checking the time on the tablet he kept tucked under his arm. He swiped a finger across the screen activating the device and typed in his password. "Ready to ascend?"

The older man took a long scan of the dome and nodded. Then he cupped his hand around the younger man's shoulder and gave it three small congratulatory pats. "This is good, son," he said. "This is very good."

"It's coming along," the younger man answered and slid out from under the touch. "But my concern is not with the shelter. Come on, the call. We can't miss the call," he turned to the vertical lift, a metal box with exposed sides, and climbed aboard. He entered a secondary code, pushed a bright yellow button, and they rose—foot-by-foot—back up to the bright morning sunlight, which was spilling over the yellow grass and porous dunes of the Sand Hills.

The two men stood together—not speaking. Beneath their feet, the younger man thought he felt the rumble of their generators, but he assumed he was imagining phantom vibrations. Everything was secured underground, meticulously hidden away from all detection and threats of discovery.

The tablet beeped with a chipper *ding ding ding,* and the young man answered without delay. "Hello, good morning," he said to the man whose face materialized on the screen.

"Good morning," the clean-shaven man with gray on his temples replied, delivering a perfunctory smile before reaching down to adjust his screen—his hand looming large in front of the camera, springing out at them then retreating. He sat at a desk, his white lab coat opened to expose a blue and green plaid shirt, a red Pilot pen stuck in the front pocket. "Calling in for confirmation meeting at an undisclosed location, employee code on your command."

"Go ahead," the younger man repeated with a

glance backward.

"Seven Two Four Eight Three Zero."

"Validated. Hello, Scott, hello. Sorry if you tried to catch us a second ago. We were touring the system and the service underground is lacking. By the time we reach the release date, however, we should be wired for all communication needs. Our best men are on it. The dome is coming along nicely. It's an impressive work of art."

"Sorry, *art* is not my area of expertise," Scott replied, putting his hands up in mock surrender, then dropping them to the desk, a nervous laugh covering his failed joke. "No, no; I caught you on the first try." Scott paused and then cleared his throat. "Well, I have good news this morning. We've made significant progress. I can brief you again at our next scheduled conference...to confirm...but as of this morning, control group six has responded successfully to the release."

"That is wonderful news," the older man answered.

"We've been pleased, yes. It appears that our initial projections were not far from reality."

"Incubation period?"

Scott nodded and consulted a yellow legal pad in front of him. "Our observations seem to put it anywhere between twenty-four hours and six days. The average around thirty-six hours after exposure."

"Any immunities?"

"None in the first six control studies, but it will be impossible to know for sure until we graduate to a more representative sampling."

The younger man turned and stole a look before focusing back at the screen. "Does that mean we are ready to begin the next phase?"

Scott scratched at the corner of his eye. He blinked and nodded. "Yes. On your word, my team will begin to test the subjects your company has procured for our next stage." Scott closed his eyes and sighed—the deep exhale of breath rushed against the microphone and was audible to the gentlemen. The younger man bristled and glanced backward to the older.

"Scott," he said, his voice tight and terse, "I hope that sigh does not indicate that you are having second-thoughts about our work? Because you guaranteed me…" the man's voice rose, but then he paused. Stopped. "Your work with us is invaluable. We never said this would be an easy road…but—"

Leaning closer to the screen, Scott waved his hand to silence the impending speech. "May I talk to your father please?"

The younger passed the tablet off, his arms crossing over his chest, his dark eyes storming.

"Hello, Scotty," the older said.

"Huck. Good morning."

"Are you for our cause?" Huck asked. "This is what I asked you when we met the first time and this is what I ask you now. Every other question is of no consequence to me. Are you for the cause?" He waited and the wind rustled the grass.

"I am," was the reply.

"Then we are united in good. We are bound in blessing," Huck said with a grandfatherly smile. "Now, do you have a concern to address?"

"None with my work...our work, I mean. I am only making sure that our agreement—as you move to the final stages—is still good. You see, as my job here becomes more," Scott paused and searched for the appropriate word, "*trying*...I need validation that when the time comes we will be protected."

Huck knit his brows. "I will ignore this question of my integrity, Scott. The worry that I would betray our agreement is alarming. I am a man of my word. Our agreement stands," the man said with swift decision and handed the tablet back to his son without a formal goodbye.

"So, then. All set?" the younger asked to the man in the lab coat, his jaw tight.

"Yes, we will begin tomorrow morning with control group seven," Scott said. "Conference in one week to go over results. Same time?"

"As always."

The screen faded to black and the man tucked it under his arm. He turned to his father who faced the horizon with his eyes closed. "You are too generous, Dad," he said. "It would be easy to dispose of him after his work with us is complete. Especially considering his tenuous grasp on the importance of our next few stages. You *know* he's only concerned for himself. What good will that do us when we move into the dome?"

"He has earned his freedom."

The younger snorted. "Freedom? Don't be foolish."

"If I thought *you* didn't believe in our cause, I wouldn't hesitate to end *our* partnership either," Huck drew out every syllable. "But I know that is just my *paranoia*, right? "

"Please, Dad, I'm your biggest fan," the son said without missing a beat and turned toward their waiting car, a sardonic smile spreading across his thin lips.

CHAPTER ONE
Release Day

Lucy King leaned her right hip against the side of Mrs. Johnston's metal desk. She held her black and white composition notebook with both hands and re-read the signs and posters taped to the wall for the sixtieth time since September: Shakespeare's ubiquitous portrait with scripted letters underneath proclaiming, "*Lord, what fools these mortals be who don't turn in their homework!*" and a picture in the shape of a dachshund, Groucho Marx's famous inside-of-a-dog quote twisted along its insides.

Concrete poetry.

If you write a poem about a light bulb, you make the whole thing look like a light bulb.

Lucy might not have remembered the definition except Mrs. Johnston had crafted a giant red arrow pointing toward the dog and written "Concrete Poetry!!!" with three exclamation marks. Loose-leaf notebook paper hung precariously next to the Marx quote; it was a gathering of student samples with poems about cats that in no way resembled cats and a horrible poem about rainbows written in alternating gel-pens.

The names on the papers were from students who had graduated years ago. Whether Mrs. Johnston failed to take them down from laziness or admiration was anyone's guess.

A redheaded boy in a baseball hat and athletic shorts sat with Mrs. Johnston as she mumbled superlatives and then passed him back a notebook.

"So, let's rewrite that topic sentence, AJ," Mrs. Johnston said as he rose, stretched, and shuffled away. Then Lucy sank into the available chair and passed her own notebook to her teacher. Her English teacher didn't even glance up at her as she poured over the pages, scratching them with red marks that looked like a star-circle crossbreed of a shape.

"Good, good," Mrs. Johnston mumbled. A flourish. A star. A circle. A plus-sign. An ink blot where she had rested her pen while reading a passage. "Okay. Good. Thank you. Nice comments," she said and then handed the notebook back with a smile.

"Thank you," Lucy replied, but she stayed seated. "Um, Mrs. Johnston...I was wondering if I could grab my work from you?"

For a moment, Mrs. Johnston looked confused and then she grimaced and clicked her tongue. "That's right, that's right. Mexico? No, wait...it was more obscure. Tahiti? Fiji?"

A flame crept up Lucy's cheeks and she lowered her head. "Seychelles."

Mrs. Johnson put up a single finger and pointed at Lucy as she pivoted on her ergonomic office chair;

leaning over a pile of paper, she brought up a search engine on her computer. When the results materialized, she whistled low and loud, shaking her head. "Wouldn't Fiji have been closer?" her teacher asked attempting a joke, but the result just made her sound bitter.

"My dad won it," Lucy answered.

"How?" Mrs. Johnston asked, curious and hopeful.

"Through work."

She wrinkled her nose and waved a hand around the classroom without comment then turned back to Lucy. "Two full weeks? Jeez. Maybe this job would be better if they sent us all away for tropical vacations during the winter break!" Mrs. Johnston said with a boisterous laugh and the students raised their lazy heads to glance at her before huddling down over their notebooks again.

Lucy nodded and picked a piece of lint off her jeans; she rolled it into a tight little ball and then tossed it to the ground.

"We're starting this," Mrs. Johnston said and procured a tattered paperback from a stack by her desk. Its spine was reinforced with yellow tape and Lucy took the book from her and idly flipped through the pages. Someone had left a series of lipstick kisses across the title page in various shades next to the declaration: Derrick Chan Forever.

"*Fahrenheit 451.*" Lucy ran her hand across the cover. The image was bizarre; a man made of pages from a book buried his head while flames licked at his limbs. The title sounded vaguely familiar and she wondered if the novel sat among her family's bookshelves in her father's study, tucked between his science textbooks and National Geographic magazines and her mother's beloved hardback editions of stuffy 19th century British authors: Dickens, Austen, the tragic Brontes.

"A classic," Mrs. Johnston launched, her trademarked pout spreading across her plump lips. The bottom lip made an appearance when a student demonstrated an act of disrespect or before her lectures about their poor performances on tests. Like a moody second-grader, she would jut her lip out in protest. Lucy prepared herself for a lecture by taking a deep breath and dropping her eyes to piles of paper on the desk. "And, frankly, while our lessons will be no contest with *Seychelles*...I really wish you could be there for them. It wouldn't be fair to extend the amount of time you have on this unit because you're leaving on vacation. I hope you understand." She pulled two papers out from a pile by her desk and handed them to Lucy. "An essay. Due when you return."

"Not a problem," Lucy replied in a faux-chipper tone, a rote and mandatory response to each of her teachers who handled the news of her vacation with a mixture of jealousy and anger. Those who opted for straight admonition usually said something along the lines of, "Don't your parents value education? There is a lot of learning that takes place in two weeks." At which point, Lucy would feel the heat rise to her cheeks, her unavoidable blush making its embarrassing appearance, and she would say, without a hint of impertinence, "If you're upset about the trip, please call my father. I understand that my absence is a hardship."

All teachers, with that line, would mumble surrender, handing her legitimate or bogus work, waving her away, wishing her well, encouraging her to have fun—despite their clear desire that she have as little fun as possible.

Lucy held *Fahrenheit 451*, the essay assignment tucked into the center pages, and rose from her seat. Another student slithered behind her to present his notebook for grading and Lucy scooted out of the way; she walked back to her seat in relative silence.

The bell was minutes away, but her classmates were actively shoving papers and pencils into backpacks and messenger bags and lining up outside the door decorated with a "What are you reading?" sign and a pocket-chart where students were supposed to write the names of books they would recommend to other classmates. Someone had recommended "your mom written by me" and another had just drawn a crude picture of a penis, but two students took the task seriously with favorable endorsements for Harry Potter and some book about teen pregnancy.

Lucy's cell vibrated in her pocket and she glanced at the screen. Salem. Like clockwork. She answered it and held it to her ear, unafraid of reprimand.

Salem's voice carried on mid-argument with someone in the hallway. "I said just put it in my locker! Lula? Lula? You there?"

"I'm here, I'm here," Lucy replied, answering to Salem's nickname for her—an endearing take on the alliterative hell her parents saddled upon her at birth: Lucy Larkspur King. The Larkspur was generously hidden between two normal names, but she shivered to recall that the obscure moniker had almost been her first name. That was before her parents came to their senses and settled for something cute, simple, and normal.

"Meet me at our locker now," Salem instructed and then ended the conversation. Lucy rolled her eyes at her own blind allegiance to Salem's orders and elbowed her way to the front of Mrs. Johnston's door, stopping long enough to remove the two offending reading suggestions and stuff them into her back pocket. It was a small gesture, but it was the right thing to do. Jealousy over the Seychelles notwithstanding, Mrs. Johnston was one of the good guys.

Salem opened and shut her locker in an animated fury—her dark curls, placed in ringlets around her shoulders, moving with a small bounce. "I hate getting in the middle of *dra-ma*," Salem lied. Drama found its way into Salem's everyday existence. It wiggled there and nudged its way into any open space it found, creating nests and reproducing at an alarming rate. If it wasn't Salem's personal drama, then it was her magnetic attraction to the drama of others—breakups and hookups, infighting among social groups, who had a crush on which teacher, who had slept with a teacher, whose parents were getting divorced, who was flunking algebra. Inside Salem's brain was a catalogue of crisis covering their classmates from kindergarten to the present.

She remembered that:

Haylee Hij peed her pants in the third grade during that field trip to the Aviation Museum and that was why Jordan Warner didn't ask her to prom: Because when he thought about asking, all he could remember was sitting next to her on the way home and she was wearing athletic shorts that were three times too big and holding a freezer bag filled with her wet and pee-ripe clothes.

Or that Tristin James bought his then-girlfriend, Jackie, a golden bracelet that had "together forever" engraved on the inside. Then, post break-up it was Salem who noticed Cassidy Blaga wearing the same bracelet—jangling it with pride to her girlfriends during physics and swooning over Tristin's unbridled commitment. And while she could've let it go, turned a blind-eye, and let teenage love run its course, it was Salem who tore a picture of Jackie and Tristin out of the yearbook, Jackie clad in her telltale bracelet, and sent it to Cassidy.

Salem knew about Craig Moss, all-American water polo player, and his secret Internet boyfriend, Pedro, for months before the rest of the school even began to whisper about the scandal.

If something bad happened to you, Salem Aguilar

would find out.

If something good happened, she would know too. But she might not tell as many people about it.

"Explain," Lucy commanded, shifting her black and white herringbone book bag up on her shoulder. She shoved her books into the open locker, her three-ring binder, and the mounds of work that would inevitably ruin her vacation.

"Grant Trotter."

Lucy shook her head. The name didn't mean anything to her.

"Oh, really? Tall. Blonde-ish. Pole-vaulter. Dated Bianca-dad-buys-everyone-beer-Nelson?" She paused for a second. "Anyway, he dumped Holly *during* their first date. Just told her that it wasn't going to work and took her home. Right then and there. That's like some serious movie crap right there. Who does he think he is?"

"A guy who knows what he wants?" Lucy replied, feeling her phone vibrate against her leg and ignoring it.

Salem stuck a bony finger into Lucy's face. "Don't get cheeky with me. That's a major self-esteem deflater. She's going to require so much coddling now just to get out of the house! Boys are so stupid. Lie. Right? Just lie like the rest of them? Hey, Holly, I'm totally into you. Kiss her. Then don't call. Am I wrong here? Wait," she hushed her voice and drew her mouth close to Lucy's ear, her breath warming the side of Lucy's face in short bursts, "that's him. Look. Look."

With a furtive glance, Lucy followed Salem's line-of-sight and spotted the offender; leaning against a locker, his hair flopping to the side, haphazardly whisked away from his eyes and his hands shoved deep inside a Pacific Lake High School hooded sweatshirt, shoulders rounded as he slouched. His group of friends laughed at someone's joke, but Grant only smirked, rolling his shoulders forward even more and eyeing the ground. When he glanced up, he looked straight to Salem, pulling his hand out halfway for a noncommittal wave.

And just like that, the war was over. Salem waved back and twirled a long curl between her ring and middle finger. "I guess he's not *so* bad," Salem declared. "Holly's a total bore one-on-one anyway, and she does have that misshapen nostril."

Lucy snorted. "What are you talking about?"

"Just wait. Next time you see her, check it out? It's freakish."

"You notice her nostrils?"

"Bike accident." Salem shrugged as if this common knowledge disinterested her.

When Lucy turned back toward the group at the lockers, Grant was still looking in their direction.

She smiled. A crooked-tight-lipped smile and then cast her eyes toward a neighboring bulletin board, exercising an interested stare at the ripped motivational posters encouraging her to "*Look to the future! Attend college!*" with multi-racial friends all sharing a toothy laugh.

The bell rang. Lucy muttered a goodbye and kissed

the air in Salem's direction, then skipped and drifted to her next class.

Halfway during Trigonometry, after Lucy had endured a short geography lesson with her Seychelles-ignorant math teacher and promised that she'd plug along through the four chapters of work, (even though she was certain that was more than they'd complete in her absence, especially considering Mr. Hegleton's tedious review sessions and a tendency to dedicate entire class sessions to discussing Doctor Who) Ethan sent her an urgent text.

"In trouble. Ride home with Sal."

A command. Not a suggestion. Ethan was a reliable ride home, so trouble was good for no one.

"Explain. Mom and Dad?" Lucy texted back.

"Anna."

Lucy's older brother Ethan had an evil girlfriend named Anna.

She may not have been the embodiment of evil, but vilifying her had morphed into a pastime that neither she nor Salem was willing to abandon. Ethan had graduated two years ago and instead of venturing to the University of Colorado where a handsome scholarship awaited him, he enrolled at Portland State and became a commuter student. He was eager to leave his part-time job and his once close-knit group of friends, but for some inexplicable reason, he was reluctant to leave his clingy, cloying, and altogether horrific high school girlfriend.

Anna, a senior, already acted like she was marrying into the King family.

She would say things like, "How are Mom and Dad?" which made Lucy's stomach flip-flop.

And Anna was popular on the basis of merely being involved in everything. A random assessment of the school day would determine that she never attended an academic class. She made posters with the leadership class, delivered notes as an office aide, sang soprano in the choir, ran the fastest mile in gym class, and made key-chains in Exploratory Metals. One thing that Anna could not do, however, was basic math or construct a passable essay.

Things had taken a turn for the worst when Lucy showed up in the library during her peer tutor hours for National Honor Society and it was Anna who needed assistance. If she hadn't hated her before, spending two hours trying to eke an intelligent thought out of her on the theme of *Hamlet* was enough to do the trick.

Lucy growled at her phone. A few heads snapped up to look at her and she ignored them. *"Jerk,"* she typed.

"Shut up," he quickly shot back.

"Break. Up. With. The. Bitch," Lucy suggested.

Ethan didn't text back.

"Thanks. Eternally," Lucy said as she climbed into Salem's decade-old Honda Civic. The interior smelled of stale French fries and vanilla body-spray; the passenger side floorboard was littered with half-full soda bottles that rolled around with each turn, hitting Lucy's feet with soft thuds.

Salem pulled out of the school parking lot and traveled past the strip mall and the Lutheran church, up the hill, and into the row of tract homes where Lucy and the King brood lived.

"Have fun," Salem said, as she pulled into the long driveway lined with well-groomed shrubbery. "I'm trying not to be jealous."

"You should just own your jealousy," Lucy suggested. "It's healthier. Besides, I'd be hate-filled and moody if you were taking off for two weeks and leaving me to fend for myself in the trenches."

"I'll keep good notes on all major events."

"I'd expect nothing less."

"When you come back it will almost be Spring Break. Do you know what happens in April?" Salem asked with mock-excitement.

"It stops raining."

"It never stops raining."

"It will be our last full month of high school?"

Salem nodded, "Yes. That. Then May. And then prom. It will be our senior prom."

Lucy groaned and reached for the handle. Dresses and corsages, awkward conversations with boys who needed remedial dating lessons from their mothers—the whole institution of prom was a frightening prospect, but at some point in her attempt to be a quality best friend, Lucy had agreed to attend with Salem. Sometimes she would lie awake at night already regretting the evening.

Salem's phone broke out into a pop ballad about feeling trapped in love. It was the ringtone she selected for her mother. She held her finger up to deter Lucy from sneaking away and answered the call.

"Hello Mom," she said. In the quiet of the car, Lucy could hear a shrill and riled voice; Mrs. Aguilar barked on the other end of the line with indecipherable syllables of anger and grief. Salem looked confused, then worried, but soon she erupted into full shock— her mouth a slack O—she gasped and bit her lip. "Ay Dios mio." She shook her head. "Mom. Wait. Mom. Are you sure?"

Lucy leaned in, concerned for her friend. "What?" she whispered. "What?" But Salem turned her face to the driver's window; she kept her back to her friend, and it was then when Lucy noticed that Salem was shaking. Small tremors rippled down her back and her hand couldn't keep the phone steady. Fear and concern overwhelmed Lucy. Instinctively, she placed a comforting hand on Salem, waiting for the conversation to end. Lucy was self-aware enough to know she was ill-equipped to traverse the delicate minutiae of other people's grief. Something big was happening with Salem, and she sat there like an awkward lump, already hoping that there would be appropriate words to say.

"I'll be right there. Mom. Mo-m. I'll be right there," Salem finally got a word in. She hung up the phone and dropped it into her empty cup-holder. Her eyes were wet when she turned to Lucy.

"Sal," Lucy started. "What's wrong? I'm so sorry. What's wrong?" She heard her own voice waver and she took a deep breath to steady it.

"It's Bogie," Salem replied. Lucy let out a slow breath. Bogie was the Aguilar family dog; he was a Rottweiler beagle mix whom Lucy had known since he was a puppy. Bogart was a prized possession, a member of the family. He was young and healthy and every night he slept curled up at Salem's feet. Salem loved that dog more than anything, and Lucy searched for perfect words of comfort while gearing up for tragic news.

"Oh. Sal. Please...don't tell me..."

"My mom came home and found him...just gone."

"Missing?" Lucy held her breath, hoping that maybe he'd just gone exploring, he'd return. Catastrophe averted. Histrionics unnecessary.

Salem let out a small sob. "No Lucy...gone. Gone. Like, dead. Just in the middle of the kitchen floor, like he was asleep. But he wasn't breathing, wasn't moving. My mom looked around, thought maybe he had eaten something bad for him."

"And?"

"Lucy, I don't know. I don't know!" She stared at her friend wide-eyed and frantic. "I mean...what's happening? What is this? Some cruel joke?"

"I'm so sorry," was all Lucy knew to say, and she reached out again to put a hand on Salem, but Salem pulled away.

"No! You don't get it! Listen to me. They just are *all* gone. All of them."

There was a pause and Lucy stopped. She gathered her hands into her lap and wrapped them in a ball; dread formed in her stomach, uneasiness replaced pity. "What do you mean?"

"My mom called the vet, but the line was busy, so she went over to our neighbor's house. She was distraught, right? And our neighbor opened the door just sobbing."

The car fell quiet. Outside a motorcycle roared passed. Its engine grew louder and then faded away.

Salem turned to Lucy. "*All* the dogs, Lucy. *All* the dogs are dead."

CHAPTER TWO
24-hours after the Release

Matriarch Mama Maxine King was short and stocky with wide hips and a helmet of full-bodied brunette hair. Her home was run with military precision; mixed with equal parts tenderness, unabashed sarcasm, and a healthy dose of profanity (usually directed at people on the television, rarely her kids, but sometimes her kids). Her kids' ages spanned fourteen years with Ethan at twenty to Lucy, the second-oldest at seventeen, followed by Galen at thirteen, and the twins Monroe and Malcolm at ten. The baby, Harper, was six years old.

Strangers liked to ask Maxine, in grocery lines or at restaurants, about the size of her family, usually to offer sainthood or astonishment disguised as praise. Maxine would smile and say, "After you're outnumbered it doesn't really matter how many kids you have. And I certainly don't deserve an award for having a well-used uterus." It was her oft-repeated line to strangers that made each kid groan with embarrassment not only because they never wanted to hear their mother say the word *uterus*, but also because they wished she would come up with a different joke.

But while Mama Maxine, as friends of the King kids affectionately called her, handled her six children with tough-love lectures, peppered with facetiousness, she was also the picture of equanimity. And love. Mama Maxine loved each child who entered her home as her own, prompting scores of Pacific Lake teenagers to declare an unyielding allegiance to the woman.

Lucy had handled the news of the nationwide dog crisis with panic. What had been deemed a "Targeted Dog Massacre" by local reporters, the televisions networks exacerbated the story even further, which catapulted the craziness to the Internet, which led to conspiracy theorists pontificating about doomsday scenarios. For dinner that night, her mother put a moratorium on discussion about the dead dogs— angrily shooting an evil eye at any child daring enough to mention the atrocities in front of Harper.

And when Lucy was caught texting and messaging Salem into the wee hours of the morning, comforting her weepy and inconsolable friend, Maxine made a surprise visit and threatened to confiscate the phone. Even through her agitation and worry, Lucy allowed her body to sleep and dream about lounging on white sandy beaches and working on her tan.

She awoke to the rambling of her mother's to-do list as her mother stood by the foot of her bed, pulling her comforter off her body and exposing her skin to the cold house.

"I need your carry-on bag and your monogrammed tote in the hall in twenty minutes. Hair-brushed, breakfast eaten, schoolwork packed. Limo arrives in an hour to take us to the airport and I will not be delayed. Lucy Larkspur King, I swear to the Lord Almighty that I will leave you behind. Do you hear me? I let you sleep in beyond all reason. Now get your bony ass out of this bed and into gear. Come child. Chop, chop."

Then she was off, her feet clomping down their carpeted hallway like a whole herd of mothers, off to rouse her next child with empty threats of abandonment.

Lucy rubbed sleep out of her eyes and swung her feet down to the floor. She leaned over and grabbed her phone—as per her morning ritual—checking for late-night missed texts from Salem, but there was nothing new from her friend.

But a second-glance at her feed made Lucy gasp. Tragedy abounded. The dogs, and now other beloved pets, were falling to some mysterious illness, and someone's grandma had passed on during the night too while a few others complained of an impending flu. Several people linked to an article about the animal deaths and someone suggested contaminated drinking water was the cause. The feed was a veritable plethora of honest-to-God sadness and bandwagon melodramas.

She heard her mom walking back in her direction and Lucy darted out into the hallway, phone in-hand, and tripped over the line of luggage—set up like soldiers marching off to war.

"Mom," Lucy said and brandished her phone like a weapon. "Have you heard about all of this? Now they say that someone poisoned our water. The water! Mom, someone thinks that people are going to die from this! Like…actual humans now? Mom! This is serious."

Maxine put her hand on Lucy's phone and pushed it down toward the floor. "I already talked to your dad. He says there's nothing to worry about. If we needed to worry, he'd know Lucy."

"He's not here?" Lucy gripped her phone tighter. His absence made her anxious—her father was a masterful voice of reason, a beacon of calm. He *never* used profanity.

"He's meeting us at the airport. Some meeting he couldn't get out of." Maxine made an attempt to scoot around Lucy, but she remained rooted, legs outstretched, hands across her chest. "Fifty-minutes Lucy. Fifty-minutes."

"Mom," Lucy repeated. She opened her mouth, then closed it. "Mom." Then just, "I'm scared."

For a brief second, she thought she saw her mother's own fear flicker across her face, but then her mom smiled and leaned in, kissed her on the forehead, and moved her out of the way. "Look, maybe some sicko poisoned all the pets. And I hope they catch him, or her, and throw them into the far reaches of hell…but when it comes to disasters, I trust your father. By the time we land in paradise, we won't be thinking about any of this fear mongering. I haven't had a vacation in six years…six years! So. Get." She swatted her hand against Lucy's backside and with a nod took off grabbing one suitcase with her.

Lucy watched her mom walk out of sight and then ducked back into her room and shut the door; she dialed her father's phone without thinking. She needed to talk to him, needed to hear the reassurance herself. It rang and rang before her dad finally picked up.

"Morning sweetie," her dad said as he picked up the phone. Before Harper arrived, Lucy was the only girl in a house of smelly, fighting, dirt-loving boys. Her father doted on her, but he never called her princess, never made her feel like she was special just because she was a girl; he always said awkward things like, "Hey, darling, I just wanted to let you know that I'm so proud of you for your eighty-six percent in math class. You're trying so hard." It was like he read a chapter in a parenting book about raising strong, self-confident daughters and followed it to the letter. It would have been more helpful if he had read a book on how to deal with painfully self-aware and awkward daughters with moderate ambitions.

"Dad? Have you seen the news? Mom is all on some Seychelles-inspired happy-juice, but Dad...Dad. This is ridiculous. Are we actually just going to pretend that this isn't happening? Did someone poison the dogs, Dad?" She took a breath.

"Lucy—"

"Does that mean that *someone* poisoned all the animals?"

"Please, Lucy—"

"It's a *big* deal, Dad. And why aren't we talking about it? And why did you have to work today? Didn't your job give you this vacation as a *reward*? Can't they let you actually have the day your vacation starts off from work?" She flopped herself back down on the edge of her bed and bounced her knee in agitation.

"It's okay to be worried, sweetheart," her father's calm voice said back to her. "I think the news is worrisome. But *you* are not in danger. I am giving you my word. And, as an added bonus, reason number fifty-two why I'm glad we don't have pets." He chuckled, but then trailed-off. "Darling, I'm sorry. But I don't know what you want me to do. You have a limo to the airport in a bit. Focus on that for me."

"Can't a poison that hurts animals also hurt people?"

Lucy's dad drew in a quick breath and then let out a sigh. "Yes. It's very possible."

"Then how can you say—"

"My sweet girl," her father was quiet for a beat. "I don't know anything that could help you here and I have to go. I do. I have a plane to catch too. Okay? See you at the airport. Vacation of a lifetime. Right?"

She grumbled into the phone a defeated growl. "Fine. The rest of the world will be in shambles," she glanced down again at her phone and scrolled through some new articles, "with some new strain of flu virus? The news is saying that...Dad?" There was no answer.

Then he said, "Lucy. Make sure you get in the limo so you don't miss the plane. Go help your mom with the little ones. Turn your phone off. Start daydreaming of scuba diving. I'm hanging up. I love you."

Lucy waited for a long moment to see if he had really hung up—but she heard the distinct click and saw the flash of their call time. He was not a dad well suited for her panic and worry; Lucy knew that if there was reason to worry, her father would tell her in calm, well-managed tones. She pushed the fear aside and grudgingly rose to her feet.

Out in the hallway, Ethan nudged her on his way to the bathroom. She turned on him. "Have you seen the news this morning?"

He yawned. "Yes," he answered.

"Aren't *you* worried?"

"No," was all Ethan replied before shutting the door with a deliberate slam.

Paranoia was a trait that Lucy had inherited from her deceased grandmother. When she was alive, her mother would always sit the two of them together at the dinner table—co-conspirators in a world where every stranger is a serial killer and mild-joint pain is incurable cancer. Her grandmother would whisper things to her, a mouth full of mashed potatoes, spittle dribbling on to her neon flowered shirt. "Your father is a spy," and then with furtive glances, "I think someone is poisoning my food."

Everyone else treated grandma like a senile pet, but Lucy loved to hear about the bears that sneaked through her apartment at night and delivered the poison for the "agents" and how her husband, a grandfather that Lucy never met, was the actual inventor of the microwave and that the government stole his plans and set "that Percy Spencer up as a puppet." When Lucy repeated the story, her father rolled his eyes. "My father did not invent the microwave. He had no knowledge of radar technology. I respect that Grandma wants to idolize him, but my dad was a mediocre scientist at best."

Grandpa King's lifelong goal was to prove the existence of time travel, but Grandma King said he failed. "A life's work down the drain," she would sigh. "I know because if he had figured it out, wouldn't he have come back to visit me? I could go for a visit with a younger man right about now." Then Lucy would blush and motion that Grandma was wearing a piece of fruit on her chin, which the old lady would brush to the floor and then say with disdain, "If your parents had a dog, they wouldn't need a vacuum."

When Grandma died peacefully in her sleep one night, Lucy mumbled something about wanting to inscribe on her tombstone: "Poisoned by bears." But the rest of the family was vehemently against the idea and Lucy was outvoted.

As Lucy dressed for the day, she channeled Grandma's obsession with conspiracy. Her heart tightened in her chest as she pondered the worldwide implications of a petless world. It seemed like an unfortunate time to board a plane. She wished she could comfort Salem and offer some semblance of a rational explanation, but none came to her. There was nothing she could say that would explain the tragedy. Nothing she could say to stop what had already happened.

With great reluctance, she began to pack her carry-on—a gift from her mom for Christmas one year. In the embroidered bag, she tossed in some books and her writing journal. But when she went to her backpack to retrieve her mountains of class work, she found a math book and nothing else.

With great dread, Lucy tore through her room. But her homework was nowhere in sight. "Idiot," Lucy mumbled and slapped her forehead. A locker drop before last period and then the distracting text from Ethan had resulted in her leaving two weeks worth of homework at school. Granted none of it actually mattered; but that was not the point—if one of her teachers had asked her to say the alphabet backwards while performing an interpretive dance, Mama Maxine would make sure it was completed before any fun was had.

This oversight would not go over well.

From downstairs, Maxine blew a whistle. It was a rape whistle that she had acquired while taking a community self-defense class; Maxine wore it around her neck for protection in public and as a parenting tool; the shrill peal was a non-negotiable call to her side. Some of her friends mocked the whistle, but no one could deny its effectiveness. Lucy tromped down the steps, depositing her half-empty bag on the landing with a pout.

Maxine paced in front of her children, as they lined up, leaning, slouching—each possessing varying degrees of excitement about their travel day. She carried a clipboard mod-podged with scrapbook paper. Some craft site on the Internet had turned their mother into a maniac, especially when she had access to hot-glue and an entire bookshelf dedicated to scrapbooking paper. She tapped a purple pen against her personalized travel list—printed freshly that morning, adorned with a stick figure version of their family in the top left corner.

"Anti-nausea pill time," she announced and pulled a white bottle out of her pocket. "Hands out." Then she tossed them all a Sesame Street juice box, watching with an eagle eye as each child gulped and choked down the bright orange pills. "Tongues out," she demanded and then nodded. "Fantastic."

Her father had stressed repeatedly that the vaccines and pills for the trip were important and that they would be facilitated without complaint. "No child is coming home with typhoid or yellow fever. God forbid you get bitten by some rabies infected wild boar," their mother had added. Monroe and Malcolm took great interest in the promise of wild boars on the islands.

In general, their father's disdain for illness of any kind had become a family joke. Maxine was the cleaner of vomit, the giver of medicine, the filler of humidifiers in the middle of the night. Their father worked on the effects of communicable diseases on living tissue—and his work had created a monster; he would visibly bristle at people who coughed and sneezed in public; he refused to shake hands and he applied hand-sanitizer by the buckets. Even though he could bring up disgusting tales of gelatinous tissue in jars and oozing boils growing on lab rats at the dinner table, one mention of a sore throat and he would raise a crucifix at you and back away in fear.

Maxine checked off the first item on her list and continued. "Let's do a carry-on check."

Ethan flipped his phone open, glowered at the screen, and with flying thumbs sent off a text and shoved it back into his pocket.

"Anna?" Lucy whispered in a mocking tone as their mom started with the younger kids, rifling through their bags and suggesting additions while tossing out a wayward pirate hat and Monroe's Ziplock bag full of mismatched Legos.

Ethan rolled his eyes in response.

"You should just dump her," Lucy said. "Then go hook up with an island girl without regret."

He turned to his sister, seeking solidarity. "She's threatening to break up with *me* because she thinks I had time to show up to the school today to say goodbye but *chose* not to."

"Has she never met Mom? Ridiculous."

On cue, Maxine was in front of Lucy, bending down for her bag. "Thirty hours, Lucy. We won't land in Seychelles for thirty hours. We're staying overnight in Dubai tonight. And all you want to bring is two books and a notebook? Wait. Wait. Where's your homework?"

Lucy grimaced. She had noticed. In less than ten

seconds.

Maxine's eyes flashed. "Oh...don't even tell me."

"It was an accident. I was sidetracked. Animals were dying Mom."

Her mother ignored the last part and raised her purple pen to Lucy's chest. "This was a condition of the trip...a condition I made with your teachers, with your dad," her voice began to rise. "I said to each of them that you would arrive back to school with your work completed, not in a state-of-completion. *Com-plee-ted*." She glanced at her watch and swore loudly. "Thirty minutes. Thirty minutes Lucy until our limo to the airport arrives." She glanced at Ethan and then turned back to Lucy, the wheels visibly churning. She swore again, then sighed, defeated and agitated.

"I can take her," Ethan offered, keys already in his hands. "Five minutes there. Five minutes to her locker. Five minutes home. I won't even shut off the car. We'll be back with time to spare."

Without hesitation, Maxine pointed to the door, as if it were the offer she was hoping for—the saving grace. "Fifteen minutes or I'll kill a kitten for every minute you're late."

Lucy paused, "A worthy threat if all the kittens weren't *already dead*."

"Are kittens dead now too? I haven't been paying attention because I have been getting ready for a trip. I will kill something. Be sure of it."

"We don't negotiate with terrorists," Ethan added.

Maxine's eyes narrowed. "You will be back in

fifteen minutes or will wish *you* were dead. So help me God."

Like a flash the two oldest King children flew out of the house—speeding down the road with manic intensity, focused on their goal and their timeframe, and fully unaware that the world was collapsing all around them.

CHAPTER THREE

Ethan pulled his refurbished 1962 Ford Fairlane up through a small gravel driveway hidden between the Pacific Lake High School's football field and the metal shop. The car bounced along, navigating the narrow stretch—the main building of the school extending out in all its beige and brown glory.

They were headed to their secret entrance—a forgotten door hidden behind overgrown trees and shrubs that led to a small staircase that opened up to a supply closet next to the defunct swimming pool. Since the pool had been closed down years ago due to budget cuts and the doors only locked from the outside, it was the perfect way to sneak into the building after the doors had been locked after the first period tone.

Their campus was a closed campus. The main entrance and two sets of double doors leading to a turnaround stayed open during the day with a security guard watching as students and visitors filed through metal detectors. It seemed like an unnecessary precaution for a school on the outskirts of Portland without a history of violence, but somehow it made the parents feel safer. After a gun-related shooting down in rural Oregon, panicky parents lobbied for hyper-vigilance. Within one year they ousted the mild-mannered, mopey, and much maligned principal and replaced him with a fast-speaking, bright and shiny wizard of Pacific Lake; he was quick with a dazzling smile and had a never ending bag-of-tricks. Principal Spencer was tall and thin with a perpetually trimmed buzz-cut, five hundred dollar suits, and perfected glower. He seemed to loathe teenagers and treated them with the exact same annoyance reserved for houseflies.

With Spencer came a high-tech camera system and intricate new security policy and a heavy duty key system that made getting in and out of the high school a challenge only James Bond could conquer.

Ethan's promise that Lucy would be "in and out" in five minutes was hindered by the closed-campus, the small army of security personnel whose main priorities were to enforce it, and that Anna had texted that *"some sort of weirdness is going down today"* after Ethan told her that she had exactly five minutes to be outside at the secret entrance or she would miss her opportunity for a goodbye.

If Lucy was caught roaming the halls without a note, she'd be relegated to In-School Suspension. Security was trained to ignore teenagers' myriad excuses; so running into a security guard would be the end of getting back on time and pacifying Mama Maxine. Eventually, the school would realize their error and set her free, but that mistake was not allotted for in the timeframe. Lucy wished that all the subterfuge and deceit wasn't just for collecting homework because it felt like a giant waste of energy.

The Fairlane rolled to a stop and Anna materialized from the side of the school. Wind blew her tangled bleach-blonde hair around her shoulders. She walked toward the passenger-side door, her arms crossed against her body, her eyes red. Lucy looked at Ethan, but he looked away, entreating her to leave without mocking him. Where Anna was concerned, Ethan was temperamental and touchy; always so defensive and irritable.

"Five minutes," Ethan reminded her.

Lucy opened the door and crawled out, grabbed her brother's black backpack to transport her work and left the door ajar for Anna, who slithered beside the door without saying a word.

"Morning, Anna," Lucy said to her as she walked away, impressed with her own civility.

"It's crazy in there," Anna replied without turning around.

Lucy pivoted and opened her mouth to ask how, but Ethan motioned her away. "Go! I'm leaving in five minutes if you're back or not. It wouldn't be fair for Mom to have to kill two children in one day." Anna mustered a weak smile before climbing into the car beside Ethan and shutting the door, a mopey argument ensuing before Lucy was even out of earshot.

Slipping in through a small patchwork of

shrubbery, Lucy walked with purpose and determination toward the door—which had been tagged some time ago with bright neon green spray-paint. She tugged on the handle and the door pulled open, leading to a damp, dark stairwell. A dim light guided her forward; the handrails were sticky with used gum wads and crushed soda cans were abandoned in the corners—the smell of mildew, dirt, and urine permeated the air.

When she pushed on the door leading to the supply closet, the door opened and then crashed back into her shoulder; she groaned. Someone had placed the old pool cover against the door. She aligned her shoulder, grabbed the handle, and pushed with all her strength—the metal cart rolled inch by inch with each well-placed body-slam. Lucy squeezed her body through the opening she had created and then, because she couldn't get back out that way anyway, shoved the pool cover back against the door. Then for good measure, she toppled some dusty chairs down too. She let her imagination play out what would happen when Anna tried to get back into the school after her rendezvous with Ethan—the daydream ended with Anna sporting a bruised shoulder while seething in In-School Suspension.

It made the unfortunate events of the morning seem a little less ominous.

While Lucy navigated the supply and the pool, she grabbed her phone. Four minutes. And still no texts from Salem. Even in mourning, Salem would make an attempt to connect. Salem allowed herself to feel no emotion unless it could be experienced with someone else. Where was she and why was she silent? No lamentations, no messages with excessive capitalization and punctuation. No farewell wishes or "Bon voyage!" or "Bring me back a necklace!"

With her eyes on her phone, Lucy checked her feed.

She stopped walking because she was unable to process what she was seeing and move forward at the same time.

All over the country, people were sending and posting alarming updates. In just thirty-minutes everything had gone from sad and speculative to real and nightmarish. A sickness was spreading. Hospitals couldn't handle the intakes of the ailing who were arriving at steady-intervals. Someone who worked in an ER posted a photo of a crowded hallway, the caption reading: "Busy day. Damn this flu." So-and-so had heard that 9-1-1 was jammed. A friend who went to another school updated her status to read: RIP Aunt Rosemary.

Lucy's phone buzzed and she almost shrieked, juggling the device before checking her text. It was Ethan: *"Anna says teachers were reporting they were going into lockdown. Get. Out. Homework not worth it. Mom will deal."*

Lockdown.

They had done a lockdown drill during the first week of school.

It meant there was an immediate threat to the

student body within, or around, the school. All students would be held in classrooms until the lockdown was lifted. Lucy took a step forward around the empty cement cavern; she could see from her vantage point the long stretch of hallway dedicated to the science department. The lights were dimmed. The entire place was clear of movement. If she could get straight down the hallway, closer to the English classrooms, she would be able to get to her locker and exit out the double-doors that opened toward the senior parking lot.

The high school was built as a giant rectangle. Students could start walking in one direction and the school would eventually lead them back to their starting point—classrooms lined the inside and outside of the rectangle. There were small hallways off the ends leading to the pool and the library on the opposite side. The science hallway ran at one end and directly down from the main office; the other end of the hallway passed by the gym, the cafeteria, the counseling center, and eventually the social studies hallway. Then came the English and math hallways. At her present location, she could not be further from her locker, but at least her exit would be close.

"Go to senior lot. By double-doors," she texted to her brother and then opened the door from the pool, aware of the clunking echo of the metal swinging open. For good measure she added a text: *"I can do this."*

She had never heard the school so quiet. On her tiptoes, she crept forward, moving at a fast enough pace to make it to her brother on time, but slow enough to watch for a patrolling guard or a teacher on-watch. But after fifteen feet, Lucy realized that the classrooms were abandoned. The lights were turned off; the desks were empty. She pressed her face against the glass of one room; there were discarded backpacks scattered on desktops and on the floor—books and papers without owners, a solitary shoe, coats still hanging on the backs of chairs. Students had been asked to leave in a hurry.

She shivered.

The clock showed that it was partway through first period. With great trepidation, Lucy moved forward, inch by inch, stepping along the white tiled flooring, her feet tapping along, the only sound in earshot.

Down the hall, Lucy heard the distinct crackle of a walkie-talkie. She pushed her body into a small opening between a locker and a drinking fountain and held her breath. Her phone vibrated in her hand. In the absence of all other noise, the vibrating seemed loud and commanding while drawing attention to her hiding space. She pushed the ignore button with her thumb and closed her eyes.

There had to be rational explanations. Students and teachers were frightened by the news and had been called to an emergency assembly. Perhaps the grief over pets and sick loved ones had impeded any valuable learning and the students were ushered into an impromptu counseling session. During Lucy's freshman year, a senior football player was killed in a car accident. The administration canceled every class and held a series of honorary assemblies and meetings with counselors—they even held a vigil out by the flagpole.

Occam's Razor.

Her father taught her that.

The simplest explanation was usually correct.

They were under lockdown out of fear, not necessity. The students were at an assembly, perhaps to alleviate or control the rising worries. The pets were dead because someone had poisoned them. People were not in danger.

Her father had told her: She was not in danger.

Back on her feed, all the doomsday prophets were broadcasting their end of the world theories as a full-fledged assault. Several of her feed items were calls to faith in the midst of judgment day. If Lucy believed in evangelical Christianity, she would have guessed her classmates had been spirited away through rapture. But Lucy shook her head and scowled—she may not be perfect, but she had a hard time believing that God would leave her behind and take the entirety of Pacific Lake High School instead.

This was ridiculous. The overreacting. The fear.

"*Bears are not trying to poison me,*" she thought to herself. "*Bears are not trying to poison me.*"

There was no way that any of this amounted to anything remotely exciting. She just needed her damn homework so she could go on vacation with her family. For a moment, she thought of just walking with confidence down toward her locker, and if a guard stopped her, she would just say with calm precision, "My ride to the airport is waiting outside. I just need my Ray Bradbury book and I'll be on my way."

The walkie-talkie crackled again, but it was moving away from her. Further down the hall it traveled. A man's voice, some security guard, sounded an "All Clear" for the science and main hallways. The talking turned a corner, toward the cafeteria, and away from her.

Two minutes.

With a deep breath, Lucy hesitated. Then, without thought, she sprinted, running as fast as her legs would carry her, shoes slapping heavily on the tile. She closed her eyes and ran; straight by lockers and classrooms, past the front of the building and the main office, they were all a blur as she sped down the wide stretch of hallway.

Then, she rounded the corner toward the English hall. Within eyesight of her locker, she slowed her pace, her heart beating with rapid thumps against her chest, blood pounding in her ears. Then her body flew forward. Pain shot up her legs and arms as she hit the tile with a crash, knocking the air out of her body. She landed on her elbows and knees and slid forward several feet before stopping. Her head caught the metal of a locker—a burning pain traveled from the top of her ear and all the way down her neck.

After a few moments, Lucy collected her composure and took in a giant gulp of air. She hoisted herself into a sitting position and then turned to see what had caused her fall.

And that was when she saw the body.

Crumpled in a heap, like someone dropped a wet rag on the floor and left it there.

She scooched herself backward, her feet slipping against the tile, until she felt her back hit the hardness of the lockers. It was a boy, his face turned in her direction, his eyes open and staring past her; one eye, one-solitary eye, was filled with blood, the blackness of the pupil still peeking through the bright red. It was a freshman she didn't recognize.

One minute.

Lucy stood up, viscerally aware of how her knees wobbled together. Her heart thumped wildly in her chest; pulsating outward all the way to her fingertips. As if walking on a small ledge, she high-stepped along the row of lockers, until she reached her own and only then did she turn around, her hands shaking as she spun the lock.

Nine.

Twenty-six.

Seventeen.

There was a dead boy in the hall.

A dead boy in the hall.

Someone left a dead boy in the hallway.

And yet she was still fully fixated on her homework and getting the hell out of there.

She couldn't shake the boy's image as she pulled up and opened the locker with a click. Lucy grabbed her big purple binder that was covered in Salem's doodles, political cartoons, and a photo of her family stuck on one side and a picture of her holding Harper on the other. She dropped the binder into the backpack and then grabbed her copy of *Fahrenheit 451*, sliding it into the bag and zipping it up. Only then did she realize she had been holding her breath and she let it in one giant hot gush. Voices down the hall snapped her to attention. Men's voices, conversational, but hushed.

Time was up.

The voices were gaining on her.

No more than thirty feet away were the doors leading outside. Lucy could hear the distant sounds of sirens traveling up the street. Ethan was out there, waiting for her, and her mother and her family were at home. They had a plane to catch. This couldn't be happening; she had a plane to catch.

Lucy struggled to wrap her mind around the evidence—the lack of students, the dead classmate. The lockdown. Her fear was intense; Lucy gnawed on her bottom lip until she tasted blood.

Her time was up.

The voices approached. To run to the door now would risk exposure. To wait would risk abandonment. She ducked into the closest classroom, grabbed the handle and shut the door without making a noise. Then she reached for her phone. It blinked with three unread messages. Amidst the panic she had not felt the phone pulsating in her pocket.

The first was a cryptic message from her mother:

"*Not what we expected. Please come home. Please come home. NOW.*"

The second was from Ethan:

"*Mom needs me. She called. She was frantic. Bawling. Screaming. Going home. Taking Anna. We will come back for you. Sit tight.*"

The third was from Salem:

"*My family is dead. They're all dead. It's the end of the world.*"

CHAPTER FOUR

Lucy collapsed against the door.

She closed her eyes and listened as the footsteps reached her and then passed her without incident.

When she opened her eyes, she cried out and then flung her hand over her mouth.

Splayed outward in the center of the classroom was another body. A man. His green Levis crept up to his mid-calf, exposing pink and gray argyle socks. The acidic smell of vomit wafted from his direction. Dried blood pooled on the floor, it had trickled down from the twisted mouth, opened wide as if in protest. His skin was yellow and waxy, and his eyes glassed over with a thin film, giving them the appearance of having cataracts.

Lucy knew that she was looking at Mr. North: Senior English teacher, recently married, advisor to the chess club. He was young and funny and impeccably dressed—a combination that added up to an adoring fan club of bright-eyed girls. She turned her head and then she saw the other bodies. A girl, head on her desk and a boy right next to her. And more. Six people altogether.

Some looked like they had sat down and fallen asleep, but others were a twisted mess of limbs and clothing.

She shook her head. A scream caught in her throat.

Lucy dialed her house number on her phone and hit send, but the phone beeped angrily at her. She dialed again. It beeped. Her screen flashed an angry *All Circuits Busy* message. Busy. Busy. Busy.

Lucy stuck the phone in her pocket and stood up; she gathered up her white shirt and pulled it over her nose and mouth—the futility of this act was not lost on her, but Lucy didn't know what else to do. She pushed her anxiety away and focused as best she could. Was this related to the dogs? What was happening? Would this happen to her? Had it happened to her family? Where was Ethan? Would he really come back? The questions flooded her brain, and ran in a loop, like a clip playing without stop.

Staying in the room with the dead was not an option, and it was not a fear of the bodies, but a fear of what killed them. Lucy peered out into the hallway and discovering it quiet, left the room with her bag hoisted up on her shoulder. She rounded the corner toward the social studies hall and froze.

Scattered up and down the long hallway were more dead students.

Like the ones before, many of these victims had thrown-up prior to collapsing. They bled from their eyes, noses, and mouths; under the bright florescent lights of the high school, their skin took on a green tint. For the first time, Lucy noticed that one boy was covered in hives. The sickness did not bother her, but the smell was overpowering. While Lucy was certain from her biology classes that decomposition wouldn't begin for hours or days, these bodies already seemed to bloat and smell like decay. Frozen in the hallway, she watched one boy, eight or ten feet away, and waited to see the subtle movement of his chest—waited to see his breathing resume.

This is what she did during movies after key characters died. She ignored all other dialogue and just watched and waited to see if she could spot the imperceptible movement of life. A short breath or small twitch. Most of the time, the camera cut away before she could see it, but sometimes she was rewarded with the slight rise and fall of an actor's chest. Then she would clap her hands and jump the scene backward, watching again, pointing out the subtle movement to anyone around.

It was a reminder that this death was not final.

But the boy in the hallway didn't move, didn't breathe. He didn't sit up and laugh and wipe away the blood—corn syrup and food coloring—from his mouth and ask if that was it for the day. This was real.

Her mother's text haunted her.

In some way, she was comforted by being at the school and staring at this lifeless body of a stranger, instead of facing the grim reality that someone at home had fallen ill after she and Ethan ran off.

Where were all the living people? Where were her friends and teachers? Why was the school achingly quiet? When would Ethan come back for her? Her nagging questions changed direction. She now had one singular focus: Wait for Ethan.

"No one can see me," she muttered to herself. "No one can know I'm here." Her hand shook as she raised it to her face to wipe away a flyaway strand of dirty-blonde hair.

Lucy glanced inside the small rectangular window of a door to a social studies classroom and found it void of bodies and movement. She stepped inside and pushed the closest desk against the door, then another, barricading herself from the multitude of unknown threats with nothing more than cheap furniture. World maps covered the walls, stuck into the thin cardboard walls with multi-colored tacks; a globe had been knocked from its perch on a front table—it had broken open and rolled a few feet and a large cavernous gash extended from the Atlantic Ocean and cut down into South America. Lucy kicked it to the side. Then she climbed up onto a table and tore down an American flag hanging uselessly next to the clock. Using masking tape, she affixed the flag over the small window— blocking the view from the outside. Security on patrol wouldn't spot her easily and that was comforting.

On the inside of the door, the teacher put up an old World War 2 propaganda poster. "He's Watching You" it read, with a shady man peering out under his helmet. Lucy turned away from the figure's militant stare.

The large canvas blinds had already been drawn over the large windows, per lockdown instructions. While everything inside of her wanted to peek out and catch a glimpse of the parking lot, Lucy worried that even the slight rustle of a curtain would give away her position. So, she steered clear. With the lights off, the room was dark. Heat funneled through large vents above her, creating a warm, womblike atmosphere, which made Lucy feel claustrophobic.

Creeping on her tiptoes, Lucy reached her hand up and flipped on the television in the corner. She pressed her pointer-finger on the volume button instantly, lowering it to just barely above mute.

Then she stumbled backward and watched the images flood the screen.

The emergency broadcast system ran below—a ticker of bright red, following by instructions. *Stay inside your house. Threat origin unknown. Do not drink water from the tap. Avoid all fruits and vegetables. Avoid contact with infected people. Stay away from populated cities. This is not a test. Stay inside your house.*

Above the warnings, a young woman sat behind an anchor desk; her hair pulled up into a sloppy pony-tail; thick black glasses pushed up to the bridge of her nose; she was wearing a college sweatshirt, a coffee stain in the shape of the state of Florida above her right breast.

"*I'm getting word…*" the girl said tentatively. She squinted her eyes—they darted back and forth as she tried to read the teleprompter, her lips curling around letters she hadn't yet said. "*That…*" she leaned forward, adjusting her glasses, "*the…center for disease control…is linking these attacks to several sources.*"

Attacks.

"*There is no…clear indication…of how the…vi—vi—virus,*" she stopped and sighed. Then she glanced off camera, her eyes pleading.

"*I can't do this, I'm sorry.*" She started to tear at the microphone hooked on her sweatshirt. From the left, a man with a headset appeared, shaking his head and trying to get her to stay in her seat. But the young woman pushed herself past him and left him alone on the set. He turned toward the camera, his eyes wide. He opened and closed his mouth like a fish. Someone shouted something indecipherable; the man inched his way behind the desk and sat down, fumbled with the abandoned microphone, and pinned it on his own shirt. He then smiled a non-smile; his lips pulled upward, but his eyes were frantic.

"*Sorry ladies and gentleman about that. We're experiencing some difficulties in studio. That was our sound design intern Jennifer. I am Tim…managing editor of KPSV news. Forgive our scattered delivery. We are trying to get everything to you as fast as we know it, but our communication is spotty. If you are just joining us, we can tell you, that many regions of our world today are experiencing great loss of life at the hands of a deadly, fast-acting, virus.*"

Lucy took a giant step away from the television. She lifted herself upon a desk, her legs swinging over the edge, and watched as the screen bathed her in a blue and green tint.

"We are posting your updates and pictures now...if you can, keep sending them in. Our audience is our...are our...men and women in the field today." Tim gulped, the microphone picking up on the sound of his swallow.

Then the screen went blank for a long, agonizing, second, and an electronic hum replaced the frenetic voice of the newscaster. The silence was jarring, but Lucy didn't move; she remained planted on the desk, sitting on her hands, her legs twitching.

An image popped up. A familiar man. A nightly news anchor from some East Coast station—he was in his seventies with two hamsteresque eyebrows and a bad comb-over. Studio lights cast a yellow pallor over his face, and he wiped his brow while the sweat beads dripped down the side of his face. He addressed the camera, his voice strong and steady, and the familiar tone of it put Lucy at ease. In a world falling apart, here was something she knew and something recognizable she could cling to.

"Good morning," he said. "It is with a heavy heart that I address our nation today. The news is grave beyond these walls."

From outside the school, Lucy heard the unmistakable blast of a shotgun. She jumped, her heart pushing out painfully against her ribcage. She reminded herself to breathe and sucked in a shaky breath. She checked her phone. No new texts. She pushed her call log and tried to dial, but her phone would not relent to her request.

The anchorman continued.

"It appears our nation is under attack. Details, at this time, are few and far between. And we do not present this information to you to frighten you and your loved ones, but to express the importance of binding ourselves together to fight this unknown enemy."

A scream. A siren wail. From the street outside, a crash of glass breaking, tires squealing. Then nothing. An eerie disquiet followed. Lucy glued her eyes to the man talking to her, just her, from the box on the wall. A country away, he sat and addressed her fear. His authority comforted her and she was happy that he had answers. She felt a hot tear roll down her cheek.

"It appears that over twenty-four hours ago, our water systems and the very air we breathe was contaminated. By what, we don't know. By whom is only conjecture. While the sickness claimed its victims, nations began to place blame. It appears that some of the loss of life today is based on retaliation from our political enemies as well as the initial biological threat. But to be honest, viewers..." The man dipped his head. Lucy saw his grief in the wrinkles around his eyes, the quivering of his chin. And then his heavy brows lifted and sank, but he continued.

"We are a nation at war with several enemies. The bioterrorism is our first threat. The government is asking that you stay inside. Do not leave your house. If you find yourself away from home and need shelter, then schools and churches are our sanctuaries. Find one. Stay there. Our…"

Thunk. Thunk. Lucy jumped. Someone was pushing against the door and sliding her carefully positioned tables forward. The flag came unfettered from the tape and drifted downward and an angry face from one of the school's security guards peered through the glass, his eyes darting around the room—landing on the television before finally locking on Lucy. She dropped off the desk and rushed to the window, throwing wide the curtain, before realizing that these windows would never grant her an escape. But her eyes caught a glimpse of the world outside for one brief moment. It was long enough to see a tower of smoke billowing into the sky, and even the clouds looked yellow and green and hazy. This vantage point had her looking across the football field where a storm of people gathered huddled in masses, their tiny bodies approaching the school like a death-march.

The security guard gained access to the room and he placed a hand on her shoulder and pulled her toward him. She stumbled into his grasp and felt her hopes of reuniting with her brother slipping away from her.

On the screen, images from around the nation and around the world surfaced in a slideshow. Nurses in biohazard gear treating the sick, a man slumped over a steering wheel in the middle of traffic, the wreckage of a downed plane, and a young mother carrying a small bundle out of her house, agony written on every angle of her face.

Lucy looked away.

How had so much happened in such a short amount of time?

The man caught a glimpse of the TV too, and his face collapsed a bit, softening in all the right places, before he toughened himself, shook the image from his mind, and tightened his hold on her. "All students in the auditorium. We're in lockdown," he stated.

"I just got here," Lucy said.

"School is secure. Has been since ten minutes into first period. So, no way, darlin'. Come on," he pushed her forward, pulling a walkie-talkie from his waistband. "McGuire here. Got a hider in Havs old room."

It took a moment before someone radioed back. "Is she symptomatic?"

The guard looked her over. His finger rested on the button. "You feel sick?" he asked Lucy. "Feverish? Nauseated?"

She contemplated a snide reply, but then thought better of it. She shook her head.

"If you start to feel achy or if you start to get a headache or blurred vision," he continued rattling off a list of ailments associated with the flu, while Lucy dropped her eyes to the floor. He led her into the hallway, maneuvering past the fallen, "You tell someone immediately. Understand?"

"Are people contagious?" she asked when he was done instructing her about what to expect upon entering the school's self-imposed quarantine. She stepped in something wet and slimy; she refused to look down and tried to drag her soiled shoe along the floor to wipe it clean.

The guard shrugged.

Together they walked past a small alcove and Lucy turned her head. The doors and windows leading to the outside were covered in long strips of bulletin board paper. The guard followed her gaze.

"It's part of the lockout procedures," he offered. "Cover all windows and doors."

"The news said that schools were a sanctuary," Lucy said. Aware of her own impertinence, she blushed.

"Not this one."

She felt tightness in her legs, and she kept her head low, looking at the ground. The guard's walkie-talkie came to life with a booming distinct voice, a man she recognized as Friendly Kent, a tall man, with extreme biceps and a closet full of V-necked sweaters. He was the administrator in charge of student discipline, but his nickname was derived from the fact that Kent couldn't, and didn't, really enforce anything—excuses and sob-stories were laid at his feet and Kent ate them up greedily, walking students back to the same class they were just kicked out of and telling frustrated teachers to "give the kid a break."

"Pablo Vasquez was hiding in the staff lounge," Friendly Kent crackled through.

"Not a chance. Checked it twice," Lucy's guard answered.

"In the ceiling," was Kent's reply. "Fell through a piece of sheetrock tile trying to move himself to the edge."

Lucy's guard chuckled. The sound of his small amusement at a student's legitimate fear and panic was grotesque to her.

They approached the cafeteria and she noticed all the lights were off and the long windows along the courtyard were also covered out and blackened. The second-period bell rang out into the empty hallways. It was a sound that normally signified chaos and excitement, inciting masses of students scurrying from one end of the school to another with sounds, squeals, yells, and shoes hitting the floor with clacks and squeaks. But now there was nothing. No laughter, no eagerness. No sounds but the two of them walking down the hall in isolation.

Lucy followed in silence past another row of covered windows. Shadows approached the paper and moved carefully along the outside wall like rows of zombies in old horror movies, sniffing and nudging for a way inside, aware of the warm bodies within. Lucy wanted to rush to the paper and pull it free, but the guard edged his way between her and the windows, as if he read her mind.

They rounded the corner past the gym and finally, after opening and closing two sets of double doors, closed upon the auditorium.

Friendly Kent came into view, escorting a sullen Pablo Vasquez, who was covered from head to toe in chalky sheetrock, and he reached the doors to the auditorium before them. He swung them open and sounds and smells poured outward—a roar of energy, hushed, intense—with voices lifting in anger and worry.

And then the meaty aroma of teenage stink burped toward them. Lucy turned her head away. She could almost taste the hormones and the racing fear. Then the doors crashed closed and everything was gone. It was like the opening of Pandora's Box: Allowing the evils of that room to tease them for a moment before being contained back inside.

Lucy took a step backward, unaware that she was shaking her head.

Her guard pushed her forward, her feet tripping slightly on the outdated red and blue checkered carpet.

"Go in here. Find a place to sit. Don't be a problem," he commanded, switching tactics and grabbing her hand.

Lucy stole her hand back and shook her shoulders away from him as he reached back toward her shifting body. "Please don't touch me," she whispered. In her own mind, she had made the command with power and aggression—her words dripped with the vitriol rising within her. But instead she had sounded meek and unsure. "I'll go in by myself," she added, hoping to ease the temper she saw flare up in the guard's eyes—a flash that dared her to run, dared her to defy him.

She reached forward and grabbed the door, the smell and the sound bursting forth a second time. And with a deep breath she walked into the darkened auditorium. Even with the lights on full-blast, the whole room was dim and the corners and walls lined with shadows. The stage was in a state of half-construction

for the play *Into the Woods*. The pieces of buildings were
flat on the floor while a mural of a dark forest with
black twisty trees rising up to a yellow moon was nearly
complete. The trees kept reaching backward into a dark
unknown. Lucy resisted the urge to climb up on the
stage and crawl her way into that forest. Even though it
was black and uninviting and full of the unknown, it
seemed safer than being forced to congregate with her
peers.

All around her, people gathered in various levels of
distress. Many students sat, staring straight ahead in the
stadium seating with phones lighting up their faces.
Another group sat huddled in a semi-circle, hugging
and crying into each other. Lucy watched a girl with a
long streak of red in her hair stroke the head of a boy
bawling in her lap; she shushed him and rocked back
and forth, her eyes closed tight.

Many students cried out, but most sat in stoic
silence, waiting and waiting for someone to tell them
what to do. In the back of the room, several teachers
stood around the glow of a television. The old
newscaster was still talking, his face drawn in a
perpetual frown. The crowd spoke intensely, like a
wave rolling from the back to the front, and Lucy just
stood, planted firm, eyes wandering for a familiar face.
She was desperate to see Salem.

But Salem wasn't there.

Stepping away from the doors and up the first
aisle, Lucy meandered. She looked at every face and
tried to find a friendly one among them. There was a

girl from science class, a boy she used to know in elementary school, a boy in her math class, a girl in yearbook. This one was in band. That one was a cheerleader. She used to talk to those three girls her freshman year at lunchtime—during the year that Salem's family moved themselves to Texas and she found herself bereft of friendship—but they had all fallen out of touch. Lucy chose to distance herself from the crowd of "fakers," as she labeled them, brilliantly loyal to your face and the quickest to sell you out to anyone who would listen. Lucy responded to their hurt by eating lunch in her math teacher's room for two whole months, before, she assumed, that teacher tattled on her and Ethan came and rescued her by dragging her off to eat with his upperclassmen friends. Her entire freshman year was marred with navigating the murky waters of varying degrees of social ostracism. Then Salem's family decided that they hated Texas and they found their way back to Portland. A move that Lucy credited with saving her life.

Lucy made eye contact with one of her former friends on accident, and as if she had conveyed some social cue that she needed to talk, the girl lurched forward from her seat, stumbling over the back of the chair in front of her.

"Lucy!" the girl screamed and then wrapped her arms around Lucy's shoulders.

She had forgotten the first girl's name. Under different circumstances she might have remembered, but her brain was a mess, a total fog. The name slipped away before she could grab ahold. It was Kylee. Or Keeley. Kyra. Kiyah. There it was just hiding in the back of her brain, pushed to the side and momentarily irretrievable. "I am so glad you're here. I'm so glad to see you. I'm so glad you're *okay*." The other girls stood up from their seats and wandered over, their heads nodding in agreement, eyes wide.

"We saw you walk in. What *happened*? Were you hiding?"

"I got to school late," Lucy mumbled and then tried to extricate herself from them by walking backward. She stumbled on a backpack without an owner.

The girls exchanged glances.

"You weren't locked out?" one whispered conspiratorially. Maddy or Molly, McKenzie. Michaela.

"Found an open door near the cafeteria," she lied. It was a silly lie. Who cared now about the secret passageway in the pool? Who cared about any of it?

"Wow," one girl said.

"Unlucky, I guess," said another. "Been better if you never got inside."

Everyone paused and then sighed in unison.

"But it's chaos outside too," Lucy replied. "Maybe we really are safer here." She regretted it as soon as it left her mouth because it aligned her with their common enemy—the girls turned on her; all but baring their teeth under throaty growls.

"We're hostages," one of the Kylees said.

"They have us locked in this room."

"My parents must be worried sick, I just want to get home."

"It's awful. This is against our rights," the maybe-McKenzie seethed and glared down at Lucy. "We still have rights."

Lucy didn't want to disagree with them, but she didn't know if she agreed. She didn't entirely disagree though. Confusion overwhelmed her. But she nodded anyway, mumbling something about just wanting her parents, which sent the trio into a blubbering mess. The middle girl, short, with a sleek dark bob and peacock inspired eye shadow, buried her head into Lucy's arm, staining her shirt with a thin streak of snot and tears.

"I'll be right back," Lucy said, pulling herself away.

She noticed Mrs. Johnston in the back, her arms crossed over her shirt. She was shaking her head at the television and wiping away tears. Briefly, she conversed with an older male teacher, and he leaned a protective arm around her and she collapsed against him. Then, as if she knew she was being watched, the English teacher turned and spotted Lucy.

Lucy took three giant steps toward her teacher, and for the first time since setting foot in the school she began to feel untethered. She watched Mrs. Johnson's shoulders shake with the heaviness of silent sobs, her legs trembling under her. This adult was falling apart. Her whole face was swollen and puffy from crying; her eyes, normally outlined in the perfect balance of liner and mascara, were now bare, giving her face a thinner, paler look. Lucy almost looked away, as if she had caught Mrs. Johnston naked.

Mrs. Johnston stared at Lucy with a lost expression. She didn't smile warmly or beckon her closer. Instead, she just lifted her hands from her chest and dropped them to her side, letting her arms dangle next to the pockets of her jeans.

And only then did Lucy notice that Mrs. Johnston's entire shirt was soaked with dark, dried, streaks of someone else's blood.

CHAPTER FIVE

"Oh my goodness," Lucy said and she walked forward toward her English teacher. But before she could maneuver herself closer, a burly Health teacher, still wearing a whistle around his stump-like neck, swooped forward with his hands out.

"No students in this area. Back to your row please," the man said, swollen with self-importance.

With no energy to protest, Lucy turned on her heels and turned her back to Mrs. Johnston, who probably had no memory that Lucy wasn't even supposed to be at school at all. Pulling her phone from her pocket, Lucy had no new messages. The time broadcast itself in large block numbers at the top of her screen. Their initial domestic flight to the East Coast would be in the air within the hour. Lucy entertained the notion in the back of her mind that sunny island weather and fruity drinks in coconut cups were in her future. She clung to those images as a last thread of hope that anything familiar could be salvaged. Halfway down the aisle, Lucy found a clearing of seats and wedged her way to the middle of the row, plopping herself down.

Lucy watched as their principal Spencer took the stage. He sauntered forward, leading with his forehead, one hand shoved into the pocket of his pants, the other one holding a wireless microphone. A pimply theater tech student assumed command of the follow spotlight and flooded the stage with a bright white light. The principal blinked into the orb and then blew into the mouthpiece of the microphone, a whoosh of sound shrieked across the seats. Like sheep, those standing, chatting, and crying filed into empty rows, all eager to hear the news, to hear the plan.

There wasn't an ounce of compassion on their leader's face as he stared down at them with flat eyes, gnawing on the inside of his right cheek.

"Sit down," he commanded, his mouth close to the microphone. "Find a seat and sit down." He pointed to the group of sobbing and cuddling kids near the front rows, so engaged in their own dialoguing that they had ignored his initial call to disband. "Get up and sit in a seat. You have sixty-seconds," he barked at them. When it was clear they had tuned him out, he motioned angrily toward the school's Resource Officer, a city of Portland policeman, his cop uniform bright and clean and his badge shiny.

The officer nodded and with quick precision, stalked forward and grabbed the closest boy to him by his back collar and tossed him backward like a ragdoll. Then he began to pull each of the students apart by force, throwing them toward seats, stepping around their huddled masses without regard for toes and fingers or long-braided hair. Only then did the kids begin to migrate toward the red cushioned seats, nursing their sore arms where the officer unceremoniously pulled them to their feet. A young girl began to wail and a boy, who had seconds earlier been cradling her, hushed her.

"Shut up," their fearless leader hissed, his voice echoing up the aisles.

No one dared to breathe. The officer crossed his arms and glared back out at the students, now huddled like potato bugs against armrests and seatbacks, all curled up into balls of arms and legs and messy hair.

Principal Spencer cleared his throat into the microphone. His speech started in a soft voice, and despite the microphone, some auditorium congregants leaned in to hear. While he spoke, he paced up and down the length of the stage. The follow spot moved with him, bouncing slightly and catching the dust particles floating like snow across the auditorium.

"You will follow orders. You will follow orders the first time we ask. There is no room for argument, for disagreement. There is no protocol for this and we are not writing futile referrals. We cannot simply call your parents to take you home," he said with disgust instead of empathy. "In order to function, we will operate with absolute obedience. And understand that the decisions I am making on behalf of the student body and the staff is for our mutual benefit. Whether or not you agree is a non-issue. My goal is protecting the people in this building." He paused.

Someone raised a shaky hand, but Spencer didn't notice.

Then a teacher called from the back, Lucy thought the same power tripping man with the whistle: "No questions."

And the student lowered the hand with resignation.

Spencer continued. "As you are aware, lockdown is in effect. We will open the outside doors for no one. No one out. Absolutely no one in. Am I clear?" he asked rhetorically.

Pockets of protest erupted around the auditorium, but teachers began to move toward the noise—silencing people and demanding attention.

"The major threat is *outside* these walls. Until we know more, I will not needlessly endanger you," he said.

"Himself," a boy behind Lucy said in a quiet non-whisper. "He will not needlessly endanger himself."

Lucy turned and saw Grant Trotter sitting behind her; his sandy blonde hair a mess of tangles, with bangs falling into his eyes. He half-smiled at Lucy—the facial equivalent of a shrug. And she acknowledged him with a nod and a sad smile-like response.

As Spencer droned on about expectations and rule following during this "fragile moment in our lives," Grant's body fell forward and his head hit against the back of the seat where Lucy was sitting. She could feel the pressure against her back, the bump of flesh hitting plastic. She turned again, her arms going rubbery, as she braced herself for the worst. She peered down at him and resisted the urge to reach out and grab his shoulder while she looked intently for the rise and fall of breath.

"Hey," she whispered, leaning toward him, but still keeping her distance. "Hey…are you okay?"

Grant's head snapped up, his eyes red, bloodshot, but his cheeks pink. He smiled an actual smile, one small dimple forming in the center of his cheek. "That's sweet," he said to her. "You thought I died."

"Yes," Lucy replied. "Don't say it like that. Don't say it like it's strange that I would think that." She blushed out of embarrassment.

"I feel fine," he said. Then he shook his head. "No. I don't. I don't feel fine. But I feel alive. Very much alive."

Lucy wondered if *she* felt alive. Certainly she could feel her heart, her heavy limbs; her head ached right behind her eyes and her stomach growled. She exhibited all the signs of a living human being, but something wasn't right. Were the crying kids in the corner more alive than she was? Because Lucy couldn't bring herself to sob or yell—instead, she felt lost, trapped in perpetual murkiness. Fear hovered just below the surface, but it hadn't created a stronghold yet, hadn't clawed its way in and nested itself among the hunger and the hope.

"I guess I don't feel alive," she said. "I don't feel real." Lucy didn't even know if that made sense, and after saying it out loud, she felt foolish. Grant didn't respond, only looked at her with his dark brown eyes in an assessing way.

She turned away from his gaze.

"Numb," he answered to the back of her head. "You feel numb."

Lucy couldn't even bring herself to nod.

Two rows in front of her, a boy leaned in to kiss his girlfriend on the cheek. A sudden sloppy decision, uncoordinated, and initially unnoticed. The girlfriend turned to him as he leaned in and then screamed loudly, a mixture of complete alarm and blind disgust as blood rolled down his cheeks. Dripping from the corners of his eyes, like a stream of tears, staining his shirt with growing circles of crimson. Even under the dull auditorium lights, Lucy could tell his skin was fading from pink to a pale, grass-stain green.

"I'm just...I'm a little queasy," Lucy heard him mumble to the girl as she scrambled away, her head turning in every direction.

"Help him! Help him!" The girl shouted, scooting backward as he reached for her, on his knees now, stuck between the chair and the row in front of him, cupping his hands around his mouth and heaving into them. Her squealing interrupted Principal Spencer's continuous droning about the consequences of insubordination.

It was the first time she had seen someone fall victim to the virus, and the instantaneous nature of this silent killer filled her with such dread that she buried her face in her hands—pleading with herself not to look. How could it work like that? One minute he was fine, just a teenage boy sitting next to his girlfriend, hoping, even among death and destruction, for a kiss, a sign of unwavering affection. And the next minute he was sucking for air, losing control of his bodily functions, spilling blood in pools like ink stains on the carpeted floor.

Teachers flew in from the corners and launched themselves over seats and into the row. Each one donned rubber gloves, pulling them from pockets and snapping them on in haste. They approached him with speed, but without worry. They would go to him, lean him back, exit others away from his body, but their faces told the truth they couldn't say aloud: *This boy is gone. There is nothing we can do for him.*

This had been their entire morning, and this student was just one of many. Already they had adjusted, adapted, and molded themselves into their new roles. Earlier their focus might have been mitosis-labs and Steinbeck-essays, parent-emails, and Special-Ed-meetings, but now they were body-collectors and lockout-supervisors. How easy it all became the new normal.

"Let's move him back," a large math teacher told the others, his belly exposed, bursting through bulging buttons. After some maneuvering around the row, a male teacher and a male counselor grabbed the lifeless boy and paraded down the aisle. Lucy only then noticed that someone in that madness had been generous enough to close his eyes. Or maybe he had closed his eyes in the end—she could only guess as she had kept her own eyes trained away from the boy in his final moments. Working together, the adults hoisted the body on the stage, and then carried him off behind the set. It was as if it were all a giant play and the boy was an actor, the charade nothing more than directions in a script.

"Where are they taking him?" Lucy asked to Grant, not bothering to turn around, just leaning her head back.

"They've been taking everyone to the dressing rooms, I think," he replied. "Confining the bodies for the uprising."

Lucy swiftly turned. "What?"

"Zombies? When everyone comes back as zombies?"

"This can't possibly be a joke to you. Is this a joke to you?" Lucy asked. "That boy *died*. I just watched that boy die!"

Grant ran his right hand through his hair, mussing it up near the crown. "First time you've watched someone..." he made a face as he trailed off. "Yeah, well, you'll get used to it. Watching it all morning will make you...what did we say? Numb. Right."

Lucy bit her lip. "This morning I was at home." She wanted to explain, but the thought of her mom— her frantic, unexplained text—and of Harper with her lopsided pigtails, her brothers and their own unique smells and smiles, was too much and she couldn't go on. There was no place she would rather be than with her family. She couldn't bear the thought of them suffering. In her mind, everyone was still packing for the trip and her mother was still pacing with her clipboard, irate at Lucy's thoughtless tardiness. Ethan was furtively kissing Anna goodbye while Galen argued that his lucky-never-been-washed Beatles sweatshirt had a place among the lavender infused suitcases. The twins were off to run reconnaissance for each other while sneaking the plane snacks.

This is how they were right now.

At her house.

Safely supported in a bubble protecting them from the chaos she heard—the gunshots, the loud crashes, and foundation rocking, earth shattering booms. Whatever was happening outside of this school was not happening at her house because it could not be any other way. It just simply could not.

"I wasn't trying to joke," he replied with a sigh. "I'm well-versed in zombies. It starts with some unknown sickness that wipes out the population and ends with the walking dead." He paused, waiting for Lucy to chime in. She just looked at him, softened, but incredulous. "I've been watching everyone at school fall all morning," he told her, leaning closer, eager to share. "Spanish class, first period. Mary...Mary?" he paused, waiting to see if Lucy knew the name.

"Bishop? I know her."

"We were watching the news. Just glued to the news, right? Senora Cochran was just sobbing and we were all just...sitting there...and Mary gets up and says she doesn't feel so good and can she go to the bathroom." Grant pauses and closes his eyes. "I'd never seen anyone die before. Before that moment, you know? It was so fast. We didn't even get up out of our seats. We thought she had fainted. Or that she was just being stupid and dramatic. Some people actually laughed. At first. They laughed at first."

Lucy didn't know what to say. She looked down to the back of the seat. "I'm really scared," she admitted.

While it could have seemed like a non-sequitur comment, Grant didn't miss a beat. "Yeah, I'm terrified too."

The body-collection team reappeared empty-handed, and Spencer demanded the attention back as he tried to calm the escalating conversations through the microphone.

"You will be escorted by a teacher into their classroom," Principal Spencer said. "You will not be allowed to leave the classroom until we have a better understanding of what we're facing or until we have support from local law enforcement." Groups began to talk with rushed anxiety. "Remain seated until a teacher comes to collect you."

Voices of dissent carried through the auditorium.

"Remain seated!" Spencer instructed again straight into the microphone.

But the panic was escalating. A teacher made his way up on the stage and whispered into Spencer's ear and as he did, a boy, a tenth grader, slipped up onto the stage and crawled over to him. It was clear to everyone that the boy was ill. He vomited near the edge of the stage, but despite the fact that the virus was taking hold, he kept trying to work his way to Spencer. By the time the student had reached the principal's pant leg, he was already starting to shake.

Lucy could hear Spencer scream to get the boy away from him.

"Remove him. He's infected! Remove him now!" came the screams, increasing in intensity as the child moved closer to death. But the boy didn't relent. He kept a grip on Spencer's pants, keeping the principal rooted to the ground even as he tried to tug and pull himself away.

Then they all saw it.

And the auditorium gasped in unison when Principal Spencer, in one swift motion, kicked the boy with his free leg. It was a solid, well-placed swipe at the dying boy's jaw, and the boy's head lopped to the side after impact. Whether or not the child was already close to death did not matter, Spencer's kick had demolished him, and his head flung backward and then hit the floor with a sickening thud.

Everyone stopped and watched as the man looked out over the crowd, his face contorted in a mixture of alarm and growing defensiveness.

"Get *it* out of here!" he cried, but no one moved. "Students…listen…your lives are in danger. And you will follow my directions or suffer the consequences."

Lucy stiffened and shifted uncomfortably in her seat.

He called the names of some of his cronies—other

administrators with whom he could form an alliance of power and hatred. But none of them stood forward immediately, and for one long moment, Spencer was left standing alone, the dead boy at his feet. He dropped the microphone to the stage, and it caused a loud crash that reverberated through the speakers. Several people threw their hands up over their ears. All around the auditorium people grumbled their resignation or agitation.

Without amplification, Spencer yelled, "Follow the orders! Just follow my orders." And then, as he noticed other children coughing and slumping, reaching out to him for assistance and reassurance, he shot down the stairs of the stage and flung the auditorium doors open wide, running quickly away from the kids with whom he was instructed to protect.

For a second everyone looked at each other with confusion. But then the teachers moved into position— determined to follow the protocol even in the absence of their leader. Some walked swiftly, stern faced, and eager to take charge. It was not surprising that even amidst the turmoil outside, some of the adults found comfort in supervision. They could push aside their own fear and assuage their growing worry with a false sense of control. Lucy closed her eyes and sent up a prayer, a hope, that she would not get stuck with some adult with a superiority complex.

When her eyes fluttered open, it was Mrs. Johnston standing next to her. Blonde hair loose in wavy curls that fell to her shoulders; she was playing with a silver chain around her neck, twisting it around the fingers of her right hand, dropping it, twisting it again. Her normally bright skin was dull and pale, and a dried glob of mascara had latched itself near her cheekbone. With a shaky hand, she ran her hand over a section of five rows.

"You all. From here to here. Follow me," she called to them, but her voice was small, absent of authority.

Ten of them, Grant included, rose from the chairs—the seats swung backward with repetitive whack-whack-whacks until they slowed to a stop. Lucy grabbed Ethan's backpack, still weighted down with the textbook and binder, swung it high on her shoulder and stood beside her English teacher. Mrs. Johnston reached out as if to pat Lucy on the arm, then dropped her hand, a shuddering sigh escaping before she turned and began to walk down the aisle, each of the kids in her charge falling into single-file line, the old elementary habit returning.

"Mrs. Johnston?" Lucy asked when they had left the auditorium and were making their way back up the long hallway toward the English hall. The other kids from the auditorium disappeared into other hallways, other classrooms, out of sight. "Mrs. Johnston?"

"Yes...Lucy," she answered, breathless, slowing her pace, dropping back to walk side-by-side.

"How long can they keep us here?"

"*They* can keep me until the end of my contract hours and then I'm gone," Mrs. Johnston responded through clenched teeth. "I have a family."

"But what about *us*? They can't keep us here. Right? They can't force us to stay against our will."

Mrs. Johnson hung her head. "You don't understand. I have to go. I have to go home. But principal Spencer isn't wrong...it is safer in this building." She glanced back at the ten students following her as each one sped up to walk in a huddle, hungry for news.

Grant leaned closer, "Before...when we were watching the television? Someone reported that military planes were flying over cities and dropping a green gas into heavily populated areas. Is that true?"

"I don't know anything," she said and put her hands up in surrender. "No one knows anything." Her heels clipped on the tile, picking up her pace to a brisk walk.

"Who attacked us?" said a sophomore girl toward the back of the group—she clutched her bright red leather purse in front of her like a shield, knuckles turning white. "Do they know who?"

But Mrs. Johnston had decided she was done answering questions, so she did not acknowledge the growing bombardment of worries. As each student lobbed up a theory or a snippet of news, she just walked faster, until the whole group shuffled along at a near-run to keep up with her. It was clear that she was taking the group to her own classroom, steering back through the trail of bodies that Lucy had traversed earlier. As they hit the long corridor littered with the dead, some of the students slowed. This carnage was new to them, and some of these people were their friends. The sophomore girl closed her eyes tight and stopped moving entirely. She just stood there in the middle of the hallway, her red purse covering her stomach, her feet shoulder width apart, unmoving. She kept her eyes scrunched closed, her mouth grimacing, her teeth showing.

Lucy recognized a boy named Clayton from her biology class among their small group. He called down the hallway. "Mrs. Johnston! Wait up!" Then he walked back and stood next to the girl, touching her purse and gently leading her forward.

"I won't. I won't go," she said and stiffened her body even more.

But Clayton was patient. "I'll lead you. But you have to take my hand. Like those trust walks, right?" But she wouldn't lift her hand up, wouldn't take it off the purse, and wouldn't open her eyes or budge.

By that time, Mrs. Johnston had noticed half the group wasn't keeping up with her quickened pace. She stopped and turned, eyes red, new rivulets of black running down her cheeks.

Then Lucy felt it.

Not the quick *buzz-buzz-buzz* of a text.

But the long and sustained *buzzzzzz* of an incoming phone call.

At first she thought she was imagining it—that all of her hoping and daydreaming had turned into an auditory hallucination accompanied by phantom vibrations. Frantic, she dug her hand into her pocket and retrieved her phone. The phone slipped, but she caught it against her jeans, and her sweaty fingers attempted to grab ahold.

As the other students noticed the action, each one looked to their own phones, scampering to send a text, place a call. Hope. Lucy saw it in an instant in all of their faces. Technology was back, so there was hope.

Without even looking, Lucy answered. A lump rose in her throat as she waited for her mom's voice to hit her ear. Please just tell me everyone is okay, she thought. Please, Mommy, please.

She pleaded for the news to be good.

"Lula? Lula? Are you there? Are you there?" The voice was high-pitched, rushed, and jumbled. Voices swirled in the background and there was a distinct gunshot again—it was louder in the phone, but the blast echoed in the school too.

From outside, this call was from somewhere right outside.

Salem.

"Sal? Sal?" Lucy answered. "Where are you?"

"I'm at the school," Salem said and Lucy hopped up and down when she heard the news.

"Thank God! Sal, I'm here too! It's a long story…but I'm inside Pacific right now. No one can get *out*, Salem. They have everyone locked inside! It's a total nightmare."

"Lucy, listen. I'm *outside*. I'm right outside the cafeteria, by the big doors. We can't get in Lucy. No one can get in!'"

"No one can get out!" Lucy said overlapping. Then she paused and processed their conflicting wishes.

Another gunshot. Again, she could hear it both in the phone and in her ear. There was a slight delay between one and the other—a small disconnect, as if two shots were ringing out upon each other.

"Salem? What the hell is going on?"

"They're trying to shoot the card lock off. They're trying to shoot the glass. I tried to tell them it's bulletproof, but it's madness here. God, Lucy, help me! Help me, please!" Salem's voice was beyond begging, her sobs shot through the phone in short bursts of pure panic.

"I'm coming! Okay, okay! I'm coming," Lucy yelled into the mouthpiece and, with only a quick look to Mrs. Johnston and the rest of the group—all of whom had frozen to listen to her conversation—she took off running back in the other direction, her phone still pressed to her ear, her backpack rising and falling as she ran, the gravity of it threatening to pull her to the ground. She didn't know what she would do when she got there, and it only occurred to her that she was running toward gunfire as the cafeteria doors came into view.

"I'm almost there, Sal. I'm almost there," she said into her phone.

"Lula. You have to get me inside the school. You have to get me inside the school right now."

CHAPTER SIX

Lucy slowed to a stop in front of the windows and doors in the cafeteria. They were covered in thick black paper, and even though she couldn't see the people outside, she could hear them—yelling and crying and pounding on the glass. Part of the district's safety plan included upgrading all the windows to war-grade fortification, thick, resilient, bulletproof glass. Before the update, an angry student on a rampage after a suspension broke an entire windowpane by throwing a metal garbage can into the center of the cafeteria door. It shattered during the school day and wasn't replaced until the following evening at which point an assistant principal found a homeless man curled up in the waterless pool.

In an instant, Lucy reached as high as she could and grabbed hold of the paper and tore it down. The strip slid to the floor and bathed the area in light. She tore another and another, swinging each discarded piece to the side.

Then she stepped back.

Forty. Maybe fifty—she was never good at

estimating—people congregated outside in the alcove beyond the cafeteria doors. They were everywhere, pressing up against the glass, their fists pounding in earnest. A woman near the door was pushed forward, the side of her cheek flat against the smooth surface, and in her arms she held a toddler. The child was wearing a blue backpack, and his face was stoic, shocked, and he clutched to his mother out of necessity, trusting that she was leading him to safety.

Lucy scanned the crowd and finally saw Salem a few people deep near the door, waving at Lucy with wild abandon, tears streaming down her face. Salem was still in the clothes she wore yesterday. And for a moment, Lucy wondered if perhaps Salem had never gone to bed. Perhaps she had laid in wait, pondering Bogart, crying with her mother, and snuggling in her mom's bed. Salem's mom was a large woman and the soft folds of her body were perfect for hugging. Or maybe, Salem had merely thrown on the first clothes she saw this morning—the ones she had shed the night before near her laundry basket.

The crowd breathed in and exhaled as one, so Salem seized her chance and pushed against the flow, rushing forward to reach the door. Against the glass at last, she reached her hands up and placed them flat. Lucy sprinted forward and matched them—the two-inch thick windows separated them, but their hands touched nonetheless.

"What can I do?" she asked. Her voice was loud, booming in the cafeteria; she was shocked by the sound of it. Salem couldn't hear her, but she understood.

"Please, please, please," was all Salem said in return. Over and over she said it, begging for Lucy to do the impossible. She took a step back and the crowd surged and what Lucy saw scared her. She could feel her classmates, Clayton, Grant, and the group, assembling behind her, but she dared not turn to look at them. She knew she would see on their faces what she already knew in her heart: There was no way to open that door.

Lucy felt a hand on her shoulder, but she didn't look to see who had approached her. She stayed staring straight ahead, her eyes on Salem and the others, her stomach twisting.

"Lucy—" she heard Grant say in a voice hovering above a whisper.

"I know," she replied without looking at him. But her heart ached for everyone who left the pandemonium of the outside world and turned to the high school for shelter and help. The people arrived there hopeful and scared, seeking solace and aid. Some of the people outside, relegated to the perimeter of the crowd, sat huddled with suitcases and other mementos. What had they expected to find? No place was protected from death.

But this was her friend. Her best friend. This was the girl who convinced her to sit on the uppermost part of the jungle gym in the third grade, a book of mythology in their hands, and pretend it was a book of witch's curses. They sat for an entire recess casting down spells on unsuspecting second-graders. This was the girl who first introduced her to nail polish and told her, in a whisper-voice one night during a slumber party, to be proud of her laugh. Salem was in every major memory from her childhood and into those petrifying and awkward junior high years and into their high school. College was next—shared dorm rooms, double dates: These were the things they dreamed about. And as she watched Salem's body ebb and flow outside like a wave, Lucy just assumed that it would be her and Salem forever.

She rushed forward to the doors, not even sure of what she would do once she got there. But she stumbled when she felt a rough hand latching on to her upper arm, forcing her backward. Lucy tripped and ended up on the cold tile of the cafeteria—the floor was littered with dried ranch dressing, crushed corn chips, and strings of wilted lettuce.

Before Lucy could get up, she felt Grant kneeling down next to her. "I'm on your side, Lucy," he said into her ear. "But this is not the way."

She paused. Lucy hadn't even known Grant knew her name. She looked up at him, pleading. "What if there is no other way?" she asked.

"This *can't* be the way," he repeated and he gestured toward the mob.

Lucy crawled back to the window. She was still clutching her phone in her hand and she sent Salem a text.

"Pool door?"

But her phone kicked back an error message.

"Send. Send." She willed it to go through, but it was no use. The phone gave her error message after error message every single time.

Lucy decided to press her phone against the glass, only for a second, while Salem, and others scrambled to read the message.

Then Salem froze. Her face fell, her shoulders slumped, and she allowed those around her to toss her around.

Blocked. She mouthed. *Or locked.* Then distinctly—*No.*

Salem stared directly at Lucy. She motioned around the chaos and someone bumped her. An arm hit the glass, then Salem's head, and she rocked backward, reeling away. Salem's body was pitched downward and someone pulled her arm behind her back and flung her to the ground.

Salem cried out. Then she shut her eyes tight; she tried to wiggle upward, and when she opened her eyes, she stared right at Lucy.

She shook her head. Just once. Fear flooding her face, defeat and worry settling around the dark pockets of skin under her eyes.

It was just a small look, but Lucy's insides twisted with guilt.

"I will get you inside," she called, squatting to put herself close to Salem's face. She pointed at her friend and then put a hand on her heart. "I will." Lucy tried to communicate dedication and strength with her body and facial expressions alone; she tried to send Salem comfort instead of fear. She could not open the door, but she would not leave her friend outside to die. "I will!" Lucy screamed and she pounded the glass.

And that was when Lucy felt heavy hands upon her, closing in around her collarbone and dragging her away from the window. Not the gentle redirection of Grant, but strong adult hands that dug into the flesh on her shoulders. The security guards poured around the windows, armed with duct tape and the discarded black paper. Working swiftly—place, tape, repeat, place, tape, repeat—the men covered the windows again and the cafeteria succumbed back into the shadows, the muffled shouts from the people outside emanating from beyond the blackness.

Salem was lost behind the partition.

"I'm sorry," Lucy sobbed into her hands, even though Salem couldn't hear her. She kicked her legs and tried to pull away from the hands that held her. "Sal…I'm so sorry." Fingers dug deeply into her bone and the pain radiated down her chest.

The mother and her son. The faces of that mother and her son burned into Lucy's brain. Salem. Everyone. It was unfair.

"Those people…all those people…" Lucy mumbled. She turned to see that it was Friendly Kent who held her back. He loosened his grip, but kept his hands on her, wary and watchful. Seeing the anger flash across Friendly Kent's face, Lucy felt doubly betrayed.

Grant watched Lucy from a few steps behind. And

it was only now that Mrs. Johnston made an appearance, the staccato clip-clap-clip-clap of her heels full of reprimand.

A larger security guard, who had helped place the paper over the windows, pivoted and turned toward Lucy. He raised an angry finger, poised to launch. But Grant raised his voice instead, preventing the verbal onslaught. "That's a Pacific Lake student out there. And I bet she's not the only one," he took a step forward. "Principal Spencer said his main concern was keeping students safe. So, then why aren't we keeping *all* students safe?"

"Enough," Friendly Kent said. "Back to your rooms."

"Those people didn't look infected," Lucy added. "They're just scared."

"They're *armed*. Are you out of your minds?" Friendly Kent replied. Then he settled back and crossed his arms across his chest. "I've waited my entire career to say this. You teenagers are idiots. Complete and total scum of the earth. Everything we're doing is to protect you, but you think you've got a better plan? Of course you do. Look, I'd be happy to unload the lot of you right back out into the fray."

"We aren't protected in here either," Grant responded. "Look! Look around." Two more students emerged from their original group of ten, but no one else. Four had succumbed to the virus in the last ten minutes.

"We're not keeping anything out! The sickness is

already here. Don't you see that?" Grant continued.

Friendly Kent raised his eyes to Mrs. Johnston and pursed his lips. "Get them back. Now." His command was swift. He yanked Lucy to her feet and shoved her forward, Grant followed behind.

Even their teacher bristled from his tone, but she nodded and obeyed. Mrs. Johnston grabbed Lucy by the arm and turned her toward the group, then she motioned for Grant, Clayton, Purse Girl, and the others to line up, follow along. They exited the cafeteria, back to following the letter of the law without question, and everything about the situation made Lucy sick.

"Don't you see?" Mrs. Johnston asked when they were out of earshot. "Isn't it clear by now?" She waited, for an answer, but no one answered. "There is no *great* master plan. It's chaos. Inside and outside."

Slower this time, they walked the long corridor. Purse Girl's eyes were wide open as she shuffled along, but Clayton still kept a firm hand on her elbow, propelling her forward.

"Those people will find a way inside," Grant muttered. "Two administrators and a small team of failed mall cops?"

Mrs. Johnston nodded. She took several steps forward and stopped, her voice shaking, "Everyone's lied to you. Your whole lives. See what happens when the world falls apart...see what happens when everything you know crumbles?" Her eyes were wild. "You realize. You will see. It's the assholes who inherit the earth."

Room 126 felt like a tomb. Mrs. Johnston kept the lights off, and she huddled at her desk, refreshing the Internet browser on her computer religiously and keeping her phone situated in her line-of-sight, next to a picture of her husband and her kids. For the most part, she ignored the students in her charge. If anyone tried to talk to her or lean over her shoulder, she shooed them away, relegating them back to the uncomfortable chairs or coarse carpeting. Pretense melted away—there was no time for comforting pep talks. They could tell they were in danger and no one was trying to spin it any other way.

Every ten minutes a security guard popped his head in and did a quick head count, then he shut the door and moved on. Every ten minutes. Like clockwork.

When Mrs. Johnston taught her English classes, she was like a puppy dog—full of boundless energy and eager naiveté—and it was something that Lucy always appreciated. This notion that someone still woke up enthusiastic about Jonathan Edwards' "Sinners in the Hands of an Angry God" and would read it in dark and somber tones, burning plastic spiders over open flames and then erupting afterward into joyous giggles, making them, with hands over hearts, promise to never tell the administration about her fire hazards. She was light and bright, and she was counselor and coach. They taught her new slang words, and she snickered with embarrassment, unbridled, genuine.

But since they had locked themselves into her room, Lucy couldn't find any of that Mrs. Johnston left in the space where they once held spirited slam poetry competitions and waxed philosophical about Emerson's Transparent Eyeball. The new Mrs. Johnston was taciturn and cold; she barely spoke a word and didn't try to hide her disgust toward each of the children in her care.

After an hour, they were down to five.

The security came by and took note of bodies and survivors; then a group of surviving teachers carried the dead away. But even the number of adults seemed to dwindle as time passed. Six teachers, now only two, continued to act out their roles despite the futility of it all. Mrs. Johnston never moved from her desk; her eyes never wavered from her computer screen as she clicked and clicked and willed the news on her screen to be different. She moved between the news sites, their updates slowing down as the time slipped away from them and then on to her own feed and her email. Lucy watched as she went through her pattern. Site one. Site two. Site three. Wait. Look. Repeat. As if it was not the intake of information that interested her, but instead the cathartic nature of the ritual.

A phone buzzed in the room.

The sporadic nature of sending texts and receiving calls made it impossible for her to communicate with Salem, but Lucy looked down at her phone, disappointed that her screen was blank. Even so, Lucy's fingers flew into action. She fired a note, "*Stay strong friend. Working on a plan.*" And she watched, stomach in knots, until the little green arrow indicated success. If Salem could read it, if she was still out there, she would know that Lucy had not abandoned her. Lucy would never abandon her.

Even if that was not entirely true because she had abandoned her—she had left Salem crumpled on the ground with hoards of scared people tearing around her. Scared people with guns. Lucy took a deep breath and held her phone to her chest. She felt it apropos to pray, but specific requests eluded her, so she just repeated over and over inside her head: *Help me, help me, help me, help me.* Less like a prayer and more like a mantra.

"I have to get home," Mrs. Johnston said. It was the first thing she had said in hours. Everyone turned to look at her and gawked, as if she had grown a tail and barked wildly. She looked at the students in the room, assessing their faces and then to the clock. Jumping up, her chair crashing backward behind her; she rushed to the window and pried it open—the bottom half was designed to open only an inch, and she ran her hands over the metal. Unless they could remove the entire pane of glass from the window, that was not a viable escape route. "Can't. I can't. I can't!" Mrs. Johnston hit the metal radiator beneath the window in frustration and immediately cradled her hand. She spun around and leaned back, breathless.

Clayton, who had been slumped in the corner of

the room, using his backpack as a pillow and drawing doodles in a notebook, sat up. "I've been thinking," he said.

Grant had moved himself under the television and he turned his head. He'd been watching the news without saying a word for most of the time they were trapped in the room, but at one point he had sidled up to Lucy and put a reassuring arm around her shoulder. She shrugged him off and then apologized. It was easier to think Grant had single-handedly stopped her from rescuing Salem than to accept that any course of action was futile.

"You have an idea?" Grant prodded and Clayton nodded.

Purse Girl, who also hadn't said a word since they got to the room, raised her body off the floor, alert. They each stared at Clayton expectantly.

"You have a master key? You know, from coaching?"

Mrs. Johnston's shoulders slumped as if she was already preparing for this plan to fail. "It doesn't unlock the main doors. They have control for the locking mechanism in the security office and outside the main office. My keys are worthless," she said. She took out a rubber band and tied her hair up into a high ponytail, her blonde hair cascading down her back. Lucy marveled that somehow throughout the entire day it had not lost its curl.

"No. I'm not interested in using them to get outside," Clayton answered. He stood up and brushed his hands off on his jeans. "Does your key unlock the doors in the East wing?"

Mrs. Johnston clamped her mouth tight for a minute and peered at Clayton curiously, as if she were trying to guess what he had in mind. Then she reached into her pocket and produced her keys, turning them over in her hand. "Yes," she nodded. "They do."

Clayton broke out into a huge smile, and he flipped his long blonde hair forward over his shoulders. "If you can get me into the metal shop, then I think I can get you out of this school."

"Wait!" Lucy popped up from her chair by the desk, forgetting she was holding her phone and it skittered away from her across the floor. "Can you get someone *into* the school the same way?" She bent over to retrieve her cell and admired a fresh crack across her screen. It seemed, even amid everything else, a tragedy worthy of tears, but she pushed them away and tried to keep her head clear and focused.

He nodded. "Yes," he replied. "Trickier, but yes. But if we don't want to get caught, we have to work in shifts. I've been plotting it since they trapped us here. Do you trust me?"

"What choice do we have?" Lucy answered and then realized it sounded harsh and unfair. She opened her mouth to add something softer, nicer, but Mrs. Johnston stepped forward—her open palm extended toward Clayton, handing him her keys.

"Just tell us what to do," Mrs. Johnston said. "I'll do anything." Her eyes were supplicating and she walked right up to Clayton. Standing next to each other, she looked so tiny, fragile, and afraid and he towered above her, a man-child, with massive, calloused hands, broad shoulders, and a smattering of acne.

He turned to Lucy. "If you can get your friend on the roof, leave everything else to me."

CHAPTER SEVEN

The East Wing was entirely its own entity. Separated from the rest of the school down a long and often forgotten-about hallway, the tiny square plot of school that held the metal and wood shops, the art studio, and the journalism lab, seemed to function as an independent school within Pacific Lake. Many students didn't even know the wing existed—it was easy to miss the narrow hallway leading to the classrooms. The East Wing was so independent and often ignored that it took administrators two years to notice that the teachers had converted an abandoned storage room into a sitting lounge complete with couches and a coffee maker.

The metals kids were their own group; funneling in and out of the metals room at all times during the day, dressed in dark hooded sweatshirts and skinny jeans, sporting lip-rings and tattoos, half-inch ear gauges, and congenial dispositions. They made electric cars after school and entered robotics competitions and their skills with blowtorches, drills, and the foundry unparalleled in the entirety of East County. And often they were outcast, huddling at the periphery of the other social groups, always humming along toward escape. They smoked weed in their cars in the parking lot of the LDS church next door and respected their mothers.

Metals kids were different from those who took woodshop. That class attracted football players on the hunt for an easy elective and entire collections of skinny little Romeos who wanted to make velvet lined jewelry boxes for girls on their buses.

The art studios were brightly painted and cluttered with decades of abandoned projects. There were bookshelves shoved with forgotten pottery and closets stuffed with unfinished canvas portraits. Mobiles dangled from the ceiling and the desks were covered with a rainbow paint splatter. The art students were shy and unassuming with their own inside jokes and general disdain for those without appreciation for the French Impressionists.

Lucy was familiar with this area of the school from Salem, who, not surprisingly, had found a niche in journalism early in her high school career as she channeled her penchant for gossip into a career as the Living Editor for the Pacific Lake newspaper *The Herald*. She would go and collect Salem from the journalism lab after school hours, meandering into the dimly lit East Wing with trepidation. It was the only section of the school exempt from the last remodel: The roof was leaky, the linoleum flooring was tearing up at the seams and entire banks of florescent lights blinked on and off, which made the entire area feel like the set of a campy 1980's horror film.

But despite its cosmetic deficiencies, there was something powerful about the East Wing. It was the only place in the school entirely dedicated to creation. A birdhouse. A watercolor. A ceramic vase. Key chains. A newspaper.

Immediately after the last round of security, the whole group left the confines of the English classroom and darted up the hall with Clayton leading them down the hallway, left toward the art studio, up to the woods workshop and the metals room. They twitched eagerly as Mrs. Johnston opened up the door and led the group inside, hushing them, and pushing them, until she could close the door without a sound. Then Clayton hit a switch and the room tumbled to life—overhead lights flickering, the room awash in a golden glow, illuminating shiny metal from one end of the room to the other.

The room was large, expansive. Row after row of long workbenches and tented workstations, each equipped with tubes and wires, stools, machinery. A staircase at the very end led to a narrow walkway where large sheets of metal were stored, each placed upright against the wall, reflective and bright. The entire room echoed as the group walked around inside, and when Lucy ran her hand over the nearest table, small shards of aluminum collected on her skin, and she brushed them off on her jeans.

"I've never been here," Grant said, peeking his head into a work station, the large green plastic curtain crinkling loudly as he pulled it back. "Four years in this place and I've never had a class back here. I didn't even know it existed." Lucy understood—she hadn't known about the East Wing either until Salem joined journalism.

"I live here," Clayton replied with pride. He walked over to a section of the room and pulled back on a white bed sheet, exposing a fiberglass body of a racing car. "I've been working on this for my electric car competition. Hours and hours," he said with a touch of sadness. He ran a hand through his long hair and then shook away whatever was going through his head. After a prolonged glance at his handiwork, Clayton threw the sheet back over the car body and turned to the group.

Mrs. Johnston's foot tapped by the door. "Get what you need and hurry!" she instructed.

Clayton pointed toward Grant. "In that closet, grab the ladder. You," he pointed at Lucy, "help him carry it to the hallway."

Then Clayton disappeared into the belly of the workshop, and after a moment he emerged carrying wire-cutters and a cordless blowtorch. He motioned for everyone to follow his lead back out into the hallway and Grant and Lucy lugged the full-sized ladder after him.

"Alright," Clayton said as the door to Metals clinked closed. "Open up this room. Hurry," he instructed, nodding toward the journalism lab.

Lucy raised her eyebrows, perplexed, but she followed them inside all the same, shuffling her feet along the tile, the ladder heavier than she had originally assumed it would be.

The lab used to be a drafting classroom. It was large with heavy cement walls, which the journalism students had painted pink and green. She had been in the room dozens of times, waiting aimlessly for Salem to finish a column or meet a deadline, and she had made a home of the dark blue couch in the corner and perused the journalism teacher's books out of boredom on many occasions. And once, while Salem argued about her advice column with her adviser, when no one was looking, Lucy stole a book of Joan Didion essays. Her intent was to read it and return it, but the book was lost somewhere—it had wandered off and adopted a transitory lifestyle, which Lucy always thought was better for books anyway.

Trancelike, Mrs. Johnston walked inside and straight into the center of the room, not even bothering to flip on the lights. There was no need to engage the overheads because the room was bright enough from a giant skylight in the ceiling. Made of milky plastic, the skylight served an aesthetic rather than functional purpose, and Lucy remembered when it rained the sound of water hitting the material amplified the drops to an alarming degree, making conversation with someone right next to you nearly impossible.

"Of course," Mrs. Johnston said as Clayton and Grant hoisted the ladder upright and stood it up on top of the long tables under the skylight. One leg on one table, the other leg on another table, and when it wobbled, Lucy sucked in a breath. Clayton climbed up onto the table and grabbed hold of the ladder, sliding it this way and that way, and testing its ability to hold someone's weight as it towered to the ceiling.

"She didn't even come to school today," Mrs. Johnston said, crossing her arms over her chest, and wandering to the journalism teacher's desk. "Yesterday we talked about starting herb gardens and taking the kids on a play date." Mrs. Johnston trailed off. She sat down in a big squeaky black chair and leaned back, and she trained her eyes on a row of pictures in frames— smiling faces on the beach, a Pomeranian dog licking a little boy's face.

Lucy remembered that Mrs. Johnston and the journalism teacher had been good friends, always huddling with their heads together at assemblies, sharing class adviser duties, bringing each other lattes in the morning.

It was strange that people were lost instantaneously and their lives released from the world in a moment. Those people were held in memories and nothing more. Best friends absorbed into bedlam in a single breath and simply—poof—gone in one startling second. Lucy was most alarmed by the fact that so many people had died and not any of them could be properly mourned. She grieved for mankind and for herself, but she knew the individual people were already turning into a collective.

Clayton climbed up the first few rungs and held the blowtorch and wire-cutters in his hands. Grant and

Purse Girl each held a side of the ladder while Lucy
looked at the clock. She watched as Clayton reached his
hand up until he could touch the plastic segments, and
when he pushed up on them they gave slightly under
the pressure. He put the wire cutters down and grabbed
the blowtorch, turning it on so the blue flame sprouted
up a few inches and hissed angrily. He began to work
on the plastic around the edges of the first panel,
melting away the sides—they curled under the heat—
their edges turning black. The room began to reek of
burning plastic, but if anyone cared, no one said
anything.

"Are we going back to your room?" Lucy asked
Mrs. Johnston. "We have three minutes."

Mrs. Johnston stood up. The chair turned in lazy
circles behind her. "Clayton?" He turned the blowtorch
off and looked down.

"Five minutes?"

"Keep going," she instructed and she sat back
down.

Lucy took a tentative step forward. "Why risk it?"
she said. "Let's just go back. Then we've earned
another ten minutes."

No one answered her.

She hadn't heard from Salem, but she had sent
three texts about getting to the roof in the East Wing.
Lucy hadn't thought through the next stage of their
plan. If they could get Salem inside, that would be
fantastic, but what happened after that? One thing
seemed clear: The entire plan would be easier if they

didn't already have security looking for them. The journalism lab didn't have windows and the entire room was isolated, and while that worked to their benefit as they plugged along, burning the plastic ceiling away, it seemed to be a detriment if they couldn't plot an escape.

Her tendency to overthink and dwell in restlessness was a trait inherited from her mother. But at least her mother was strong enough to transform anxiety into action. She wondered how her mom would have organized the troops if she were here and she couldn't help but smile at the thought of Mama Maxine swooping in and taking charge, charting their course without room for error. Mama would have already set up camp somewhere, hunkered them down and have them eating an elaborate lunch. She would have found a way to help the people trapped outside while still protecting herself. She would have all the answers. But she was not there; Lucy had not heard from her since her frantic text. All the text messages sent to her mom and Ethan remained without reply.

Her apprehension grew as the second hand on the school's wall clock made its rounds.

They were zeroing in on the point of no return.

Around. Around. Mrs. Johnston circled in the chair. Her face appearing and disappearing in even intervals. Then she threw her foot down and the chair stopped. "Are we close?" she asked and, from atop the ladder, Clayton said he only needed one more minute. He had burned around the perimeter of the whole first panel and now his hand was the only thing keeping it in the air. With impressive dexterity, he handed the blowtorch to Grant and then grabbed the piece with both hands and lowered it down.

Everyone looked up. They had a perfect view of the sky—blue, virtually cloudless.

A mesh of chicken wire covered the four-foot by three-foot hole, but in a moment, Clayton was snipping the metal into pieces, where it fell with small plinks on to the table below. He seemed to sense the question before anyone asked, and he turned to his audience. "Last year, I almost got suspended for climbing up onto the roof during metals class. We spent over an hour up here exploring," he shrugged. "We could hear everything from this classroom on the roof and that's when I realized it was just plastic. I kept thinking, if the wires weren't there and I stepped wrong, I'd just fall right through. It was kind of a funny thought." With a final snip, Clayton had created a large enough space for any of them to fit through.

If they stood on the very top of the ladder, it wouldn't take much to grab the side of the roof and hoist themselves upward to freedom.

Clayton looked down at everyone. "Well?" he asked. "Do we just...go?"

Grant looked at Lucy. She marched over and climbed up on the table, swinging her legs off the floor. She stood and stared up at the hole, frowning.

"Someone should go and check for Salem." Lucy pulled out her phone and punched in Salem's number.

The *All Circuits Busy* message beeped at her. Frustrated, she sat atop the table and felt the cool wind rustle down through the hole.

Then as loud as an air-raid siren, the two-tone announcement bell jolted them into attention.

They all froze.

The microphone clicked and Principal Spencer's voice filled the room.

"Nikki, Nikki. Where'd you take your room of kids?" He cleared his throat, and the noise crackled through the temperamental sound system. "Either you *defied* my instructions or dead bodies just learned to get up and walk away. Whether you like it or not, you are still under my leadership. You have one minute to get back to your rooms…or…"

He paused, baiting them. Lucy stood up. Clayton remained motionless at the top of the ladder. Mrs. Johnston rose from her colleague's chair and walked over to the room's speaker. She stood directly beneath it with her hands on her hips. She looked up at the box expectantly as the intercom hummed.

Then Principal Spencer hiccupped, his words slurred together. "Never mind. Forget it. Forget *you*. You don't want my protection? You don't want my *help*? Then leave. Go ahead. Come to the front doors and I'll let you out myself. I want everyone out of this building. DO YOU HEAR ME?" He screamed so loudly that the intercom clicked off, obscuring the end of his rant.

Mrs. Johnston shook her head. "Moron," she

muttered and rolled her eyes.

"Is he drunk?" Grant asked.

"Absolutely. He keeps a bottle of single-malt scotch in his coat closet," Mrs. Johnston replied and then turned swiftly and climbed up on the table, where she just looked at Clayton, her big eyes wide and waiting. "Well, Clayton, you heard the man. He *wants* everyone out of the building now."

"Sure would've saved me some work if he'd just invited us to go out the front door ten minutes ago."

"You want to go out the front door, be my guest. I'm not holding that man to his word. I'm going up." Mrs. Johnston started to climb the ladder, but she stopped when she traffic jammed with Clayton. "Are *you* going up?"

Clayton looked down at everyone and saluted. "Best of luck comrades," he mumbled and then climbed the rest of the way up the ladder. He grabbed the edge of the exposed roof and using all his upper-body strength pulled himself to the black tarred surface.

"Do you see Salem?" Lucy cried out, grasping the ladder's leg and peering up into the sky.

Clayton didn't answer.

Mrs. Johnston took her turn next. She reached the top and swung herself up. Then she popped her head back down. "Everyone," she started and then her voice broke. "Take care of yourselves," she told them all and then was off. They could hear her footsteps trailing away with the creak of the ceiling and the steady thump-thump above them. They could make out every other word of Clayton's instructions as he directed her to get down. "That way…a dumpster…you…jump."

Purse Girl ascended next. Lucy took over holding the ladder as she wobbled upward—throwing her purse on the roof and then taking Clayton's hand as he helped her past the lip. The girl ran across the roof toward the edge and her running shook the tiles above them.

Grant looked at Lucy and held out his hand.

"I'll hold it steady. Promise," he said and grabbed on to the ladder with both hands.

Lucy stared at the sky through the ceiling. She looked at Grant and patted his arm. "No, you go first," she said.

Grant dropped his hands to his sides. "It's okay. I don't mind. Just go. Clayton can help you up if you're worried. I don't mind climbing up without someone holding the ladder. I'm a pole-vaulter," he paused. "*Was* a pole-vaulter? Look, I'm good at balancing, so I'll go last, and I don't mind. Let me hold it for you." He reached up and grabbed the side, giving it a little jiggle to show that it was sturdy.

She narrowed her eyes. "I'm not *worried* about falling. I'm not arguing chivalry. I'm just…" Lucy looked at him and her shoulders slumped. "I'm not going."

He let his hands slide from the sides of ladder. "Not going?"

"My family knows where I am. Ethan said he'd come back for me…what if…we miss each other. What if he comes back and I'm not here? Plus, Salem." She motioned upward, "She was scared out there and she was trying to get inside. Maybe it really *is* safer in here."

"But...Spencer…?"

"He's one guy. And this is a big school."

Grant looked upward; Clayton popped his head back down. "Hey, are you two coming? You should see it up from the roof. The whole world is just eerie. And it's quiet," Clayton said to them in a hushed voice. "The world is really quiet." He disappeared again, his long hair sliding up and out of sight.

Then they heard it.

A distinct knock against the door. Softly at first, tentative, and then more aggressive. Building, building, and escalating in intensity and loudness.

"Oh great. Just what we need," Grant mumbled and motioned to the ladder. "Okay, no more arguments. Just get up there now."

Lucy looked from the ladder to the door.

The knocking was growing and it sounded like flat fists against the metal door.

Grant looked torn.

"I'm not leaving you here," he said. "It's not chivalry...it's like basic human kindness. But can you please climb this ladder. Right now." He reached out to touch Lucy's arm, but she pulled away, slid down off the table, and took tiny steps toward the door.

"Wait. If it were Spencer, he'd just open it. He has a key."

"Lucy—" Grant banged his head against the ladder. He sounded panicked now. "It may be...there's a possibility that it could be…"

Lucy spun and looked at him. "Please tell me you were not going to say zombies."

"It is a very *real* threat and I wish you would stop thinking that it couldn't happen," Grant said in a long rush. He hopped down off the table and followed after her.

"Zombies knock?" She couldn't help but smirk.

"Nothing good is on the other side of that door, I promise you," he said and he took her hand and tried to pull her backward.

"Stop!" Lucy hushed him.

A voice was calling through the door—its tone hurried and hushed. "Dios mio. Abre la puerta. Lucy? Lucy? I am going to punch you if you don't let me in right now."

Salem.

CHAPTER EIGHT

Salem tripped into the room as Lucy yanked the door open wide. Her eyes traveled from Grant and Lucy to the ladder standing on the table. She took a tentative step forward and raised a finger. "Oh," she said. "You wanted me to come down that way?" Then she smiled. "Thanks, but I found a door."

"A door?" Lucy asked as she wrapped her arms around Salem and gave her a giant hug; she could hear Salem's vertebrae crack as she squeezed.

"Easy, easy. Yes. There are all these large metal chutes up on the roof, they are large enough for a person, and for a while I thought maybe you wanted me to slide down those? But then I found this door and when I opened it there was a staircase bolted on to a wall. Dropped me into the boiler room."

"No one saw you? No one followed you?" Grant asked.

Salem looked at him, her mouth closed, assessing his presence and then realizing there was an absence of anyone else in the room. "Grant Trotter," she stated matter-of-factly.

"Hey Salem," he said back and then: "And no one saw you?"

"Jeez, the inquisition. No one saw me." She collapsed on to the couch and rubbed her eyes with her heels of her palms. "You have no idea how happy I am. I am really glad to see you two," she said, with her eyes still covered.

And then her chin began to quiver.

Lucy sat down next to her friend and watched as Salem let loose and her shoulders shook with rolling sobs. Salem hardly ever cried. She got angry and scared and she yelled and kicked inanimate objects, but she rarely turned her sadness, fear, or nervousness into tears. It was Lucy who was the crier—misting up when teachers corrected her in stern tones, spilling tears over poor exam scores or if her parents wouldn't let her go to the movies. But these twenty-four hours had turned Salem into a blubbering mess. No one could blame her.

Salem turned. "I walked to school, you know? Walked here. I tried to drive, but after I got off my street, it was a total traffic jam. People were getting out and just abandoning their cars. Sirens everywhere and yet the ambulances couldn't get through." She let out a small gasping hiccup and wiped her nose with the back of her hand. In a swift motion, Salem clutched at her crucifix necklace and held the small golden Jesus tightly in her hand. The necklace was a prized possession given to her by her father at her quinceañera. Her mother had wanted to give her a locket, but Salem helped pick this necklace out herself. The icon was a rich gold, the cross, encrusted with tiny diamonds.

Ethan once mocked the necklace one day while Salem lounged on their couch after school. "You're wearing a dead guy around your neck," he said. "And that doesn't make you creepy?" But Salem's response was quick and ruthless; catlike she pounced, slapping Ethan across the face with an open-palm. Not hard enough to hurt, but he recoiled and rubbed his cheek.

"Que dios tenga pieda de tu alma," she spouted as he nursed his wound. "I can forgive a lot. But never blasphemy."

"My God is better than your God," he replied, standing up and running behind their couch. Reckless teasing always turned into a game for him. But Salem wasn't laughing.

"The Kings have no God," she muttered. Then sulked back to the couch; staring blankly ahead, waiting for Lucy to intervene, but Lucy never knew what to say. Salem's faith was a novelty in their household and they tolerated it like she was an exotic pet, allowing her bizarre rituals out of curiosity.

Out of the hole in the ceiling, Clayton lowered his head, his hair tumbling downward and obstructing his face. Salem screamed when she saw him and scrambled off the couch toward the door, continuing to let out worried cries until she saw Grant and Lucy's confused stares.

She put a hand over her chest and inhaled. "It has not been a good morning for surprises," Salem said between gasps. "Next time. Warn me. If you know there is a guy *in the ceiling*."

"Thought I'd check again. Y'all coming?" Clayton called. "I didn't know if I should wait or not?"

Grant made a move toward the ladder. "Yeah, wait up," then he turned back to the girls. "Coming now?" he asked, looking first to Lucy, then to Salem.

Lucy stared at the ladder and she stood up as if she was ready to go. She paused, looking back and deferring to Salem.

Salem let out a low whistle. "I'm not going back outside there. Took enough effort to get *inside* today, I don't think I'm up for a repeat attempt."

"Lucy?" Grant asked expectantly.

Lucy shook her head. "I'm with Salem. I stay with her."

"This place is a prison. And Spencer said he wanted everyone out," Grant replied.

Without saying a word, Salem lifted the side of her shirt. She held it high enough to expose a patch of skin along her ribs and then she tucked the loose end into her bra. Running from her stomach, up her side, was a long red stripe; her skin puckered at the end, a dark hole covered in dried blood.

"What is that?" Lucy asked, rushing over. "Sal! What happened?"

"A man tried to stab me today," Salem responded.

"What the—" Grant muttered and took two steps back toward the girls. "How? Why?"

"Over my water bottle. When I got out of my car, I took a water bottle for the walk. Halfway to school and this guy comes from nowhere and demands I give it to him. I refuse and he tries to grab at my clothes, we struggled, I don't know what happened, and then I just feel this pain in my side. When he was gone, I looked down, and I had this long scratch."

"A scratch?" Lucy looked at Salem her mouth open. "My friend Salem would never call this a scratch. You'd have called me and told me you were bleeding to death."

Salem moved away from the door and back to the couch, she untucked her shirt and let it fall back over the slash mark. "You weren't out there when the news broke today. You didn't see everything with your own eyes…the bodies, everyone so afraid…" Salem choked on all her words.

"Go," she motioned toward the ceiling, "go if you need to. But the threat outside is unknown…the sickness, the fear, the fighting and rioting and the looting. It's *war* out there. There are guns and fires. People are assaulting each other." Salem's eyes went vacant, remembering. Then she rolled on to the couch, tucking her knees up along her belly.

Lucy sat down beside her. Grant hesitated.

"Grant, the threat inside is known. One man. Honestly, the fact that he wants people out of here is helping us. Maybe that's what we want." Salem closed her eyes and then continued, "We can make it work here. You weren't out there today, Grant, Lula. You didn't see it. You survived the hardest part and now we just need to survive the next part."

"Survive what?" Lucy asked. "What are we surviving?"

Salem pointed a shaky finger at the room's TV and Lucy walked over to it and stood on her tiptoes and hit the power button and then she took a giant step back. Grant looked at both girls for a long minute and then he climbed up the ladder; he rested at the top, closed his eyes, his shoulders slumped. Then he motioned for Clayton to continue on without him, and he descended back down to join Lucy and Salem as they glued themselves to the footage of a world descending into mayhem.

The emergency broadcast ticker still scrolled its perpetual warnings.

The pictures were from around the world. Houses in flames, bodies in the street. The US military sprinting into action—armed with gas masks and semi-automatic weapons.

But the picture that made Lucy sick was that of a downed plane; its tail was upright and the body was almost fully submerged in the Columbia River with waves licking and slapping the sides in poetic rhythm. No survivors, the caption read.

They wouldn't have.

They wouldn't have boarded that plane without her.

Maxine King would never have allowed it. There was solace in that single thought—her mother would never leave a child behind. She shook away the image of her family in that plane with their terrifying last moments and life flashing before their eyes. This was not the way it ended, not for her, and not for them. Lucy felt like she would know if her family was gone because she would feel the loss inside her. And she didn't feel hollow and empty; she didn't feel limbless and alone. In her marrow she knew the King family was thriving, and they would come for her as Ethan promised. But knowing that didn't cure how much she missed them. It was an ache so powerful that her legs started to give out, and she tumbled to the floor, the coldness of the tile seeping through her pants.

"Sal?" Lucy asked, turning toward her friend. "Momma and Dad Aguilar?"

Salem didn't move a muscle; her hand still glued to her necklace. After a long moment of silence, she looked down to Lucy. "I'm not ready…I can't." Then Salem turned to Grant, wiping her nose, "How about you? Your family?"

He shook his head. "Normal when I left."

"Nothing was normal," Lucy replied. She pointed at the screen. "This was a planned attack against us. It was totally calculated."

The screen skipped and buzzed—a jolt of static, a mechanical purr. A stark studio appeared and the newscaster from before faced the audience. Again, there was comfort in his appearance, by this small idea that something out there was still up and running like it was supposed to; the world had not quit yet. Here was someone, someone familiar, who was not gone.

But when he opened his mouth to speak, his voice

wobbled dangerously.

He addressed his audience.

"We are in a dire place my fellow Americans. We are at a place untraveled before in our history. By the time the sun sets tonight, it is estimated that over ninety-seven...perhaps ninety-eight percent of our earthly population will have succumbed to the act of bioterrorism unleashed upon us. No group has come forward to take credit for the attack, but it is clear that this group was not trying to send a message. They were simply trying to destroy the earth and everyone on it. The loss of life today has been staggering either through direct contact with the virus or as part of a side effect. That means...if you are watching this...you...me...we are one of the few. The very few."

Salem reached out and grabbed Lucy's hand, sliding her fingers between all of Lucy's fingers until their skin melted together with body-forgetfulness—as if their hands didn't know where one person started and one person stopped. Lucy let those numbers sink in. Ninety-eight percent of their city was dead or dying? In Portland, that meant there were no more than twelve thousand people still trying to cope in the aftermath of the virus. Not enough to fill up even half of the city's soccer stadium. The statistics were overwhelming.

"It is the decision of our dwindling numbers to cease broadcast. Whatever was released upon the world was a well-executed attack by a patient and cautious enemy. Our crops are contaminated, our water supply no longer safe to drink. The misting of some cities with a live virus was a secondary attack. I ask you, those of you here and with me, to remain aware and kind."

Grant slumped against the back of the couch. Lucy saw him wipe his eyes and she turned to look at him. Then with her free hand she reached out to him too, enveloping his clammy hand into her own. They sat there, connected in a line, bonded together with sweat and pain.

"Whatever is left of our grieving earth will be divided into two. Victims of a senseless genocide and those who perpetrated this crime against humanity."

Off-camera someone spoke and a row of lights flickered and the newscaster's eyes watched the studio dim. The TV station's soundstage rumbled and the anchor desk swayed.

"Earthquake?" Salem asked.

"As we speak, this city is under attack. Fires are sweeping up streets destroying what is left. What you hear are..." the desk shook again, a facade of a cityscape toppled backward. *"...bombs. It is unclear from where this particular..."* A resounding clap; the camera shook and glass broke. *"...attack is coming from. But we call to you to be ever vigilant and kind. We will rise from the ashes, but we cannot rebuild on the back of evil."*

The screen erupted with golds and yellows, oranges and then nothing. Only blackness.

The trio sat in stunned silence before Salem peeled her hand free and disappeared to the computer. She tapped the mouse and watched the screen come to life; then she opened a browser and scrolled.

"It's like there aren't any journalists left," she said. "None of the news sites have been updated in hours."

"But the feeds?" Grant asked. They hoped the Internet was not gone completely, although they all knew it was a matter of time before that piece of their world disappeared too.

And Salem's head moved up and down slowly. "People are still updating as they can. And I can't even process it. Come read this stuff."

Together Lucy and Grant walked over to her, peering over her shoulder. They read the statuses and saw the pictures. Each of them gasping or turning away as the realization dawned on them.

Someone had dropped a nuclear bomb on New York City.

The virus had decimated the city first. And the fires and the fallout wiped it off the planet.

CHAPTER NINE

Ding-Dong.

The group jumped at the interruption.

The intercom clicked on.

In that nanosecond between the end of the tone and the start of Principal Spencer's slurred voice, each of them raised their head in anticipation. There was a sharp intake of breath, and then he launched, his breath hitting the microphone like a punctuation mark.

"If anyone is out there…if anyone is left…you have five minutes to reveal yourself at the front office. After that time, I am closing the gates. Do you understand? I am closing the gates. You will lose access to an exit, to food, and to protection. And this will be *my* fortress. And I will not *allow* or tolerate intruders."

There was a loud crash. A shuffling. And then he returned to the intercom.

"Am I clear? Five minutes. And if you don't believe that I'm serious about protecting this place…my health…my building." A shot rang out.

Grant pointed at the ceiling speaker, "Did he just fire a *gun?*"

Lucy nodded.

"Please show yourself at the front office…because I am very welcoming with this gun!" Grant mocked, but his eyes were wide with shock and disbelief.

Lucy nodded again.

"A gun."

"He wants the school all to himself and if he can't do that then he wants supreme rule over the minions," Salem said. "Megalomaniac Spencer till the end. I never trusted that moron and I'm not about to deliver myself to him on a platter."

"I don't think he's crazy," Grant challenged. "I think he's scared."

Lucy looked at them and grimaced. "A man who is afraid for his own life is way more dangerous to us than just some power-tripping jerk," she said.

Despite the warning, they didn't move.

The metal gates were thick metal garage-like doors that descended from the ceiling and locked into the floor with the help from powerful magnets. They were impenetrable; designed to herd students like cattle away from classrooms and into community areas like the gym or the cafeteria. Once Lucy had attended a football game and wandered into the school during halftime. She didn't get very far, stymied by the metal walls. Each time she tried to work her away around them, she encountered another and another.

From the East Wing, the gates would lock at the start of the English hall and math halls and end just past the computer labs before the main part of the school. They would be left with a 'U' shape of accessibility, and Spencer's warning rang true: The cafeteria, the teacher's lounge, the front office—areas with access to food and water—the nurses station and the security office, all would be behind the gates which made it infinitely more difficult for them to sustain themselves for long periods of time.

As the minutes ticked down, none of them made a move until Lucy rose from her crouched position in front of the screen and walked over to the door where a school emergency disaster plan booklet hung in a plastic cover. She took it out and walked back to the journalism teacher's desk, rummaged for a highlighter, and then slapped the paper down in front of Salem and Grant.

"Look," she said and took the cap of the highlighter off with her teeth. "The gates will come down here and here." She drew a line separating the hall to the gym and the auditorium and from the pool to the main office. "And here." She highlighted the gates' locations separating the English hall and the computer lab. "We're locked in."

"Right," Grant said. "Clearly."

"It's to *our* benefit," Lucy replied. "Spencer is keeping himself in the main office. And why not...he walks down the middle hallway and he has cafeteria access and with the exception of the cafeteria courtyard doors and the main entrance, he's isolated himself from intruders too. But—" Lucy ran the highlighter over the English and math hallway and the East Wing. "He doesn't have access to *us* either."

"That's fine, but how will we eat?" Grant asked.

"Easy," said Salem. She pointed at the Boiler Room on the map. "Boiler Room. Next to the cafeteria. The gates going down don't affect us. We have no reason to let him know we're here. It's a big building. We can hide."

Grant looked up to the ceiling and then down at the girls. "How long before he figures out we have open access to the roof and shuts us down?"

"We'll have to be careful, of course. And quiet. Figure out the best times to sneak in and back without detection, but it's entirely possible to hunker down here and fly under the radar," Lucy added. "I'm a little concerned about the roof though. We've created open access for anyone to get inside and people seeking shelter here won't be deterred easily."

"I wouldn't worry about that," Salem said sadly. "If what the news guy says is true, then there won't be many people left wanting to get in. Even by the time I climbed up, the numbers outside were..."

"It's about resources," Grant interrupted, "not how many people are still alive. People will know the school has food. Eventually people will want inside."

"Then we make it hard for them." Lucy walked over to the gaping hole and pointed at the ladder. "Without the table and the ladder, it's a what...twenty foot drop? If we move everything away from the skylight and...I don't know...glass shards?"

At this suggestion, Salem laughed. "Glass shards?

You been watching action-adventure movies in your spare time?"

Lucy sat down on an empty chair and plopped herself into it and stared ahead. "It's not like I'm good at this. It's not like I woke up this morning and suddenly I'm an expert on how to booby-trap the journalism room. None of us are equipped for this. If we even live until morning, I don't know how we'll make it to the next day or the next." Her tone was sharp, cutting in all the right places. Little daggers of truths wrapped in fear.

It was Grant who approached her, standing next to her knee, waiting for permission to speak or help her up.

The tone sounded again. This time they had expected it and they calmly waited for the announcement.

"Ten…Nine…Eight…Seven…Six…Five…Four …Three…Two…One…Zero." Spencer counted down in a lazy drawl. "So. If I'm the only one standing…" he trailed off. "Or if those of you still here don't feel a need to *coexist*." He spat the word like a curse. "This is where I leave you." The intercom did not click off, but Spencer got up from his seat, humming an incoherent melody that trailed away and then came back and then trailed away again—they imagined him pacing along the length of the front office—the microphone for the intercom situated on a box at the front secretary's desk.

Lucy knew that Spencer couldn't hear that he was still broadcasting his movements to the school. There was no speaker for the intercom in the office, so there was no way for him to hear himself. It was to their benefit that he could not detect this because it provided them a distinct advantage.

Students at the school were aware that sometimes the intercom system remained on blast when the people around it thought they had turned it off. Their cheerful and grandmotherly school secretary was most famous for forgetting to shut off the intercom. Once she was overheard calling a particularly rude parent a "douche bag" to a fellow teacher while the intercom still broadcast every word.

Grant, Lucy, and Salem heard a distinct click of a door opening and then a slam as it shut. Spencer was leaving the main office.

Then, in the stillness of the school, they heard the rumble. From the security office, Spencer had flipped the gate switch and the metal bars tumbled downward.

Without fear, they sprang up and ran out of the classroom, Lucy remembered at the last second to shove the doorstop beneath the door before it slammed shut and locked them out. Then they rushed to where the East Wing met the English hall and peered into the openness of the hallway. To their left, they could see the gate hit the magnetic metal locks. Then they braved exposure and wandered down the hallway to their right, peering around the corner only long enough to see that gate shut them in and lock with a distinctive click. Hearts pounding, they scooted back away into the safety of the English hall. Now, unless the gates lifted, they were sealed off from Spencer.

Lucy looked at the empty floor where the young boy's body had been that morning. Someone had moved it. Dried blood and vomit remained stained on the tile, but the boy himself was gone. Moved to his final resting place without fanfare.

And then Lucy noticed something shift in the corner of her eye. Subtle at first, a small twitch, and then a longer sweep: The security camera above them was rotating and scanning the hall. Spencer, sitting in the security office, was on the hunt. Unaware of the camera's range, Lucy grabbed at Salem and pushed her backward into the wall, then pulled Grant's shirt.

"What?" Salem asked in a whisper and Lucy pointed above them. The red light was pulsating and the purr of the lens rotating around was barely noticeable.

"This complicates things," Grant mumbled. He watched the camera and took a step. "Wait," he said. "Wait." The camera whirred to capture the other end of the hall and they had a second to move—the girl's bathroom was mere feet away. While the camera could easily capture the bathroom entrance, it was common knowledge that the bathrooms were free from video. Which was why in her four-year tenure as a student, Lucy had witnessed three girl-fights and two drug deals during routine bathroom breaks.

As the lens scrolled over the top of them, in the second after it could no longer see the bathroom, they bolted and scrambled inside and shut the door, leaning against the back of it, holding their breath and waiting.

"How will we know if he saw us?" Salem asked.

"He'd say something," Lucy whispered. "Call us out on the intercom."

"Maybe not," Grant replied. "Maybe he'd just come for us."

Salem moved away from the door and walked over to the mirror. Someone had scrawled, "You are beautiful to someone" in Sharpie on the expanse of wall between the two mirrors above the sink. Salem put her finger on the writing and traced the words. "We'll hear the gates go up," she replied. "Simple. He says he sees us or he puts the gates up and comes to get us."

"There are three of us and one of him," Lucy noted. This gave her confidence.

"But he has a gun," Grant reminded them.

"He has a gun," Salem repeated.

"But maybe it's just for show," Lucy said.

As soon as she said it, they heard a second shot as it echoed down the hallway and rang out over the intercom.

Spencer's voice yelled and called as he retreated back into the office. "Stop, stop where you are!"

A group of voices called out, distant at first, but then getting closer to the office.

"Get him!" someone shouted.

"Go around! All sides, all sides!"

There was the sound of breaking glass and then a struggle.

A mob had moved in and Spencer was shouting,

his tone vacillating between wrath and sheer panic.

"What's happening?" Salem pushed herself against the bathroom door, as if the fight was bearing down on her, getting closer.

Grant's eyes landed on a spot on the bathroom wall, and he stared at it as he listened intently. It was just noise raining down from above; and it was the noise of things falling apart. "Students. Has to be. I think other students are on the *attack*."

One of the voices, female and young, screamed something indecipherable before someone else yelled, "We're losing Sarahi. She's down...oh no, help her...Somto...wait! Wait! Don't..."

There was another shot and screams. And then they all heard Spencer's voice clear above them. "Get. Out." He was breathless and angry. Something scraped along the floor; there was the sound of muffled shouting and doors opening. "Get out!"

Then: Nothing.

Each of them paused and then at once they let out long breaths.

"Why?" was all Salem said, she looked to each of them.

"This is not good for us," Grant added. "Any kid is now a potential threat to resources and his life. Was it too much to ask for everyone to just *hide*?"

Lucy walked to one end of the bathroom and back—peering into the stalls, with their graffitied walls and dwindling toilet paper supplies. A deserted binder perched precariously against one of the toilets and the wall. There was a picture of a baby taped to the front that reminded Lucy of her binder, which was still in Ethan's backpack left abandoned in Mrs. Johnston's classroom. She made a note to retrieve it when it was safe to go in the hall again.

"There could be others still in the building," Grant continued.

Salem's shoulders slumped. "But maybe *they* don't have roof access?"

"And maybe they do. What do we know?" Grant kept his back firmly planted against the door. His feet fell outward, his toes pointed up. He stared at his shoes.

"I realize this is neither the time nor the place to announce this, but I have to pee," Lucy said. She turned to face them and then shrugged.

"Well, *I'm* not stopping you," Salem replied as if the act of urinating annoyed her and she motioned for Lucy to head into a stall.

Lucy glanced over at Grant. He smiled, his single-dimple appearing in a flash. "I'm definitely not going outside to wait if that's what you want. I'm not getting shot over girly privacy issues."

"I have four brothers. So, I'm not embarrassed to pee in front of *you*." Lucy marched into the stall and slammed the door, locking it for good measure. She pulled down her jeans and underwear, careful not to pull them too low so that Grant, if he were so inclined, would notice the bright blue and pink argyle pattern of her undergarments. After a second, Lucy sighed. "Salem...can you turn on the sink water or something?"

"What? Need inspiration?" Salem asked and soon the sound of the sink filling with water echoed in the small bathroom and Lucy allowed herself to go to the bathroom—she realized as her bladder released, how much better she would feel and she rested her elbows on the exposed flesh of her thighs and closed her eyes. After she was done, she just sat for a long second. It was a second that belonged only to her.

Then she felt wetness hit her exposed flesh; a gush of lukewarm water bubbled up, pouring over the sides, spilling at her feet.

Lucy shrieked and scrambled off the toilet, pulling up her pants and underwear in a quick motion and clawing at the door, yanking it with force. The water had pooled below her feet and Lucy slipped, sliding forward into the side of the bathroom wall; she turned to look as the toilet overflowed—the water was clear at first, and then it turned a murky brown, and it began to spew like a geyser, sending a spray of water and sewage into the stall, drenching the wall and the floor—creating a stream that ran down into the drain in the floor.

Then the other toilets followed suit by gurgling and belching up waste and water. Salem and Grant sprang up and huddled together on a tile near the door while the water crept slowly toward them. But every time Lucy tried to move, she would slip and tumble back down into the wetness. When the water calmed down to a mere trickle, the explosion subsiding, Lucy regained her footing and stood sopping wet in the middle of the bathroom. Her jeans clung to every inch of her skin, scraping along the inside of her thigh like a razor as she took a step forward. She lifted her arms up and watched the water drip with a repetitive *plop-plop-plop* to the floor.

Salem cried out, "Oh no, Lula!"

She wanted to laugh—her instinct encouraged her to let out a giggle. Embarrassment usually garnered this type of response; she wanted to laugh and blush while she wished for reprieve. Her pants were still unbuttoned and she reached to fasten them, but as she looked up she saw Grant and Salem huddled in the bathroom corner, close together, pushing themselves as far away from the water as physically possible. Lucy stifled her smile when saw the fear in their faces.

Lucy took a step toward them, her shoes swishing.

"No, Lucy, wait," Grant said and put up his hand. "Just wait."

The water was contaminated.

The water was poison.

They stared at her as if she were already dead.

CHAPTER TEN

They stood there for a long moment and then Lucy
lowered her arms a bit, feeling the weight of her clothes
pull her body toward the floor. The intercom right
above her broadcast the banal sounds of an empty
office. Then they heard a door click and Spencer started
to hum again. Not happy, jaunty humming, but a
focused and intense hum. There was an edge to his
musical interludes, a hardness to the melody that
seemed entirely for show.

It unsettled her.

Lucy opened her mouth to speak to Grant and
Salem, but as she opened her mouth, she saw Salem
flinch and draw back and place her hand immediately
on Grant's arm with her long fingers wrapped around
his biceps. Grant regarded Salem's grip for just a
second and Lucy saw his eyes flit to his arm and then
back up at her, as though even among the tragedies of
the day, he was still aware of being touched by the
opposite sex.

"No," Lucy replied to a question that hadn't been
asked. "No. This is not the way it's going to happen."

Grant took a tentative step forward, "How do you know it's not contaminated?"

"I don't!" Lucy answered him and her eyes locked in on his. "But we've been around the dead all day. All day! All of us, all day, and we're still here."

"We're allowed to be worried," Salem said in a small voice.

Lucy's eyes flashed to her friend; she swallowed hard and blinked back tears. "Worried for me?" Her eyes flashed. "Or worried for *you*?"

When Salem didn't answer, Lucy bit her lip and nodded. "Right. So, we're all just still alive because we haven't been exposed yet? The bioterrorists polluted our water, our food supply, our air and we just *lucked* out?"

"I don't know how it works," Salem's hand still held on to Grant. Lucy took a giant step forward, her legs stiff. "We just don't know."

"Fine," Lucy tore off her shirt, exposing a thin white camisole beneath. She balled it up tightly and then tossed it into the sink. Bending down she held the heels of her swollen canvas sneakers and slipped out of them too, picking each one up individually and throwing them over to the wall. One hit the wall and bounced back, and it landed on its side, empty and ownerless.

Then she walked right past them, while Salem buried her head into Grant's armpit and cowered as if she were expecting Lucy to hit her, and stormed out into the empty hallway.

Waddling, Lucy walked to her locker and opened it without taking her ears off of the hum, which was now some bizarre arrangement of a familiar Mozart Waltz, and as she approached it, her eyes zeroed in on the camera—the red light was still blinking, but the angle of its lens was abandoned in the other direction. She knew that the cameras were live-feed only. There was a master record of the camera feed, but it was a convoluted series of tapes and buttons and memory cards. Spencer would figure out how to watch the recordings eventually, but they were safe for a small, limited, finite amount of time.

She knew about the camera's issues with recording because last year she had been an unwitting helper in Anna's quest to recover a stolen cell phone. Over an hour she wasted in that tiny security office, the bumbling men scrambling over the camera system struggling to locate the right disk that recorded the right hallway during the right time. It was a total mess and eventually the effort and Anna's prized possession were relegated to paperwork and nothing more.

Lucy knew that an old pair of yoga pants and a tight leopard print exercise shirt, from her first semester PE class and purchased by her mother, who had no sense of style, were stuffed down under the weight of unused textbooks and discarded papers. When she felt the soft fabric hit her fingers, she grabbed and yanked, sliding them out, and catching anything that fell in the process. Her eyes scanned the hall. Grant and Salem were still holed up in the bathroom, no doubt discussing her septic state. Grant, perhaps, bringing up his undead theory to her and bravely volunteering to be the one to attack Lucy with the wire cutters from metal shop if the need arose.

Maybe turning into a flesh-eating monster wasn't the worst thing that could happen. For a juicy moment she realized the idea of attacking her friend and burying her teeth into her arm or leg sounded deliciously evil. She wondered if Grant and Salem really were going to avoid her until they knew if she was infected. It seemed childish and born of irrational fear. Or maybe it was rational fear; maybe their decision was smart and cautious. Either way, it hurt. Then she let the thoughts slip away and slammed her locker shut, the echo bouncing down the hallway. Arguments between close friends were always riddled with personal hurt. Salem, out of all of them, probably had the most exposure to the virus—she arrived from a diseased house and was outside among the infected. Those barbs could have stung, and she wanted them to sting, but she would have never said it out loud to her friend. What good would it have done?

Living would have to be her giant middle finger to them both.

With the clothes in her hand, Lucy walked slowly back to the journalism room and once she was alone, she shed her jeans and her underwear, and pulled the stretchy black fabric of the pants over and up her legs. She took off her bra for good measure and put on the tank top. Then she sat with her back against the couch, her knees drawn up to her chest, and waited. Goosebumps prickled her skin.

Her toes were cool on the tile.

She concentrated on her body. Did she feel sick? What would it feel like? Did people know they were about to die or did it just happen suddenly? If it happened to her, would she have time to say goodbye?

Lucy found a discarded hoodie with their school mascot on it and used it as a blanket. She stretched along the couch and listened to the background noise of the office. She felt her brain pulling her body toward sleep and she resisted. The room was getting darker and she realized she didn't even know what time it was now. Her phone was still in her jeans pocket and it was possibly wet and beyond repair. While her thoughts spun with worry, all her energy left her body and Lucy couldn't even bring herself to check if the phone had survived the flood.

She closed her eyes. Her body sunk into the cushions of the couch.

Sleep claimed her.

Her eyes snapped open.

The room was bright and light.

Lucy tried to sit up, but her body resisted, pulling her back down into the comfort of the fabric. The inside of her mouth was dry and she smacked her lips together and swallowed. It hurt to swallow and she needed water.

Lucy was totally disoriented, forgetting where she was and what had happened to her in the past twenty-four hours. She reached out to silence her alarm clock and felt nothing but air where her bedside table was supposed to be. She tried to tug her comforter around her body, but the fabric slid off and wouldn't cover her shoulders or reach her feet.

"Mom?" she called and then she cleared her throat and sat up. Rubbing her eyes, she looked around and recognized the journalism room and her brain began to make sense of their surroundings. Tossing the flimsy Spartan-themed sweatshirt to the floor, she put her feet on the tile. For a moment she sat with her head in her hands as her stomach growled, and she put her hand over it to silence it.

It didn't take long to reconnect to her reality. She was in the journalism lab at school and she had been sleeping on the couch, there was a hole in the roof, and outside the world was dying. She was cold and shivering, hungry and confused, and to make matters worse, she was alone.

Grant and Salem were not asleep in a corner of the room and they were not awake and waiting for her. If they even came back to the room that evening and had seen her sleeping, she didn't know, but they weren't there now and the anxiousness and heaviness in her chest felt oppressive and unmanageable. The terror of day two was here and Lucy woke up abandoned.

Lucy stood up and stretched. For good measure, she walked to the computer and tried to refresh the

Internet pages, check on the status of the world, but it was futile. Not only would the news pages not refresh, they simply did not exist.

They were off the grid.

She tried to check her feed. Nothing. In that moment, more than any other, Lucy felt her brain grow fuzzy from the realization that she was cut-off. There was no way to connect with the outside world and without the news, status updates, feeds, her endless salvo of human contact would come to an end. Now she realized how much she needed Salem and Grant, without them she would be left with only her overactive brain.

She hurried back over to her pants and found her phone in working order, but empty. Void and lifeless. Not a message, not single a notification. And to top everything off, her battery life was diminishing fast. With a fast-building fury, Lucy tossed the phone to the couch and let out a primal growl.

It was then she heard the journalism door slide open. In the silence of the morning, it was impossible to disguise the subtle squeak and she spun her head toward the sound and eyed a tentative Salem poking her head through the doorway, the rest of her body planted in the hallway. Salem's eyes were wide with worry, but Lucy recognized the look—it was not the fearful expression of someone expecting to find a dead body, but the hesitant mien of someone who was guilty and afraid of being yelled at.

"Good morning," Lucy said, her words clipped

and dripping with as much sarcasm as she could muster. She would not yell at Salem, but she didn't feel like acting particularly warm toward her either. Salem looked behind her, nodded to an unseen lurker and then ventured inside—she was frowning as she walked back over to the couch. Her clothes were wrinkled and her hair matted in the back; her lips were void of her trademark lip-gloss. Salem collapsed upon the couch and leaned her head back and closed her eyes. Her hand found an errant thread, and she began to pull at it mindlessly.

"I'm alive," Lucy said. "Not what you were expecting?"

Salem's face collapsed and she tipped her body over on the couch and she let out a giant, far-reaching wail. Lucy rushed over and sat herself down beside her and stroked her hair. All her plans for stoic and coldhearted responses leaked out of her and Lucy felt only compassion for her crying friend. It was, she supposed, a consistent reaction based on the last few days; there was comfort in knowing what was expected of her.

"Lo siento. Lo siento," Salem said over and over. She sat up and her eyes were bright red, a thin stream of snot dripped from her right nostril and she let it fall until it passed her lip. "Forgive me. Please?"

Lucy looked down. Then she took Salem's hand and held it. "I didn't leave this school for *you*. I stayed with you."

"I know, I know," Salem said. "I was afraid. I can't

lose you Lucy don't you see? I've got nothing else."

She sat up. She had wrapped the thread around her index finger until the skin around it turned white.

"Yesterday, when I woke up, my dad was just hovering over my mom. He was just screaming at me and screaming and I didn't understand. And I ran to call 9-1-1 and the recording said that the hold time was over an hour to reach a dispatcher," Salem looked at Lucy, pleading. "He wouldn't let me near her. All I wanted to do was just touch her...feel her for myself. But he just grabbed me and shoved me."

She grabbed her shirt and lowered it over her shoulder, exposing her collarbone, where a deep purple bruise in an abstract shape materialized. When she was sure Lucy had seen it, she pulled her shirt back up, hiding the pain. Knife wounds, colorful bruises: Salem's adventures seemed so violent compared to her own. Here was her friend and every comfort in her life had been violated.

"Whatever happened to you yesterday...you didn't see your own parent scared, Lucy. I could just see it all over his face, this fear...this total fear. And I said, 'Papa, que pasa? Que pasa?' And he just sat down. In the middle of the floor. Sat down. He sobbed and sobbed because she was already gone...Lucy...there was nothing we could do. She was gone and he thought I was next. But dear God, I wasn't next. And there's no way you can understand that."

From somewhere outside, they heard a crash and a boom. The boom shook the school and the leftover plastic on the skylight rattled.

The girls jumped. Lucy picked the sweatshirt up off the ground and wrapped it around Salem.

"I was afraid."

"I know," Lucy answered.

"Don't let me watch you die."

"That's out of my control." Lucy didn't say it meanly, but she realized as the words left her mouth that it was the truth. Nothing was safe.

"I *can't* watch you *die*," Salem said and she grabbed Lucy's hands.

"I'm not going to die," she said and she smiled to help cover the unease she felt in saying it out loud. She wondered if it was like birthday wishes: Saying it out loud ruined the chance of it happening.

"It's just us now," Salem continued. "It's always been us and now it's *just* us." Then she looked over to the wall and smiled. "Well, us and Grant Trotter."

Lucy leaned her head back. "Strange," she muttered. "Grant Trotter."

"Strange," Salem echoed.

In a swift motion, Salem tucked her feet up under Lucy, connecting their bodies in a tangle of limbs.

It was an apology.

Lucy accepted and she reciprocated by lifting her right leg and laying it over Salem's body. She reached over and tried to untangle a mass of her hair with her fingers, but she didn't get very far; her fingers latched themselves into Salem's waves and got stuck, so she released her grip and then tried to smooth her own hair instead.

"And where is Grant?" Lucy asked. "And how long did I sleep? Did I miss anything?"

Salem gave a half-chuckle and closed her eyes. "Did you miss anything?" She repeated the phrase, amused. "Let's see…Kelsey asked Domo to the prom and that made Kevin Yourn, you know, from ninth grade bio, really mad because he'd been planning to ask Kelsey. Made a video to put online. But she jumped the gun…poor Kevin."

"You don't say."

"Mercedes works at Safeway and told me that she ran into Mr. Russo there and he had Magnum extra large condoms in his cart."

"That's really gross."

"And…I know this is going to come as a huge shock," Salem said in a calm voice, "but I spent the night with someone last night."

"I'm riveted." Lucy didn't even blink.

"It's not what you think," Salem continued with a sly smile.

"It never is."

"Lucy," Salem said, her voice changing—softening, switching, allowing the genuine to poke through. "I think I could like him someday. When everything calms down. When I can get my head straight, you know?"

"Sal—"

"No. I'm just saying it out loud. I know it doesn't mean anything." She closed her eyes and put her head against the back of the couch. "I think he's a good guy."

"Yeah, I know," Lucy answered and grabbed Salem's hand. "So, if you two didn't come back here last night…where'd you go?"

Salem's eyes opened. "You know that little teacher lounge across the hallway from here? The not-so-secret secret one?"

Lucy nodded.

"Unlocked. And there are couches and a minifridge. Bottled water in there too. Not much. We worked for a bit last night trying to get it situated as a more permanent hideout. Even started the morning with coffee and some stale crackers."

The news that Grant and Salem had let her sleep in a cold drafty room while they waited for her imminent demise by equipping a more suitable living space across the hall created a heavy cold ball in the bottom of her stomach. She tried to look excited, but she could tell her mouth was drawing into an inadvertent frown. Salem noticed.

"We thought we'd let you sleep. I didn't think it would be all night," she replied in a quiet voice.

"It's okay," Lucy said. She gave up the moodiness as quickly as it had arrived. There was no way it would do them any good.

"We should've come to get you." She untangled her feet and swung them to the floor. "I was a jerk," Salem leaned her head against Lucy's shoulder. "Lo siento, por favor perdóname mi amiga."

"No, really. It's fine."

"It doesn't have to be...and it's my fault too. Grant asked if we should go get you like a million times—"

"Stop," Lucy said and put her hand up. "It's over."

Salem let out a long sigh. "Then I propose breakfast as a peace-offering."

The crackers were stale and mushy, but Lucy ate them ravenously, shoving one after another into her mouth and swallowing them without tasting. She had not had a bite to eat yesterday and Lucy couldn't remember what they had eaten for dinner the night before; something frozen and overly processed—not because her mother didn't care about her health or about their rapidly-disappearing family dinners, but because trip preparations and concern over dead dogs consumed their evening instead.

She longed for her mother's sweet and sour meatloaf and goat cheese mashed potatoes, honey-drizzled asparagus spears. It was the dish, along with a smooth as silk lemon-lime cheesecake, Lucy requested for her birthday dinner every year. With six children, birthdays were not large-scale affairs. Instead, every child received a dinner menu of their choice, without snarky side comments from siblings and the fear of complaining.

A lump formed in Lucy's throat and she bit back tears. She would not cry over eating mushy crackers and drinking cold instant coffee made from bottled water because she did not want to appear ungrateful.

The room was a find. Windowless with a thick wooden door that blocked out most of the speaker sound, which was currently broadcasting Principal Spencer's throaty snoring, emanating through the speakers in evenly paced intervals, interrupted by jolts of snorts, then settling back down, consistent as clockwork.

The walls were decorated with tacky inspirational posters. A scared looking teacher holding a math book, the message below: *Teachers are people too.* A young girl with tears in her eyes holding out the remains of a broken vase: *Take RESPONSIBILITY for your actions.* Another one reading: *Effort, not excuses, is the key to success.*

Lucy rose from the one of the couches, it smelled vaguely of citrus scented air freshener, and walked over to the first poster. She examined it and then yanked it down off the wall, and the loud rip filled the small space with a big sound. Then she tore each one down, ripping the paper at the corners, leaving little remnants stuck under the imbedded staples.

"There," she said. "Better."

No one replied. Spencer's snores still persisted.

"How can he sleep like that?" Grant asked and he rubbed his eyes, which still looked heavy from sleep, with bags forming in the sockets, the skin tinted black and blue like bruises. "I didn't sleep at all last night." He looked over at Lucy with a questioning gaze.

"I can sleep anywhere," she replied. "It's a defense

mechanism. When my grandma died, they found me asleep in the back seat of our van. I had just crawled there and fallen asleep…"

"I couldn't shut off my brain," he said and closed his eyes. "Wondering if I made the right decision."

"About?" Salem questioned, taking a sip of their cold coffee and grimacing as she swallowed it down.

"About what's going on out there," he said. "Maybe I should go home."

"No!" Salem looked stricken. "We decided to stay. Together."

"Salem—" Grant started, but he stopped himself. He walked to the door of the room and opened it a bit, peering out into the hallway. "Have you thought that maybe we're just taking longer…to die."

"That's an awful thing to say," Salem said softly.

"It's what I've been thinking about all night."

Lucy ate another cracker. She had thought the same thing, but she abstained from entering the argument. Grant's decision to stay or go was his own, and she could not begrudge him his desire to leave. They were relegated to eating leftover teacher food in a glorified closet while a principal with a gun lurked nearby. It was far from ideal.

"We're not helping anyone in here," Grant said. "I feel like a coward. There might be people who need us."

"No one out there needs us," Salem pleaded her case. "How many times do I have to tell you? There's nothing out there but corpses, car crashes, chaos and crazies."

"Maybe my family is out there," Lucy said after a long moment.

Grant looked down at his shoes and kicked his toe against some invisible object.

"Is that why you want to go? Grant?" Salem asked. "To look for your dad?"

"I already told you I don't care about that!" Grant snapped and it was the first time Lucy had ever seen him get upset. Then he hung his head, remorseful. "I'm sorry. But no. I just feel like I could be doing something."

"You *are* doing something!" Salem replied. "You're surviving."

"It's not the same. You don't understand," Grant said and he moved back an inch, half his body in the hall, half of it in the room and he leaned against the doorframe.

"You're absolutely right it's not the same!" Salem was getting fired up. And in typical Salem fashion she had shifted the argument right out from under him. Like a brilliant chess player, she had maneuvered her pieces without anyone noticing and then went in for the kill. "You still have the *possibility* of a family out there somewhere. You're scared and worried, but you don't know. Maybe a friend died yesterday or someone on the track team, but you didn't see your parents take their last breath. So…what then? You want to go be someone's freakin' hero? Go be a hero. But we are not the same. You're not completely demolished yet." She took a breath and pointed a finger to Lucy and Grant. "When *you're* a shell of yourself…then you'll see. There's nothing to conquer out there but more loss."

Lucy's heart beat in her ears as she contemplated replying. Grant looked close to tears, or close to throwing a punch, Lucy couldn't tell which. His whole leg twitched and he bounced it up and down. She knew Salem. Knew that a little pushback would calm her down.

"I won't speak for Grant," Lucy interjected, glancing in his direction, and he nodded his thanks. "But for me? Don't you dare make me feel guilty for having hope that my family is alive. That doesn't take away from *your* grief…"

"I'm not a monster," Salem interrupted, lowering her finger, her voice still on edge. "I'd never take that away from you. I *want* you to be right. I *want* them to be alive. Who do you think I am?"

Lucy stood up. "I don't think any of us know who we are anymore. And maybe we should be allowed some time to figure it out."

It was truth, spoken in kindness. This sudden detour from the ordinary unmoored them from reality and thrust them into a disquiet about the future too difficult to digest. Underneath it all was a permeating worry that their time too was short and that they were treading water until the next wave of loss and horror crashed down on them. Lucy could see it on all their faces, playing out in the blank-glances, the dark circles: The sagging weight of loss.

Grant opened his mouth to respond, but then he turned his head and he opened the door wider. The snoring had stopped. There was rustling on the speaker and they knew what that meant. The man was waking up.

"Food is our first priority," Salem said. "We can stay put and away from the cameras if we have food."

They had listened to the office sounds for fifteen minutes. Spencer left and came back twice. He hummed and mumbled to himself, but the specifics of his one-way conversations were indecipherable. None of his current actions struck them as alarming or worrisome; he had not fired the gun again or sent menacing messages out over the intercom. In many ways, they hoped he stayed away from the intercom, lest he should ever notice it was helping them track his every move in and out of the office.

"So, we need to get to the cafeteria," Lucy stated. "And we can't just waltz through the hallway." It had been a bit since Lucy had checked her phone; she had set it on one of the couches and she grabbed it, but the low battery light blinked and blinked, warning her and threatening her. But there was still nothing but silence. Lucy shoved the phone in her pocket and willed it to keep itself alive for a little bit longer. She didn't even know if cell phones were working, if her wish was wasted.

"Go up the ladder," Grant instructed. "Boiler

room is on the inside of the gates. It'll be easy, as long as Spencer doesn't leave the office. If he goes on the move, we should abort the trip and head back."

"Agreed," Salem said.

Back they trudged to the journalism room where the door was kept ajar with the doorstop. It was easily ten degrees cooler in there with the open roof funneling in wind and elements. The trio worked to move the tables back under the skylight and then drag the ladder upward.

Grant went first, pulling himself up to the roof with sheer upper body strength, his legs following after. Lucy went next, bracing herself each time the ladder wobbled under her weight the higher she climbed. When she reached the top, Grant lowered his arms and pulled her up and she scrambled to the hard surface the second her legs could catch the side of roof. For a prolonged moment, she rested on the cool roof, flat on her belly against the tar. Then she stood and blinked.

Scanning the landscape, Lucy's shock caused her to nearly stumble backward through the hole in the skylight. She regained her composure and took a step forward. The sky was altered, filled with the bright yellows, purples and pinks of an early-morning sunrise even though the sun had been up for hours. Above the colorful hues, the rest of the sky was dark and dense with smoke, and as Lucy opened her mouth to call down to Salem she could feel a sharp taste on her tongue and in the back of her throat. Everything around her took on a subtle orange tint—as if she were wearing thin filtered glasses. The effect of the colors and the smoke and the orange created a dreamlike atmosphere—otherworldly.

She clamped her mouth down and took a tentative step forward. Then another. Walking to the edge of the roof and peering down on to the parking lot below to the dozens and dozens of deserted cars, dead bodies, discarded backpacks, and other personal items littering the area. It was then Lucy realized the earth was strangely quiet, just like Clayton had said. There were no planes in the sky and no cars rushing down the street. The screams and torment of the survivors from yesterday were all gone. Only a few sporadic sounds remained—a crash, a sudden car alarm—and their appearance was jarring, unexpected, frightening, causing each of them to jump and seek out the source with their hearts pounding with fear.

She closed her eyes and listened to the wind. From miles and miles away, she heard the distinct sound of a dog barking.

Then she realized with sadness that she must have imagined it.

CHAPTER ELEVEN

They climbed down into the boiler room and out into the small walkway that connected the room with the main hallway. With their hearts racing and their ears trained on the intercom, they moved with cautious precision. And when they rounded the corner to the hall, Grant leading the front, Salem huddled at Lucy's elbow a few steps behind, they all stopped short and gasped.

Splayed out on the tile was a dead man. He had brown hair and was wearing a blue button-down shirt, jeans, and a walkie-talkie was still in his hand. A thick key ring with at least fifteen silver keys dangled from a belt-loop. The man still looked like a man, but his skin had a greenish and cloudy quality along his bloated cheeks and extremities, as if he had been submerged in a vat of soured milk.

This decomposition was not normal. Not even the Ebola virus could arrive without symptoms, kill in minutes, and reduce the body to rotting tissue within an hour. Lucy knew if her father was around, he would be looking at this virus with curiosity, examining it with a scientist's eye, and she longed for his strength and whatever answers he could give her. Not having him within reach was alarming—she had questions. Who would answer them?

It was difficult to look away, despite the disgust. Grant coughed into his shoulder and then leaned forward, inspecting and assessing the body. He dropped down and squatted, turned his head away from the stench, and started to reach forward, his eyes watering.

"What the hell are you doing?" Salem asked.

With one quick motion, Grant unhooked the silver key ring and swiped it off the belt-loop with a small tug. The keys jangled in his hand and he held them up triumphantly. "Master keys. Locker keys. All keys. *This*," he jangled them, "is a treasure."

"I wonder why his body was left here," Lucy said out loud.

"One of the last adults to get sick, probably." Salem crossed her arms over her body and looked up and down the hall with nervous, shifty eyes. "Come on, I feel exposed."

"Wait," Grant said and his shot up to the cameras. "Where's Spencer?"

They all strained to listen, but the office was quiet.

Then they heard the ring of a telephone. One long ring, another long ring. Then Spencer answered it—off somewhere in the office, away from the microphone.

"The phones!" Lucy exclaimed and she reached her pocket, scrambling. Pulling it free, she stared at the screen, waiting for dormant text messages to start pouring through. A beep signaled that she had a message and Lucy clicked on it quickly. Salem's name popped up. *I'm in the building. Journalism room?* But that was all.

"What? What did you get?" Salem asked, leaning over to look at the screen.

"Just you. From yesterday." Lucy didn't even try to mask her disappointment. She dialed Ethan's number. After five long seconds, the call clicked in. "It's ringing! It's ringing!" she said and she took two long strides back down the side walkway toward the boiler room, shoving her left hand over her left ear out of habit, even though there wasn't any noise to drown out in the background. After four rings, it kicked her to voicemail. Ethan's voice on the message was bright and chipper— and so clear, like he was standing right beside her. She wanted to cry.

"Ethan? Ethan. It's me. I'm at the school. I haven't left. I'm still here. If you make it here, I'm in the—" the phone kicked her off. Lost signal. Lucy growled and shoved the phone back into her pocket. Salem was looking at her and she tried to smile.

"He'll hear it. He'll get the message," she encouraged.

Grant had positioned himself directly beneath a speaker in the hallway; his head upturned, his eyes squinting.

"Who could he possibly be talking to?" Grant said as Salem and Lucy joined him, stepping around the dead janitor in the process.

"Family?"

"No. He's angry. Can you hear the tone?"

Grant was right. The conversation happening halfway around the school and just out of range of their intercom was not a happy one. Spencer's voice raised and lowered, with growing levels of intensity.

Occasionally they heard a snippet.

"*I will control that. Only me,*" Spencer had snapped once. Then a few seconds later, "*No. I will not help. But we can talk.*" Lucy, Grant, and Salem exchanged puzzled glances.

Then there was nothing. A lost signal, an angry hang-up, they could only speculate what ended the discussion and who was on the other end of it. But they now heard Spencer opening and shutting drawers and files with a fury, shouting to himself as he went: "*No. My school. My rules.*"

Salem lowered her head from looking at the ceiling and scowled. "I don't like this."

Grant took one look at the camera. "Me neither, but while we know where Spencer is…" he pointed to the red light blinking at them, "let's get what we need and go."

The three of them bolted into the cafeteria—running together against the wall; trying to stay on the outskirts as much as possible, crawling behind tables and using stacked benches for cover. Out of all the areas in the school, the cafeteria was most covered with cameras. Every corner boasted a device—sometimes several—and there were limited blind spots. Ducking behind a metal food cart, the trio the scooted to the back of the cafeteria, where the industrial refrigerators hummed.

None of them had entered the kitchen before and they stood in awe of the prep area and the pantry, the freezers, and the endless rows of stainless steel pots and pans. Sterile and polished, everything gleaned brightly.

"I never actually thought any *cooking* happened in this kitchen," Grant mused. "Like these have to be just for show." He pinged a hanging saucepan with a flick and drew back, rubbing his nail.

Lucy walked over to the walk-in freezer and unlatched it, opening the door wide—a cloud of cold air billowed up at her as she walked inside. She was instantly freezing as she rummaged around boxes of frozen peanut butter and strawberry jelly sandwiches, the kind with the crusts removed, all the ingredients jammed into a bread pocket. The frozen options were limiting: Meat patties, chicken nuggets, pre-cooked French fries, burritos. Lucy didn't know how they would cook the frozen items or if there was some cooking rule on letting a frozen meat patty defrost in a refrigerator for an unspecified amount of time. That was a question for a mom or the Internet and neither of those things were readily available.

"Take what you can carry," Lucy instructed the others.

A drawer near the back yielded industrial size garbage bags and Grant handed one to each of them so they could start collecting food. They flipped them open, spreading the top wide and started filling it with anything that could be stored, consumed, and transported with ease. Salem grabbed milk cartons and sandwiches and then she turned her attention to a metal rack that held small bags of pretzels and corn chips.

"What about the fresh stuff?" Salem asked, palming an orange.

Grant shook his head. "Too risky."

"How long does it take to get scurvy?" Lucy asked.

"Like sailors or whatever?" Grant shrugged. "Months?"

Salem dropped the orange back into the crate. She took a few steps and opened up a refrigerator and examined the shelves stocked from top to bottom with juices and water in plastic bottles. She smiled and started dumping then two at a time into her bag.

The bags began to drag on the floor, heavy from an abundance of food, snacks, and bottled water.

"This should last us. What a goldmine," Grant said excitedly.

"A statement that has never been said about a school cafeteria in the history of school cafeterias," said Salem. She hauled her bag over her shoulder and started to walk forward, hunched over from the weight.

"I wish we could get into the vending machines," Lucy said. "Swedish fish and red vines, chocolate chip cookies, and peanut butter cups."

Spencer's voice erupted above them, the cafeteria speakers echoing in the empty space. They jumped and it reminded them that their time was limited. Each heaving their loot, they began to work their way back to the boiler room—taking slow and deliberate steps, like cartoons figures tip-toeing away from a snoring enemy.

They climbed back up the metal ladder embedded into the boiler room wall and pushed open the small square on the ceiling that allowed them roof access. Then they skipped and ran back to the skylight in the East Wing, keeping their bags hoisted on their backs as they slid down the opening, their feet blindly searching for the ladder, kicking this way and that until the wooden steps materialized and guided them back down to safety. Then Grant carried the ladder down and shoved it up against the wall and slid the tables away as well. The skylight still offered a wayward outsider entrance, but they still hoped the long drop on to the tile floor was enough of a deterrent.

Without a word, they meandered across the hall like weary roommates arriving home from a shopping trip. Grant swung the door wide, the girls sliding inside as he fumbled for the light. Lucy dropped her grocery bags and walked to the far corner. She sat down on one of the small red couches, her bag between her legs, and she opened it wide, rummaging around, counting and assessing.

Her cracker breakfast left much to be desired and Lucy couldn't resist the thought of thick peanut butter and sweet jelly; she grabbed a sandwich, still partially frozen, and began to gnaw on it, succeeding in breaking off pieces of bread and hardened jelly between her teeth, and she rolled it around her mouth, warming it with her tongue.

As if she had reminded each of them that they were hungry, Grant and Salem also descended upon the bags like a pack of wolves. They crouched over their plundered food and began to eat it on the spot. Grant opened a bag of pretzels and a water bottle and Salem downed a bottle of juice, each of them depositing their garbage in the corner.

"We'll dump our garbage next door," Lucy suggested. "Grab a bag and then lock it up in the wood shop or something."

Grant dangled the keys. "This might help," he replied. "Locker keys."

"Nice," said Salem, making a grab for them, but Grant whisked them out of her reach.

"What do we need?" Lucy asked. She surveyed the room again. They had two small couches and a big leather chair, a small wooden desk with the coffee maker, a half-empty bookshelf, a large built-in cupboard with paper cups, a stack of computer paper, and a box of old t-shirts advertising a canned food drive from six years ago.

She turned to Grant. "I want a classroom key. I want my backpack." Grant wiggled a key free and slapped it into her upturned palm.

"I'll open all the lockers in a section and we can go through them piece by piece. Save anything essential, right?" Grant asked.

They nodded.

They made the trek down to the English hall. Lucy

let herself into Mrs. Johnston's room and went straight
to Ethan's backpack, slipping it up over her shoulder,
holding on to the strap tightly. More than anything,
Lucy wanted to be reunited with her pictures. She
looked around the room and assessed the familiar
quality of it. Everything now seemed so foreign, so
strange, and so empty. Pausing by Mrs. Johnston's desk,
she scanned the pictures, the notes from students and
the ungraded papers.

She hoped that Mrs. Johnston made it home.
Hoped that her family was waiting; hoped that she had
water and food and a plan. Some people deserved a
happy ending, Lucy thought. And Mrs. Johnston was
one of those people. She stopped for a second and
opened up Mrs. Johnston's desk drawers. She nabbed a
bottle of ibuprofen, but couldn't find anything else of
use—various office supplies, a thank you note, a tube
of lipstick, and a nail file. She left the remaining detritus
undisturbed.

When Lucy exited the room, she saw Grant
opening lockers wide with the key and Salem swooping
in to plunder. They worked as a team, standing side-by-
side, yanking and pulling, flipping things over and
tossing it to the ground.

It felt so wrong. But it was also so necessary.

Maybe the items in the lockers were important, but
these were still artifacts of someone else's life, tucked
away for them to discover and judge. Within minutes
Grant and Salem were tittering over some of their finds:
Packs of condoms, a locker turned shrine for some

overly auto-tuned pop star. Salem unearthed a collection of phones and music devices, treasure trove of technology, stuffed in a shoebox under unused textbooks and half-eaten sandwich.

Grant spun to Lucy. "Hey, I unlocked a row over there," he pointed to a section that included Lucy's own locker. "Want to start on those?"

Lucy gave pause to the instructions; she took a long look at Grant and Salem's tag-team duo. Right then, Salem shrieked as she pulled out a pair of bright pink thong underwear and held it between her pointer and thumb fingers and she tossed them at Grant, who sidestepped away from them as if they contained the virus. The chumminess bothered her, but she couldn't put her finger on why. She couldn't command them all to stay morose and depressed, it wasn't healthy. It was fine to smile, find distraction, but still Lucy couldn't escape how tactless the playfulness felt.

Stewing, Lucy walked over and pulled the first door open wide, letting it crash a little louder than she might have wanted. Then she went to the next, then the next, and then the next: Garbage, books, binders, chewed-down pencils, magnetic mirrors. Love notes from boyfriends, girlfriends, lunch bags, rotten fruit. The more lockers she searched, the more she realized how unsurprising the items were. When her classmates were reduced to things in a locker, they were impossible to differentiate from one another.

She stopped and leaned her head against one of the doors. It moved under the pressure and she could feel the metal digging into her forehead.

"Find anything? Salem called to her. Then without waiting for an answer, "Oh, gross…Grant…look at this one…"

Lucy raised her head from the door and sighed. She went to the next locker and rummaged through the usual assortment of items. Then she shoved a paper bag out of the way and realized that it didn't budge. She picked it up, unnerved by the heaviness, and looked inside. It was then she caught the shiny flash of silver and the black handle. Roaming around at the bottom of the bag was a handful of copper bullets, clinking against each other.

In the background, Grant and Salem expressed amusement and intrigue over someone's large collection of American flags. They found a small pill bottle filled with Vicodin and high-fived at the find.

Lucy reached into the bag and took the gun in her right hand, and she let the bag fall to the floor where it fell to her feet. It was a revolver, like the cowboys in Westerns used to shoot. She examined it, rolling her hand over and she noticed the tremors in her fingers. She had never held a gun before, never felt the weight of it against her skin. Lucy recalled, with embarrassment, when her mother first dropped her off at Salem's house for a play date, she took Mrs. Aguilar aside and asked brusquely if they had any guns in the house. "No. Of course not," Mrs. Aguilar had answered in return, her face struggled against showing her offense. Only then did Maxine leave Lucy, kissing her for a second too long on the forehead and whispering instructions to call if she got homesick.

They did not own guns. Her father did not hunt.

And here she was, holding this gun and wondering—what did it mean? Why was it here?

Hidden in a lunch bag, with bullets.

Who did it belong to?

Lucy pondered the danger of it all, and she tried desperately to place a person at this locker mere feet from her own. Who opened it? Who sat under it in the morning? Had she ever been in danger?

But then the realization poured over her: Whoever brought this gun to school was likely dead now. Their intentions—to intimidate a bully, self-harm, bragging rights to friends—didn't matter anymore. She pondered putting it back in the locker and shutting it back up, burying it under a geometry book and gym socks, hidden out of sight. Then Lucy realized that this could be a blessing. She spun and held the gun resting in the palm of her hand

"Sal? Grant?" Lucy called, aware of the rise in the timbre of her voice. "I found something," she said and turned to her friends, holding the gun flat in her hand.

"Is that a—" Grant started and he took a step. Sal turned around. She was holding a giant fleece blanket in one hand and a bulk container of hand-sanitizer in the other. She opened her mouth to speak, but then her head snapped quickly to the right.

They all heard the clank and rumble of the gates as they moved upward, unhooking from their magnetic bases. They were exposed. Lucy's eyes darted to the camera and it was trained directly on them.

"The intercom is off," Grant shouted and he scrambled forward to collect the items he had set aside. "We didn't even notice…dammit…we didn't even notice!"

Spencer had spotted them. He had been watching them and he knew they were there; knew they were hiding. But more disturbingly, he knew they had a gun.

CHAPTER TWELVE

"Shit!" Grant yelled and he tugged Salem's arm toward the East Wing hallway, pinning a collection of confiscated locker items to his side. "Lucy, come on!"

Lucy leaned down and grabbed the paper bag of bullets and darted forward, her bare feet slapping against the floor. But instead of turning up the narrow hallway, Lucy ran straight past them and down the English hall, toward the opening gates and toward Spencer.

"Are you crazy?" Grant called after her. "We gotta get out of here."

Out of the corner of her eye, she watched the camera and its subtle shift following her. She slowed at the turn and then peered around the corner.

"Wait," she yelled to her friends, her voice was shrill and panicky. "Don't go anywhere!"

Salem and Grant stood waiting at the edge of the hallway, ready to run, but Lucy kept peering around the corner. It was a long hallway to the main office and security office, roughly one hundred feet, but she had a perfect view. Unless Spencer was lying about being alone, there was no way he had time to man the cameras and also bolt after them.

"He's still in the security office, just watching," Lucy called to her friends.

"You sure?" Salem called.

Lucy nodded. "He put the gates up so we would run…so he could watch where we ran to." Her heart pounded as she kept her eyes trained on the hallway, watching for Spencer's lanky body to come barreling down upon them.

"I have an idea," she called back to them. "Go to the lab, put the tables back and the ladder up. Then wait by the door for me. Don't leave the lab until I come for you."

Grant shook his head, just once, a quick and sudden shake and stepped back out into the hallway. "What? You're bait?"

"I'm bait," she replied and then drew in a tight breath.

Salem opened her mouth to protest, but Grant saluted her. "Good plan," he said with admiration. The tone encouraged her, helped stay her shaking hands a bit. Lucy didn't have a real plan other than to draw Spencer out of the security office so she could get them safely in their hideaway without detection. And if that didn't work, she was fresh out of back-up plans.

Grant and Salem darted out of sight.

Lucy took a deep breath and with her back to the camera, she dropped the gun back into the paper bag. She crumpled up the top and then held it tightly in her hands. The gun was not an asset if Lucy didn't know how to use it. She knew that Spencer was armed and she was not, but it was a risk she had to take.

She slid back out of view and pressed her back against the wall. The camera was on her. It moved, zoomed in, zoomed out. Spencer was no doubt watching Salem and Grant lead him to the journalism room, but there was Lucy, unmoving, a sitting duck. He had to wonder why.

For a second she wondered if Principal Spencer recognized her. If he knew her name or her year in school. She wasn't an athlete or a drama kid. She never took a student council class and despite Salem's pleading, she never wrote for the newspaper. Before all of the madness started, Lucy assumed that she would graduate from Pacific Lake with relative anonymity. She would be the person her classmates years later would sort-of remember as that "one girl in that one class". People would try to pin down a list of defining characteristics, but they couldn't.

Then she heard the echo of a door shutting. She peeked around the corner and saw a flash of movement and a blur of gray and black. She glanced at the camera and stood up, she sprinted forward a few steps and then turned—the camera had stopped following her. At that moment, she could recognize the loud pounding of feet racing down the extended hall. Her breath catching in her chest, she made a dash for the East Wing.

And that was when she heard the shot.

A blast echoed down after her and Lucy jumped.

She ran wildly, hitting her shoulder against the wall as she turned the corner, her body unable to keep up with her feet. Lucy ran up the East Wing hallway, around the corner, and up to the lab where Salem stood guard in the doorway and Lucy yanked her out, motioning for Grant to follow, but he was still carrying the ladder into place, holding it with outstretched arms, wobbling forward with obscured vision.

"Who has the keys?" Lucy asked, out-of-breath.

Salem shook her head and pointed at Grant.

They heard Spencer's footsteps pound down English hall and then heard him turn into the East Wing hallway. Like a honing pigeon—he knew where they were. A second shot rang out and the blast seemed much louder and menacing than before.

Lucy ran back into the lab, terrified that they were too late. Her plan was failing, instead of leading them all into security, they were going to be caught and shot by a crazy man.

"Keys Grant! Keys!" she whispered, cognizant that Spencer could now hear their voices echoing. But Grant was positioning the ladder under the skylight with both hands and unable to grab them. "Hurry, hurry!" Lucy commanded and Grant stepped back, dug into his pants, and pulling out the jangling janitor's keys he ran toward the door.

Salem was wracked. Her face was flush with spotty red circles and her hands had gone ghostly white. Lucy opened her mouth to talk, but Salem shook her head violently to stop her. Spencer was close.

They all heard him and his shoes on the tile in the East Wing. He was walking with purpose, but no longer running, as he stopped to peer into rooms. The art room door had been propped open with a garbage can and Lucy only now registered the luck of that. As they pushed themselves to become one with the wall, they listened as he yanked the door open and then disappeared inside.

"Now," Lucy mouthed and Grant opened the supply closet door. They flew inside. Shut the door and locked it without a sound. And sank to the ground.

"He's going to find us, he's going to find us," Salem mumbled.

"Stop," Lucy said and crawled over in the darkness to her friend.

A sliver of light was all they had—illuminating a few centimeters of carpet beyond the door and nothing else. Lucy waited for her eyes to adjust to the darkness, but they never did. It reminded her of her freshman photography class, when Kyle Ingwood took her into the tiny rooms where they unrolled their film, and tried to kiss her in the complete darkness, his lips groping the air and then the side of her chin before finally landing on her lips. Photography class suffered extinction at the hands of budget cuts the following year and Kyle never spoke to her after their messy make-out session in the dark.

But she still could taste the dark in that room. With her eyes wide open, she could not register anything around her; the thickness of the dark was oppressive.

Pitch-black.

No outlines of the couches or of each other's bodies as a reference as the room pressed down on them. It weighed on them like a heavy blanket—the sound of waves inside a seashell hummed near their ears. Lucy struggled to take a breath, her head pressurized like she was in an airplane.

Spencer was done with the art room and he paused outside the woodshop. They collectively held their breath. And Lucy had to cover her mouth to keep from screaming when they heard the rattle of the doorknob into their hideout. He turned it once and then twice, pulled on the door, found it locked, and soon gave up the idea. Spencer then must have seen the door ajar to the journalism room, because they heard the door creak open, and without warning or fanfare he was walking away from their hiding spot. For a brief second, the fear of discovery left them like a deflating balloon.

They heard the tumble of the ladder as it crashed to the floor and hit the desk along the way, then the scraping of desks, the push and screech of metal on tile. And afterward: Nothing, just silence. They waited to hear him exit, waited—holding their breath—to see if he would examine every room in the East Wing. After a long moment, the journalism door swung open, hitting the wall with blunt force and then shutting with a distinct click. Spencer's heavy footsteps walked away from them—away, away—until they couldn't hear anything anymore.

"Is it safe to turn on the light?" Salem asked.

"No," Lucy answered. "Not until we know he can't see us for sure."

"The cameras in the East Wing don't show this door," Salem added. "I don't want to sit here without being able to see...it's suffocating."

Lucy waved her hand around until she felt the cotton of Salem's shirt and then felt for her hand, grabbed it, and gave it a squeeze. "He might come back."

"We'll wait," Grant said, his voice floated to them from somewhere near the door. "We have no intercom now. No way of knowing what's happening out there. So, we wait."

They listened intently, but couldn't hear a sound.

For minutes, long hour-like minutes, they waited.

Lucy curled up on the floor, the scratchy carpet rubbing against her cheek, as she felt her body melt against the fibers. Even though she struggled against it, Lucy found herself succumbing to sleep. She wished she would will herself to stay alert, but sleep dragged her down into a fitful abyss.

She dreamed Spencer found them. Yanked them out by their hair and dragged them to the auditorium where the boy who had died right in front of her was inexplicably alive, but bleeding out his nose and eyes. The blood pooled at his feet, thick, red, and sticky and his mouth was moving, but no sound came out. As they were pulled past him, his arms shot up he reached for

Lucy's kicking feet.

Defying physics, Spencer hoisted them all on stage and tried to deposit their broken and tired bodies into the dressing room, which was filled to the top with bodies like a hall closet shoved with piles of junk and clothing. But Friendly Kent sent them away. *"No room. No room. No room."*

So, Spencer grabbed them back and took them to the pool. The cement cavern was now a mass grave of tangled bodies. He threw them into the sea of limbs and blood. Lucy tried to get out, flapping her arms forward and gaining leverage against the dead, but she couldn't make any progress forward. The dead pulled her down into them and she sank, as if their mushy decomposing bodies were quicksand or a riptide. Frantic and calling for Grant and Salem at intervals, Lucy gripped a body and the head rolled over to her.

It was Ethan.

She screamed and pushed his bloated features away. Her scream echoed, carrying on for ten full seconds and it appeared to trigger something as select tiles in the ceiling slid out of the way, creating cavernous black holes.

From the ceiling, green and orange snakes descended. Their blood red fangs gripped dead rats in their mouths. But even Lucy could see that the rats were also decaying, clumps of their fur was missing, holes in their sides oozed thick white pus. Down the snakes, with their prizes, slithered, sliding in and out of the masses, appearing and disappearing and reappearing.

As Lucy tried to pull away from the creatures, she saw a mass of dark hair the same color as her mom. The body ebbed and flowed toward her and away from her. Lucy reached out to touch the hair and get a closer look. She needed to know. She had to know.

The face started to shift toward her and Lucy put a hand on the back of the dead woman's head.

But as the face rolled into view, Lucy scrambled backward. The woman had no face; there was just a giant gaping hole where her features used to be.

It was the pounding that woke her.

Vigorous strikes of a hammer against wood. *Thunk-thunk. Thunk-thunk. Thunk-thunk.*

Grant mumbled and his clothes rustled in the dark as he fumbled around, trying to sit up.

Then they heard the creaking of footsteps on the roof, the dragging of material across the tar, a crash, and then more hammering.

"He's on the roof," Lucy said, sitting up, rubbing her eyes.

"What's he doing on the roof?" Salem asked sleepily.

"He's on the roof!" Lucy said again and shot up, stumbling forward, kicking an empty juice bottle, and reaching for the lights. When she hit the switch, the room lit up brightly and they all groaned and covered their eyes, squinting and adjusting. Grant and Salem looked at her, failing to grasp Lucy's urgency. "He's blocking us in. He's taking away our escape route. Between the gates and covering our roof access? We will be stuck in the East Wing."

"You think he knows we're still here?" Grant asked, standing up and stretching.

"No," Lucy shook her head. "I think he thinks we bolted."

"Good, then we're safe!" Salem let out a long breath.

"No," Lucy said again through clenched teeth. "We're not *safe*. And we *are* definitely trapped."

"We need to get the stuff we dropped when we were running away."

Salem confessed that she had dropped the loot from the locker cleanout on to the blue couch in the journalism room. "But I suppose we can't go in there now…it's lost forever."

Lucy opened the door slowly, just a crack, and waited for the hammering to start to open it wider. "Grant…unlock the journalism lab."

"Are you crazy? Spencer's right up there," Salem put an arm out as if to stop Lucy. "I want the stuff too…but we should wait."

"You're right. You're right," Lucy nodded. Then she turned to Grant, "Unlock the woodshop instead."

He nodded and worked fast, sneaking out into the hall, with the hammering above them as a beacon of safety. Grant let Lucy into the workshop and then took off down the hall, running out of sight. Lucy turned on the lights and scanned the shop for what she was looking for: Any block of wood that could cover the small gap between the door and the floor of their hideout. She found a pile of scraps and among them a sawed down two-by-four. She estimated it was four feet long and so she grabbed it, lugging it out into the hallway and back into the closet.

Salem was sitting on a couch, her knees tucked up, waiting. Her hair was matted on one side. Lucy shut the door and set the board down across the floor. It was a perfect fit and it blocked out their light. Since the door opened outward, this was the board's only purpose, but it gave Lucy a small bit of relief about keeping their light on during times when Spencer, on patrol, could see it.

The hammering stopped, but they could still hear Spencer on the roof, his heavy feet walking around the perimeter of the East Wing. Lucy imagined he was exploring for other points of entry. If the stairs in the boiler room were the official roof access point, then Lucy knew that he would take care of that too. She had to give Spencer credit, if he wanted his school secure he was doing everything in his power to make that happen.

When Spencer resumed hammering, Grant singularly recovered their blanket and hand sanitizer, a box of Kleenex, a deck of cards, and an assortment of sweatshirts and pill bottles. He shifted in and out of the journalism room swiftly and undetected.

Then they sat back.

"What do we do?" Salem asked.

"We wait," Grant answered.

They pulled out the deck of cards and played a lazy game of Go Fish; Salem had to be told she won and she barely registered the news before dumping her winning collection in the middle of the floor. For an hour they heard the incessant pounding and dragging above them before all went quiet.

When everything had been silent for a long time and they were certain Spencer wasn't returning, they darted across the hall to assess the damage. The ladder was still on its side on the ground, the tables tossed over too. Where the room used to glow with the light from the open hole was now dark. The skylight had been covered with long slabs of wood, but not just the hole they had created—Spencer had nailed wood over the entire plastic skylight section, blocking the sun entirely, and preventing them from recreating their escape route on another section.

This time, there was no announcement—no intercom interludes to give them peace of mind. He had locked the gates, he had closed their escape and he could watch and wait for them to make a mistake and reveal themselves. They had a small gun and limited bullets and a small room with limited resources to sustain them. Eventually they would run out of food and water; and that worry nagged at Lucy most of all.

Darkness fell over their second night.

They wouldn't have known it was dark, except

their phones broadcasted the time for them. Lucy's phone had a live background that displayed an open field and a sun moving across the sky throughout the day. The background was now darkened shadows and stars, a crescent moon. Her battery life was now at 5%. The phone hadn't succumbed to its low-battery or cracked screen. It was a miracle.

Every once in awhile they thought they heard something outside, but they couldn't tell if it was inside or outside or from which direction. Their cubby was insulated.

They devoured another round of peanut butter and jelly sandwiches and drank bottled water. They discussed the problems of where to pee and decided that the faculty bathroom mere feet away was too risky. So, Grant set up buckets in the woodshop—each of them claiming a canned food drive shirt to use as toilet paper. It was disgusting and inhumane, but it was the reality of their situation.

"When should we turn out the light?" Lucy asked. "Just to be safe?"

Nobody responded.

"Patrick Miller," Salem said the name slowly as if it had just come to her—as if she had been trying to remember it for ages.

"What?" Grant asked. He stopped playing basketball with the torn up pieces of poster paper. He had been lobbing them upward and trying to land them in a paper cup on top of the refrigerator. "What about him?"

Lucy turned on her belly so she could face Salem and propped herself up on her elbows.

"Patrick Miller was a crush I had sophomore year. Right after I got back from Texas. Just this total goofball. Moved here from somewhere in the South and had this thick Southern accent. Do you remember him at all?" Lucy shook her head. "He played piano and wore a tie to school sometimes for no reason. And he was totally unpopular, but I liked him. I felt like I should maybe go on a date with him anyway, even though I was nervous, didn't know what people would say. How silly does that sound...but I thought it would be too big a risk to my social standing. So, then he started dating Brittney Phillips and I just got pissed."

"The cheerleader?" Grant asked. He resumed his paper-shooting game. Aim. Shoot. The paper bounced off the rim, the cup toppled over and fell to the floor. He looked at it like he wanted to pick it up, but didn't move.

"Yeah, that beautiful, perfect little cheerleader. Who—on top of being the only cheerleader who could pull off stunts—was also like super nice? And she took calculus. Super nice calculus taking cheerleader. Ugh. And she really liked him, you know?"

"I don't remember her dating anyone," Lucy said. Just to say something, anything. Just to be a part of the conversation, but she knew better than to question Salem's recollection of events.

"Well, it was like a *six* month thing. Went right into the summer. Then something happened and they broke it off the next school year. That doesn't matter. Brittney, true to form, never said anything bad about him. And he dropped the ties and started hanging out with the student council kids and joined yearbook. One day I had to go ask him for a yearbook photo for an article I was writing and I just felt all clammy. Like, well, here's my chance. But I mean...seriously...Brittney Phillips? I convinced myself that my first crush on him was because I felt sorry for him. But that he was gonna be alright, you know? He *survived* that first year here, got a hot girlfriend, made some friends. And I wanted to be like, you know, I liked you first. I liked you *before*. Hey, Patrick. Remember when you would sneak into the band room and play Beatles songs on the piano? I stalked you and would listen. And I kinda fell in love with you. And I'm kinda sorry you're popular now. Because I kinda, actually, want you all to myself."

Salem shrugged and picked at lint on her pants.

"You never told me about him," Lucy replied.

"Yeah, well, I thought you might tell me to go for it," the corners of Salem's mouth turned up into a soft smile. "And what-might-have-been is always easier than well-that-was-a-disaster."

"The dream is better than the reality," Grant affirmed.

"Exactly. But it wasn't entirely just in my head. He was the *coolest* kid I ever wanted to be with. And I never told him." Salem looked to all of them. She sniffed. "Here's the thing though. He was out there today trying to get into the school with me."

Grant and Lucy looked down at the floor—Lucy lowered her upper body to the floor and rested her head on her forearms.

"One minute, he was there. I saw him and I was going to talk to him. The next minute, gone. Just like that. People moved him out of the courtyard and just dumped him on the grass, like he was garbage. Patrick Miller, the boy I still thought well, maybe, in the future. After college even. Or maybe I could just say, I don't know, just admit that I liked him. And now it's not even that I'll never get to say it. It's not even that. It's this idea that he's completely gone. And I want to remember him. I just keep thinking of everyone who will never be remembered. How sad is that? And there won't be memorials or funerals or...I mean...they don't even get their own time to be remembered. Just another body."

Lucy felt the tears building. She sniffed and let them fall. "Yeah. I thought that too," she said.

"I'm sorry, I didn't mean to—" Salem paused. "It's just—" her hand went up to her crucifix and she spun it along the chain.

"I get it," Grant said. "I understand. Their lives mattered." There was a long pause and then he added, "Amanda. Amanda Starr."

"I knew her," Salem said and closed her eyes.

"Yeah. She was my first love. For a whole summer she came to my dad's farm and we swam in the little creek by my house and we'd ride horses. Then in September, the day before school was starting...she came out to me. She was too embarrassed to tell anyone. She said she always knew since she was little, but that her parents told her she just needed to find the right guy. We talked for hours. It was actually a really good moment. I told her I loved her. And she asked me not to tell anyone. She said she wasn't ready. That we'd take it to our graves."

"I didn't know that. Amanda was gay," Salem repeated the news slowly and shook her head. "What else didn't we know about people? People we saw every day."

There was a bit of jealousy in her voice; here was a juicy piece of someone's life that Salem was not privy too. Something she had missed, that someone else knew. She looked at Grant with adoration and begged for him to keep going. "What else? What do you remember? What were you too afraid to tell someone?"

So Grant cozied up, wrapping the fleece blanket around his legs and leaning his head back. "I don't know…what do I remember?"

Slowly, slowly, they brought classmates back to life with humor and anecdotes. The spilling of secrets that no longer mattered.

Lucy contributed when she could, but mostly she listened, feeling heartsick. She wondered what they'd say about her if she had been one of the fallen.

It was human to want people to remember you; human to want to feel heard. With her last remaining battery life, Lucy opened up her profile page and her fingers hovered over a status update. She typed, slowly:

I'm still alive. Then she poised her finger around the send key and contemplated if it mattered if she sent it, if anyone would see it, or if just saying it out loud made it feel like a victory instead of a loss.

Then Lucy gasped. Just as she was about to exit out, her phone buzzed in her hand.

She had a text message.

Lucy's heart stopped and her veins ran cold. Her hand was almost too heavy to click on the smiling-face icon. That little emoticon so bright and cheery and so full of hope.

She looked.

It was from Ethan.

Ethan was out there and he was alive.

His message was from mere seconds ago and it just read: "*Don't leave. Stay safe. I'm coming for you.*"

CHAPTER THIRTEEN
Five days after The Release

Ethan's imminent arrival gave Lucy hope and equipped her with temporary patience. She had tried unsuccessfully to send him a text in reply, but the network kept bouncing it back. Out of anger and frustration she just sent a message that said *Waiting!* both as a battle cry for her frustration and an exclamation of her excitement. Of course, that text slipped away and sent. The last message she could get to him was neither revealing nor warm, and she hoped that Ethan would not think her text was implying she had been anxiously expecting him for two days.

They all worried about immediate details. How would Ethan find them? How would he navigate Spencer's supreme desire for a school absent of all other life? And then the most dangerous thought of all—maybe the text had been sent days ago and only now found its way through the fickle network. Then their hope and plans would be futile and in vain, entirely rooted in misconception.

It didn't help that it had been three days since Lucy

began expecting Ethan. Her phone died not long after the text arrived and Salem and Grant's phones didn't last much longer. She was vigilant and aware, but losing confidence that Ethan was safe.

"Something must've happened. It wouldn't take him this long to get here," Lucy complained. It was day five. Grant's baby-face began showing subtle signs of fur as pale blonde whiskers poked up on his chin and under his nose, barely noticeable, but still there.

It was morning. They assumed. Hours and minutes weren't important, only daylight and darkness. Spencer periodically marched the halls, which kept them confined to their hideout for extended periods of time. Lucy had ventured to the journalism lab on two occasions to check the Internet and found that sites no longer existed. There was an endless hourglass, in perpetual thinking, never connecting to a world outside. She occasionally ventured to the woodshop to use their makeshift bathrooms, but for the most part, over the past few days, Grant, Lucy, and Salem had stayed hunkered down.

"Do you think he got here and Spencer shot him?" Lucy asked. "Possible, right?" Sporadic gunfire was now a normal sound and they regarded it with annoyed eye-rolls and when it interrupted naps or sleep and they growled in frustration. They never assumed Spencer was actually shooting at anything in particular, but they could have been wrong.

"You're being paranoid," Grant said. He clicked a confiscated zippo lighter open, running his thumb over the flint wheel over and over again.

"Am I?" Lucy paced. "*We've* been shot at."

"We don't know if he wanted to kill you," Grant replied. The wick erupted into flame for a brief second and Grant closed the lid tight.

"It takes an hour to walk to my house."

"Lucy—" Grant said her name slowly with an undercurrent of warning. "You've been having this conversation for days now. Days."

Salem, who had been watching Lucy pace, her head moving left and right like she was in attendance at a slow-moving tennis match, stood up and walked to the mini-fridge. Flipping it open, she grabbed a peanut-butter-sandwich and bottled water and she opened the package with an exaggerated rip, the crinkling of the wrapper was the only sound in the tiny space. Lucy's stomach soured a bit as she watched Salem eat, the smell of peanut butter filling their small room. At first it was welcome nourishment, but now Lucy could barely choke one down.

Salem paused, mid-bite and then she rushed back over to the fridge and sat on her haunches, legs folded under her. She began to pull out the food with both hands and sorting it into three piles. When she was done with the contents of the fridge, she moved to the garbage bags, adding whatever bags of chips or granola bars they had left. She worked with determined efficiency—pull, stack, sort—her jaw still working her breakfast.

"What are you doing?" Grant asked.

Salem, mouth full, glanced sidelong at him. "I am *seeing*," she answered.

"Seeing what?" Lucy spat, angry that her own issues were temporarily ignored and invalidated.

"Food," was all Salem said. She took the three piles of sandwiches and waters, juices and thawing chicken nuggets, yogurt squeeze tubes, and then counted. She looked to the trio wide-eyed. "If we eat three meals a day and drink 2 bottles of water a day…this will last us…only three more days." She sat back, and then sprang up, reached for Ethan's backpack and started rummaging through it, tossing out Lucy's books in distracted ambivalence.

"Stop," Lucy said and when Salem ignored her, she put her hand out, touching her friend on the shoulder. "Stop!"

Then Salem's hand landed on what she was looking for—a yellow thin-tipped highlighter—she walked back to the food and marked it: L, S, and G. After branding their piles, she stood up and crossed her arms over her chest.

"Wait, wait, wait. Wait a second," Grant said. "But *you* already ate a sandwich this morning and Lucy and I haven't had anything. So, that isn't even. And you ate three bags of the popcorn last night when I didn't have any. So, it's not like we've been equitable until now. Why the sudden concern over fairness?"

"I'm not concerned with *fairness*," Salem replied, her hand still hovering over the sandwiches. "I'm concerned about *eating*. And making sure we can eat.

And here," she hoisted herself up and walked over to her half-eaten sandwich, broke off two pieces and handed them to Grant and Lucy. "Fine. Now we're even," she said.

Lucy handed her piece to Grant and walked over to the couch and plopped herself down; she grabbed a thick chunk of her hair and began to spin it around her pointer finger. It was oily and slick. She caught a whiff of her own body odor and turned her head away.

"There's no more food. Don't you get it? We're trapped in here. This is all we have. So, your pile is your pile. You can eat it all at once or ration it out. But your pile is your pile."

Lucy looked to her stack of food and then to Salem, wondering what nightmares Salem had encountered in the dark to wake up so changed and rattled. They each had their share of waking up mid-scream. As time passed, they got closer to each other every evening, sleeping in a mass on the floor, pulling each other close for warmth and comfort. The room was suffocating and small, but the people of history had often waited for the world's atrocities to end while hiding in small attics, basements, and closets.

They would be fine.

Ethan was coming.

They would be fine.

Lucy wished she could convey this mantra with enthusiasm to her colleagues in waiting. In an act of boredom, she reached into Ethan's book bag and pulled out the copy of *Fahrenheit 451*. She read the first line.

She read the line over and over fifty or more times before moving on to the next section. The words floated before her—her eyes scanning those six simple words before she moved to the next part.

But she couldn't get her brain to focus. Lucy shut the book on her finger. The room had been silent for too long; Salem's sullen expression made Lucy furious.

"Come on, I can't let it go. Ethan is out there!" Lucy said on the verge of tears. "And I don't feel like any of you give a rat's ass about it."

"Salem would like to carve up a rat's ass into three perfect proportions for dinner," Grant quipped unsmiling and then ducked as an empty water bottle careened toward his head.

"You think he wants to get us out? Maybe he wants in," Salem said. "You haven't thought of that, have you?" She leaned her back against the wall and slid down, resting her elbows on her knees. "Then I'll have to reconfigure the food."

"Really? You're still just worried that we might run out of peanut butter and jelly? What the hell is wrong with you? My brother is *alive* and you can't even pretend like you're happy about it. Screw you, Salem. If you don't want to leave when Ethan gets here that's on you. But me? I'm out of here. And guess what, when I'm gone, you and Grant can split the food pile. Have an extra bag of Cheetos. Merry Christmas."

"Lucy—" Salem started to say, her eyes wild. Then she stopped herself and put a hand up. "Never mind. Just never mind." And with that Salem stood back up, marched over to a chair where the classroom keys were resting, grabbed them, and stormed out of the room. Grant and Lucy listened as Salem unlocked the journalism lab door and went inside, the second door shutting behind her.

"I can't handle her drama today." Lucy tucked the book under her leg and kept twirling her hair.

"That might have been a little harsh," Grant replied, he scratched the top part of his scalp and grimaced apologetically.

"Wait," Lucy looked at him. "Which one of us was too harsh? My brother *is* coming for me. He is." And she didn't know if she believed it or if she just wanted to believe it.

It took a while for Grant to answer and when he did, he changed the subject. "What does it feel like?" he asked, not looking at her, his eyes wandering to the door and then to the carpet.

"What does what feel like?"

"I don't mean anything by it. I just want to know. Ethan…he's alive…to the best of our knowledge."

Then everything clicked all at once; the last pieces of the jigsaw sliding into place. "Oh."

"I'm not being passive-aggressive," Grant replied. But maybe he was a little. Or he was tactfully steering her toward the truth. "It's just...you know...it's like we were all sitting around playing our lottery numbers. And you won."

Lucy didn't say anything. Color and heat rushed to her cheeks.

"What did I win exactly?"

"A survivor."

"Oh, come on," Lucy tried to calm herself down and she tried to push the seeping defensiveness away. "Your dad could still be—"

"No. He's not. My dad is a coward. He didn't really care for me. I mean, not really. He made it mighty clear that I was just a burden to him. If the virus didn't get him, I bet he took his own life…without a single thought about me. But hey…at least he's consistent. Didn't care about me from day one, why start now?"

"I'm sorry." But Lucy didn't know what she was apologizing for: Ethan being alive or Grant's father being dead.

"It's hard," Grant continued, "not to be hurt that you have something we don't."

They sat without speaking, Lucy resisting the urge to spill out her defenses. She sighed shakily and swallowed.

"It's not like…you know…we…me," he quickly corrected, "wanted you to have lost everything too."

"I get it," Lucy said kindly. And she did. She could understand the jealousy and bitterness, the anger. "But you're right. You were all right. Maybe he's…maybe the message was from that first morning and he's gone now too. Maybe I'm chasing a phantom. But—"

"But," he cocked one eyebrow, "maybe he's not gone."

"I can't help but hope," Lucy answered, willing herself not to cry.

Grant sighed and crawled over. Hesitating, he put an arm over her shoulders. "We don't want to take away your hope," Grant said in a whisper. "It's envy."

"I should go to Salem," Lucy said and rose on her haunches, but Grant put a hand on her knee and kept her from rising the full way.

"Nah, just let her be by herself," he told her and Lucy listened. She settled back down on the floor and eventually stretched her whole body out on the ground, staring at the ceiling. She saw her book and grabbed it, flipping through the pages, her arms stiff above her, just flipping, flipping, not really reading, but scanning the words, taking in bits and pieces.

She noticed a phrase and it caught her off guard. Spilling from the page some character asked another character about the life *before*. It was an interesting concept. Some day, maybe, people would wonder: What was life like before the virus? *Before the virus.* The world wasn't always demolished, broken, and full of fear, she wanted to scream. Lucy let these words and ideas percolate through her.

"I've read that book," Grant said. He was leaning against the couch now, his eyes closed.

"Uh-huh," Lucy responded. "Mrs. Johnston gave it to me. To read on my trip."

"That's right. Your family was going somewhere really far away, right? Some place in Africa? I heard about that."

"Kinda. Near Madagascar."

"Why?" Grant asked.

Lucy flipped through more pages. Flip, scan. Flip, scan. "My dad was leading a team that had some major breakthrough at work. And he'd worked without a vacation for like three years. So, the company got him this trip. I think my dad picked the destination. He had written some report or something about the island a long time ago...they said they'd send him anywhere."

"Nice," Grant replied. Then he opened his eyes and grimaced. "I mean—that would've been nice...it still *sounds* nice."

"It's okay," she stopped him from saying more. Let him off the hook. "It was nice." She paused. "So, did you like it?"

"What?"

"The book."

Grant nodded. "Yeah, sure. I still remember, you know, we read it in class and our teacher, Ms. Houshmand, had this one quote written on the board for the whole unit and I just stared at it. I don't remember what it said exactly...but something about infiltrating people's brains or souls. Or something like that. It was up there, like a command."

Lucy didn't say anything for a second and then in reply she repeated the quote back to him, trying to make sense of it. "Huh," she shook her head. "That's funny."

Grant raised an eyebrow incredulously.

"I mean," Lucy plopped the book on the ground. "I get it, you want control and so you limit what people think. But...look at us," she motioned around the room, "someone out there found a different way. Infiltrate our *bodies*."

He let the phrase linger and then nodded, "Maybe you want absolute power, but you know you can't control the people."

"Destroy the people," Lucy finished.

"Are we ever going to be safe?" Grant asked.

"No," Lucy answered.

Someday people would wonder what the world was like before. Someday people would dream of a world free from the memories of bioterrorism, death, and fear.

Life would never be the same.

This was the new world.

Salem didn't return right away. They gave her space and time; they set her rationed lunch outside the journalism door and knocked and then retreated. But an hour later her corn nuts and peanut butter and jelly were still sitting there and she hadn't made an attempt to come back to the room. While it wasn't completely strange for Salem to allow a perceived wrong to fester, Lucy was usually the one who had to crawl back to her with an apology—deserved or not—and this typed of prolonged nonappearance was unusual. Salem needed to make her dramatic exits, needed the weight of her absence to be felt by everyone, and then she waltzed back in, accepted apologies, and went on with life as if nothing had happened.

She was the quintessential drama-queen, still trying to cause a scene in a world with a dwindling population.

It was aggravating to be her best friend sometimes with her sense of self-entitlement and her lack of self-awareness. It grated on Lucy. But Salem's quirks notwithstanding, she was a good friend. A great friend, even. Sacrificial. Supportive. Fun. It was true Salem's inflated ego caused problems, but she at least had inflated opinions of her friends too. If Lucy needed someone to go to bat for her, Sal would be there. No doubt.

"She'll be back," Grant said numerous times. "Maybe she's sleeping. Where could she go? She'll come back when she needs to," he mentioned with softness and deference. Like he knew her and was protecting her—because they shared pain and loss and because Salem had already fallen in love with the idea of falling in love with Grant while they wasted their hours in a glorified storage closet, among garbage and stolen treasures, surrounded by the constant stink of processed peanut butter.

Lucy knew her.

Salem didn't need to say that she wanted Grant's attention or his arms around her while she cried. Somehow the ache for love's magic was made even more real by their proximity, their shared experiences, and their limited options. Throughout their entire friendship, Salem had longed for a boyfriend to sweep her off her feet. She was a romantic and a believer in love at first sight. She was the girl who needed an epic story to pass down through generations. *You'll never believe how your grandfather and I met.* There was no dose of reality Lucy could administer and this made Lucy irate and irrationally angry. But Salem was Salem.

"She's waiting for *you*," Lucy replied. She picked up her book again and pretended to become immediately engrossed in a particular passage, but she occasionally lifted her eyes to watch Grant's expressions as he processed. "Pouting probably. Just go. Get her."

Grant sighed.

He waited a few more minutes and then sighed again.

"Are you sure?" he asked. He ran a hand over his stubble. "Why me?"

Lucy rolled her eyes.

"Fine, fine. Close the door after me. Four short knocks to get back in."

"I know the drill."

Lucy sat and waited for their return. It was nice to have a small moment of total aloneness. She thought back and tried to think if she had been fully alone since the first night at the school and she realized that she hadn't. But after fifteen minutes, Lucy wondered what would be taking so long. She slid off her couch and walked over to the door and as she neared it, she realized that there were voices in the hall, hushed and whispering. Opening the door a fraction of an inch, Lucy spotted Grant and Salem standing in the small alcove outside the journalism lab. Salem's foot was holding the door open and Grant held the keys. She could barely make out their conversation, but Lucy realized that they were oblivious to her and there was something about their body language and tone that suggested to Lucy she shouldn't be privy to their dialogue. Yet she couldn't turn away.

"How long will we stay here?" Salem had asked in a whisper. "I'm going crazy."

"Is this the moment I remind you that this was your idea? To stay."

"It can be my idea and I can still hate living like an animal in a cage."

"A very big cage with a lot of peanut butter and jelly."

"Are you going to make a joke of everything I say?" Salem complained, but she didn't sound too angry with him.

Lucy's heart quickened. And even though she knew that tone, that mischievousness, and the mechanics of Salem's flirting, she couldn't turn away. She wanted to interrupt them, shout at them to get back into hiding, but she knew that it would be pointless; Salem would only get more persistent and obvious.

"I'm diffusing," was Grant's reply and he must have smiled. Salem smiled back.

"You did a good job. It's not that I don't love Lucy," Salem started and Lucy felt suddenly sick, she closed her eyes tightly, not wanting to hear what came next, but unable to shut the door and turn away, "but she can be so self-absorbed. It'll be great if Ethan is alive...but this entire thing is not about her. We have big decisions to make."

That attack wasn't even true. But she just breathed deeply. It was so plotting, so transparently manipulative, an attempt to damage her character as a precaution against Grant ever liking her instead. She was not a threat to their blossoming love affair and she wanted to yell at them to just get back inside already. Lucy wasn't even angry, she saw the gears working and knew that in many ways Salem wasn't capable of stopping herself.

"Like what?" Grant asked and Lucy felt so sorry for him in that moment. He was so oblivious to her scheming.

Salem tucked her dark hair behind her ear and leaned in. "I like you," she whispered. "So, now I've said it."

From her vantage point, Lucy couldn't see Grant's face. He hadn't moved away or said anything in return. Instead, it looked like he was frozen, waiting for her to continue, but Salem didn't say anything else. She leaned in and kissed Grant gently on the mouth and then she coyly pulled back, biting the corner of her lip.

Lucy's heart sank.

"I wasn't expecting that," Grant replied, his voice nervous. "I didn't know...you felt that way."

"Confining spaces," Salem giggled.

Grant cleared his throat. "Or maybe you just

realized I might be one of only a few teenage boys left in the world."

Salem found the comment funny and she hit Grant playfully on the arm. "It's not like that."

"It *could* be a little like that."

"Then you got me. You're the last one left and I want you."

Lucy grimaced at Salem's boldness. She wished and hoped Grant could see through the shtick.

"You're fun," Grant mumbled. But Lucy wasn't convinced that was a ringing-endorsement for dating. "I'm surprised...and wow, I guess. Just wow, Salem. Wow."

She had heard enough. As she watched Salem position herself to go in for another kiss, she shut the door again without a sound and retreated backward.

It wasn't too many minutes longer until they both entered, knocking to announce their impending arrival. Lucy searched them for sheepishness or embarrassment, but if they were feeling awkward about their interactions, they gave no indication. They didn't act particularly starry-eyed either and if Lucy hadn't spied on them, she would've never guessed that they had shared a kiss in the doorway. But she *had* seen them and now she wondered what happened next. Would they attempt a clandestine relationship right under her nose?

Salem hugged herself as she walked into the room and walked past Lucy to the corner, where she pulled up a blanket and fluffed it into a pillow. Grant closed the door shut and stood next to it.

"It's raining outside," he said. "You can hear it in the other room and it's dripping through the wood over the skylight."

Salem sniffed and looked to Lucy. "I'm sorry. For storming off. Sometimes it's just too much…"

"We all feel that way," Grant said and he smiled at them both. Lucy looked down to the ground.

"Maybe it's asking too much," Lucy started, "but maybe we shouldn't be mad at each other for things that we have control over." She had a speech planned in her head, a series of plans and procedures—places to go if they needed a break from their claustrophobic living situation, code words for expressing a desire for someone else to be quiet. But as she opened her mouth to continue, the long dormant intercom switched on with its telltale two-toned *ding ding.*

Lucy scrambled off the couch and Salem jumped up from the floor and Grant swung the door to the hallway open wide as they poured outward toward the speakers.

"Well, well, well," Spencer's raspy voice called outward. "It has come to my attention that a certain Lucy Larkspur King is a stowaway in my building."

At the mention of her name, Lucy jumped and took a gulp of air. She reached out and grabbed Salem's arm, her eyes wide.

"Naughty. Naughty," Spencer continued, the slow drawl of his voice apparent as he clipped the end syllables.

None of them dared to speak. They held their collective breaths.

"If it were up to me, I'd shoot you on site for your insolence, and for wasting my precious air and resources. But it appears," he paused, cleared in throat with a hack, "someone has *purchased* your freedom. And who am I to turn that offer down?"

Lucy finally let out a breath. Ethan. It was Ethan. The use of her middle name was a giveaway, a hint, because only her family and Salem knew of her flowery moniker. Her older brother had arrived at last. His text was not an accident and not irrelevant. She turned and hugged Salem and then turned to hug Grant, uncaring about any potential jealousies or complications.

"Don't think I didn't know about you," Spencer spat. "And your little friends—" he trailed off. "You have five minutes, *Lu-cy*." The breathy quality of her name on his tongue made her shiver. "And your friends, if they're alive and still here, should come forward too. I offer up a onetime cease-fire and guarantee of safe passage. After that, should you *choose* to trespass…I will hunt you down like the dogs you are."

Then they heard the rumble of the gates, rising up into the ceiling, beckoning them.

CHAPTER FOURTEEN

Salem shook her head. "What if it's a trap?"

Grant walked back up to the hideout and opened the door and he ducked inside, leaving Salem and Lucy alone in the hallway.

"He knew my name, so it has to be Ethan…but you're right. I wouldn't put anything past him." She and Salem locked eyes. And they both recognized each other's fear and worry.

Salem nodded. "We have to go, I guess. He's right. He knows we're here now. Staying isn't safe. It would only be a matter of time before he sniffed us out."

"Maybe we *don't* go. Maybe we find another way out and meet up with Ethan on the outside. My brother's smart. He'd find us."

Grant came back out into the hallway. He was carrying Lucy's black backpack and two other small bags, filled with supplies. In many ways the call to the front office made Grant look relieved. He handed Lucy her bag and she swung it over her shoulder. They took a moment to regard each other all disheveled and tired. Lucy was still barefoot. They each wore some article of clothing pilfered from a student's locker and they were worse for wear and drained, but still they mustered up the courage to face the man they had been hiding from for nearly a week.

"We're going," Lucy stated. She took a deep breath. "Is it weird that I might miss our little room?"

"Nah," Salem smiled. "I think I might miss it too."

Their five minutes were ticking down and they were conscious that they were running out of time.

"Where's the gun?" Lucy thought to ask.

Grant patted the waistband of his jeans.

"Good. Let's go."

Lucy walked with purpose down the English hall and around the corner. The bottoms of her feet slapped against the floor. Grant and Salem kept pace with her in a straight line, and they were silent as they moved forward.

Spencer was waiting for them. He had changed out of his trademark suit coats, and even from afar Lucy could see that he had replaced his button-shirt with an oversized athletic pullover. He had a gun trained on them. It was a long-barreled rifle and he kept the butt of it flush against his shoulder.

"Hands up!" Spencer called to them. In unison, they each raised their hands in the air.

He didn't move as they reached him. They stood regarding each other with his narrowed eyes never leaving Lucy and barely acknowledging Grant and

Salem.

"So. My trespassers," Spencer finally said after a beat. "A little predicament…what to do with the two of you who have not been mentioned by name or desired."

Lucy cringed. If her friend's jealousies over Ethan's survival were already fragile, Spencer's blatant announcement that they had no one out there fighting for them was too painful a reminder. Her heart pounded. She shot a glance over to Grant's waistband, hoping that his raised hands did not expose their one and only weapon against Spencer.

"We're not leaving Lucy," Salem called out. She sounded strong and brave. Lucy felt a swell of admiration for her friend. Whenever her relationship with Salem became tenuous, she did have a way of making it all better with a single declaration of friendship and support.

Spencer shook his head, barely, and cocked the rifle. "You will do exactly as I say."

He nodded over to the front doors.

"The doors are unlocked. Go. You two…the non-Lucys…go."

Grant hesitated. His bag slipped from his shoulder a bit and he moved to grab it. Spencer pivoted the rifle straight at him.

"Hands back up or I shoot! I have a huge cement pool down the hall filled with the bodies of your former friends, enemies and teachers. I will not hesitate to add one more to the pile."

Lucy shuddered. So, her dream had been true.

"Toss your backpack to me."

She balked at his request. "I'm not doing anything you say unless you let my friends stay."

"Slide it over." He repeated. "I am not negotiating."

"I want my friends—"

Spencer raised the rifle and fired a warning shot into the ceiling. Tiny bits of sheetrock and plaster fell to the floor. Then he fired again, this time aiming at the window that led to the athletic office. The window burst and glass shot out in every direction. Tiny shards made their way to where Lucy was standing and she looked at her bare feet.

She shed the backpack and put it on the floor, then gave it a gentle toss in his direction, it hit the ground and the sound of it echoed back down the hall.

"Lucy," Spencer said her name again, quietly drawing out the syllables. "Tell your friends to go."

Lucy turned to Grant and Salem and when she registered the fear in their faces, she started to cry.

"Where's my brother? I want to see Ethan!"

She recognized the glimmer of confusion as Spencer tried to process her request. "I don't know what you're talking about. I don't know your brother."

"You said that someone bought my freedom. That I'm free to go! Right? Right?" She began to feel panicky and weak and her head was spinning. It had been a trap; Ethan was not here, they were not going to walk out of the school and into the daylight, laughing together, leaving the small room and a gun-wielding principal behind them.

Spencer fired the rifle a third time and this time he shot at a display case a mere foot away from where Salem was standing. Salem shrieked and covered her ears and shut her eyes tight as the glass fell around pennants and trophies from athletes and teams from years gone by. When the sound from the shot died away, Salem looked up Lucy, her eyes wide.

Grant took a breath. "I can't." He nodded toward the gun. "He'll kill me before I can reach it."

"We'll go," Salem said loudly. Then she turned to Lucy, her eyes wet. "We're going."

"No!" Lucy cried out. "No!" She turned to Spencer, raising her hands out toward him in supplication. "There has to be another way!"

Spencer took two long strides forward. "There is no other way," he replied. "They have ten seconds or you can pick which one I shoot first."

Letting out a gulping sob, Lucy spun back to her friends. "Find Ethan!" she cried out. "Stay safe and hidden. And don't—"

"Five…four…"

Grant and Salem began to run. When they reached the front doors, they grabbed the metal door handle and pushed the door swung open, a gust of spring air blew into the foyer of the school. It was the first breath of fresh air, full of moisture and wet earth, that they had experienced in days. Grant pushed Salem forward over the threshold and then turned to look back at

Lucy.

"Three…two…"

Grant opened his mouth to say something, but then watched as Spencer moved the gun on him. And before he could even wave goodbye, Grant was out the door. The heavy door closed quickly with a bang. And Lucy was alone.

Spencer reached into his pocket and pulled out a pair of handcuffs. He tossed them over to Lucy and nodded. "Put one end around your wrist."

"Why?" Lucy asked, her voice shaking. "My friends are gone. When do I get to leave too? I thought you said—"

He aimed the gun at her and took a step forward. Lucy trembled. "Handcuffs. One wrist."

Breathless, Lucy obeyed. The unattached end of the handcuff dangled at her side. Then Spencer lowered the gun, his finger dropping off the trigger. He marched over to her and wrapped his hand around her upper-arm.

He tugged her over with him to the door, where he inserted a key into a plastic covered security box, lifted the lid, and then entered a seven-digit code. Metal bars and locks slid back into place over the front doors of the school; the high-tech automated system, which cost taxpayers millions of dollars, had not gone to protect the students from any real threat. The locks and bars and bulletproof glass had not kept the virus out. Instead all the bells and whistles continued to facilitate the supreme rule of a maniacal madman.

"Tell me what's going on. Why are you keeping me?" Lucy asked as Spencer began pulling her toward the office. Terror rose in her throat like bile and she wondered if she screamed if he would shoot her or if he would ignore her. He pushed her to the floor and then hooked the other end of the handcuffs to the underbelly of a table in the middle of the room. Gravity pulled her hand and arm toward the floor, and her wrist went limp against the metal.

"I don't owe you an explanation."

Lucy yanked her hand and rattled the handcuff. "You said. You said! Why am I here? Let me go!"

Spencer placed the rifle flat on a desk in the corner. He walked over to a filing cabinet and poured himself a drink out of a tall clear bottle with a brown label. Tipping his head back, he downed the drink in one gulp.

"You…Lucy…are a commodity to me." Raising his drink in a toast, he took another sip and then took a step forward. "I will not let you *go*."

"A commodity. What the hell does that mean?" Lucy adjusted her body. She slumped against the table leg. He turned his back and walked back over to the cabinet; he took a new glass and poured another, then he walked it over to her and tried to hand it to her, but Lucy turned her head away.

"Drink," he instructed.

"I don't want to drink anything you give me." Lucy pushed the drink away. But he shoved the glass closer to her face and leaned down, his rancid breath spilling over her face. She inhaled deeply and then held her breath.

"Drink," he said again, slower, his mouth leaning closer.

Taking the glass in her hand, Lucy noticed the liquid sloshing against the sides, dangerously close to spilling over. She shook her head and tried to set the drink down on the floor, but Spencer pushed her hand to her face. Then he pinched her cheeks and took the glass back and poured the burning alcohol into her mouth. She tried to let as much dribble down her chin and to her shirt as she could before she spit the rest on the floor. It burned her tongue.

"You wasted it, you little bitch," he seethed. "Do you know what this cost me? *This*," he gestured to the bottle, "was two Tasers. And twenty bottled waters."

For a second, Lucy couldn't process what that meant. Then she turned her head sharply to him, her mouth dropping open. "You're trading the school's supplies…for alcohol?"

Spencer laughed, a grotesque, throaty laugh, his unbrushed teeth bared. "And weapons. And pills. And *other* food. But that doesn't have much to do with you, now does it?"

"It does when you think you can trade *me*!" Lucy said, practically screaming.

He dropped to her level and grabbed her chin. "The moment you chose to stay in my school, you became *my* property. It's just my luck that someone seems to think you're worth trading for."

"Who?" Lucy asked while Spencer's hand still gripped her. "If it's not my brother, then who?"

"Doesn't matter to you." He let her go violently and Lucy's head snapped backward and hit against the metal edge of the table. Her head burned and a shooting pain traveled down into her neck. She took her free hand to rub the spot and realized that the back of her head was wet and when she looked down at her fingers, they were smeared with blood.

Spencer frowned. "Oopsie," he glowered, "accidental damage to the goods. Such a shame. I hope it doesn't hurt your value."

"Who are you?" Lucy asked. She was too shocked and scared to cry, but her whole body trembled.

"I am a man. A fighter."

"An opportunist," Lucy spat.

"You see," he smiled, "yes. And you say it like it's a bad thing. But I'm alive. You and me...we aren't supposed to be alive. And yet, here we are. I realized...quickly...all those people." He stopped to drink and then he walked back over to Lucy, squatted down, his eyes were bright and wild. "All those people...they wanted into *our* building. For food and water and shelter. The limited survivors need me."

"You made yourself important."

"I am important. I *am* needed."

"So you abuse that need?" Lucy's head felt thick and achy. "What about your own family?"

Spencer broke into a sinister smile. He rose and waltzed over to his office. Lucy could only see only a corner of the room. He leaned over and swiped a picture off of his desk, walked back out, and tossed it to her. In a fancy metal frame, was a wide-smiled and white-toothed brunette, the ocean in the background, wind whipping her hair into her face.

"Fake. My girlfriend, I'd say." He shook his head and laughed. "Some picture off the Internet. But teachers are kinder to you when you have a family. Paint yourself as a family man; tell people how eager you are to start a family. I was always *this* close to marrying her, settling down. Do you know how eager all the young female teachers are when they think they get to offer up some dating advice for their boss?"

"You're a sociopath."

"Opportunistic."

"You lied about having a family?"

Lucy noticed the flash, however brief and fleeting, of self-awareness passing over Spencer. She wished he would drop the act, but the drinking wasn't helping anything.

"Please." He drank. Then added, "I'd say I'm lucky." He stared off at one of the office walls, his eyes glazing over. "Who did I have to mourn?" And even though it was a fact that was supposed to have spared him pain, Lucy watched as Spencer closed his eyes and took a shaky breath.

"The world," Lucy answered in a whisper. "We have the entire *world* to mourn."

This did not even garner a response. Spencer went and drank another tumbler—his back to her. Then he slammed the empty glass down and grabbed his rifle, taking an exaggerated step over Lucy's legs, and walking five feet away to a small table. Sitting on top was the head of the school's mascot, Spartan Joe. Without an owner, the head took on a freaky vacant quality. Grabbing Joe by his foamy crown, Spencer walked out of office. Lucy could see from her vantage point the front windows, still taped over with black construction paper.

First, Spencer loosened some tape around the edges and then he kicked over a black crate to the window. He placed the mascot head on top of the crate, its empty eyes staring outward. Then he let the black paper fall around it, creating an obscured view back into the school. Onlookers from the outside would just see a giant head in front of a black background. Then Spencer yanked up on his long sleeved shirt and checked a wristwatch.

After several minutes, Lucy heard a knock on the front door. Four short knocks right in a row, then knock followed by a beat and two more knocks. Spencer raised his gun and walked forward. He unlocked the plastic covering the security panel and punched in his code again. The large mechanical bolts slid open; then Spencer hit a second key code and one of the front doors starting to swing forward automatically.

Lucy hoped that Salem and Grant would be the ones to enter the school. That somehow in that short amount of time they would have planned a rescue.

Instead, a single body ducked through the doorframe.

It was a tall, slender young woman with raven hair. A large single stripe of faded pink framed her face. Spencer pointed his gun at her as she entered with one hand and typed in a key code that slid the metal back over the doors.

The woman had a gun of her own in a holster around her hips; her hand hovered over it like she was about to engage in a duel. She wore black lace-up combat boots over black leggings and a white long sleeve t-shirt—a clear mixture of every video-game heroine Lucy had ever seen. If the new visitor was trying to adhere to some cliché of a badass female, she was succeeding in the category of costuming. She held a bulging messenger bag across her body and her eyes shifted as she watched Spencer's every move.

"Afternoon," Spencer mumbled to his guest, he lowered his gun and then walked over and kicked the Spartan head away from the door, the paper flapping back into place.

The new visitor did not return his greeting. She looked at him with nothing but suspicion and potential loathing, her big bright eyes moving quickly from Spencer to the office and ultimately to Lucy.

"You got the girl," she said. Her voice was smooth and deep.

"Just like you asked. I can see her appeal," Spencer grumbled as if Lucy couldn't hear.

The woman slid the messenger bag off and strode

with wide, far-reaching, steps into the office, where she tossed it on to the desk where Lucy was handcuffed. Without even a single word to Lucy, she began to pull out various items from the bag: A bottle of whiskey, bottles of pills, a stack of magazines, a box of bullets, and other sundry items.

"Everything on your list, plus some extras thrown in for good measure," she said as Spencer examined everything piece by piece.

"And what do you want?" Spencer asked.

She snapped her head at him, annoyed. "The girl. And two water bottles for the road. That's all. Per our discussions and negotiations. That was the deal."

Lucy saw the girl's hand itch above her gun, then she slid her hands to her hips, standing there looking at him squarely, her mouth drawn into a thin, tight, frown.

"We didn't have a deal," Spencer said. He picked up the whiskey bottle and palmed it, then he tossed it up and down, the brown liquid splashing around inside. "We were in *talks*. And now that Lucy Larkspur King...that was the name you gave me, right? Well, now that she's here, in the flesh, in my office, I feel like perhaps she's more valuable than all of this."

The woman's eyes flashed with unmistakable rage. She let out a small huff and then gracefully recovered. Taking a breath, she then gave Spencer a tight-lipped smile. "I see. You want to play a game." She said it as a statement. And then she nodded, as if giving Spencer credit for his using Lucy as a pawn. "What could you possibly want? Try me."

Spencer narrowed his eyes. "No, my creativity is limited. I want this to be *challenging*. I want to be surprised."

The girl in the black leggings laughed. "I could pull out my gun and shoot you before you even knew I had moved a muscle," she said with a smile. "Let's remember something and be real clear about it. I'd much rather kill you and get on with my life."

"Is that a threat?"

The girl dropped her voice down to a whisper. "A threat? Oh no, Spencer…it's a promise."

She even spoke in clichés and sound bites. Lucy watched wide-eyed.

Spencer was quick and he swung the rifle he had been holding a few minutes before off the table and into his hands—but the girl didn't move and she didn't reach for her gun, didn't aim it at his head, and didn't do anything. Instead, she took her right hand and lowered the gun to the floor.

"You want to keep her?" She asked.

"No. But you want her and that makes her worth more than my usual assortment of loot."

"Your lack of imagination is hindering my ability to fully comprehend what you think I can get for you…"

He took a step forward, his breath, hot and reeking of alcohol. Lucy watched as he extended his hand and swiftly tucked a long lock of the girl's hair behind her ear.

"I do have an active imagination after all," he whispered. "I can think of a few things."

The woman took a deep breath, but she remained frozen and unfazed by his closeness. "Don't touch me ever again," she whispered in a soothing voice. Then she leaned in, her lips a half an inch away from Spencer's scruffy cheek. "Or I will blow your brains out." She made the sound of a gun exploding.

Lucy rattled her handcuff against the table, annoyed and frustrated from being ignored, bartered, and a witness to their sick tête-à-tête.

"It doesn't matter what you give this man because I'm not for sale," Lucy interjected, but she sounded insecure and frightened. The woman turned her gaze downward and narrowed her eyes as if she was noticing this human for the first time. She looked disgusted at Lucy's timidity.

"Do me a favor," the woman said, turning her attention back to Spencer. "Give me another day. Same time. I think I have something that might interest you."

She then bent down and examined Lucy, pulling on the handcuffs, patting her down for weapons. When she saw the gash on Lucy's head, she shot Spencer a frustrated look.

"I need her compliant. And in good condition. Handcuffs, good, fine, whatever. Violence, bad. Are we clear?"

"Yeah, yeah." Spencer pointed to the door. "Tomorrow. And I better not be disappointed."

"That's entirely up to you," she replied. "But what I'm prepared to offer you is so rare it has no value. It might be the single most important item left on our

Godforsaken earth. And you'll take it. Eagerly. Then I get the girl in excellent condition. I mean…for the love Spencer…fix her a decent breakfast, share your deodorant." Then she turned to Lucy, looked her up and down one last time. "Tomorrow." She started to walk away.

Spencer followed her back out to the doors, his rifle raised again. He started to punch in the code to slide the metal locks apart.

"Who are you?" Lucy cried out after the stranger, her voice full of anguish and fear.

The girl spun. She paused as if debating whether or not she would answer. "I'm Darla," she called and then disappeared back outside.

CHAPTER FIFTEEN
Six days after The Release

Lucy wasn't able to sleep that night. Her mind kept spinning around thinking of Salem and Grant out there in the world for the first time since the attack. She wondered if they found it cruel or peaceful, and while she hoped they had located her brother, she was not optimistic. But more than anything, she kept imagining that kiss, and she pondered whether or not she would be rescued. After waiting and wondering, she just assumed they had forsaken her for more romantic pursuits. It pained her to think of their closeness while she was so alone.

Her hand ached above her head and she could not find an ounce of comfort. Occasionally she dozed, but when her body pulled on the chain, she would jerk awake to the sound of metal rattling on metal. All through the night, her anger and pain increased, but Lucy didn't cry. Five days ago, she wouldn't have stopped crying, but she could not find it in herself to shed tears. Spencer watched her like a caged pet—balancing his interest with both fascination and indifference.

When Spencer attempted conversation with her, Lucy turned her face away from his and stared off at the beige office walls where pictures of former students had been taped up in equally numbered columns and rows. Tiny squares of smiling faces, painted and plucked, wearing brand new outfits, without a hair out of place. Lucy's own senior photos were sitting at home, already distributed to her mother's friends and distant relatives.

Spencer never wanted to talk about anything that made sense. Instead it seemed that he was excited just to hear himself talk to a human being at all, even if that person was his prisoner. He held court in front of her and recounted movie plots and stories of crazy students and he told her the details of teacher scandals—all of which might have interested her a few days ago, but not anymore.

After he realized it would be a perpetual one-way conversation, Spencer retreated to his office with his bottles and his pills. In no time at all, he was snoring. His rattling breath kept Lucy wide-eyed and awake until the wee hours of the morning.

When Spencer rose with the sun, he was slow, grumpy and suddenly silent, but otherwise fine. He fixed them both a breakfast of scrambled eggs, sausage patties, and French toast sticks drowned in maple syrup from a collection of tiny plastic packets, which he opened for Lucy without so much as a good morning.

But even if he handled himself in virtual silence,

Spencer abandoned his antagonistic banter. He didn't have to be nice to her, but somehow Darla's instructions were weighed with authority. They spent the morning like awkward houseguests—one not sure what to do with the other—even though the reality of her situation was never far from Lucy's mind.

After hours of waiting, Darla was back. Right on time. Her four short knocks, beat, two knocks. The song and dance of raised guns, sliding bolts, mutual distrust, locking doors. When she returned, he seemed jittery with excitement, like a child on Christmas morning. His morning moodiness was lifted.

"Easy, easy," Darla said. Her messenger bag was empty and light. She set it down on the table slowly and then kicked out a chair and sat down. Plates with the remnants of their breakfast were beside her, and Darla took her pointer finger and made lazy circles with the leftover syrup. Then she brought her finger to her tongue and licked the syrup off with a deliberate smack. Lucy had left a bite of sausage and Darla ate that too. If it bothered Spencer, he didn't say. Instead, he watched her curiously and anxiously as he leaned against one of the walls, his gun at his side.

After a moment, he cleared his throat. "Enough. I'm waiting."

"I'm about to honor your request."

"I hope so. Or why are you here?"

"An unobtainable, rare, valuable product. For your own personal use, if you desire. Or for sale. I don't care what you do with it once it leaves my hands."

"My curiosity is piqued."

"Sure, sure," Darla waved him away with disdain. "Let's set the ground rules. First, let her out of the cuffs."

Spencer blinked. "I don't know. She'll bolt."

"Let her out of the damn cuffs."

"Tell me what you brought for—"

Darla pulled her firearm out of its holster like lightning and pointed it at Spencer; only her hand and arm had moved—the rest of her body had remained positioned calmly in the chair. "You'll want what I'm selling and if you don't then you lose the product and the girl."

With Darla's gun still pointed in his direction, Spencer bent down and unlocked one side of the handcuffs. Lucy's hand fell into her lap. It was numb and sore, a red, raw indent surrounded her wrist and she cradled it gingerly against her body.

"Come over by me," Darla instructed to Lucy. Whether or not she wanted to bolt, Lucy realized that fighting her request would be useless. So, Lucy slid herself over to Darla's feet and then wobbled upward. Her legs ached.

Darla pulled her messenger bag down off the table and flipped it open. She reached inside and pulled out a brown box with a lid. Dropping her bag on the floor, she lifted the lid, and Lucy saw that the box was packed with packing balls. They fell to the floor as she reached in and grabbed a plastic baggie. She ripped open the top of the bag, held out her hand, and rolled out four vials.

"This better be good," Spencer mumbled, clearly unimpressed.

"*This*," Darla held the vials in her hand, "is a cure."

Spencer looked at her uncomprehending. "A cure." He ran the back of his hand over his nose and cracked his head to the side.

She rose to her feet and held the vials outward, but when Spencer took a step forward and tried to reach for them, she drew her hand back and waved her free pointer finger at him. "Ah-ah-ah…not so fast."

"You mean…a vaccine."

Darla smiled, her large, evenly spaced teeth flashing. "Now you're catching on. I'm holding the only known and only available vaccine against the virus that was unleashed on our dearly departed Earth. Four vials. There is one for you for sure. I have three more…but we'll discuss their fate next."

She let the news settle and when Spencer opened his mouth, she continued, without waiting.

"I know you're incredulous."

"To say the *least*," was his response.

"Of course. I waltz in here, purport to have some cure for a quick-killing tool of genocide used by bioterrorists. Hard pill to swallow?"

Spencer motioned for her to continue.

Following every word with growing anxiousness, Lucy slid her body down into Darla's now empty chair and rested her elbows on the table.

Darla reached into her bag once again and pulled out a sheet of white computer paper and a digital camera. Still with the vials in her grip, she brandished the paper, like a gift, and placed it in Spencer's hand. He shifted his rifle to his back and held on to the sheet with two hands, his brow furrowing as he read. "This could be forged," he mumbled.

"Oh really? With my endless hours of available free time and design experience?"

"You could have traded for it. How the hell am I supposed to know?"

"It's not a forgery."

"It's a scare tactic."

"You're right. It's scary...but it's no *tactic*."

"What does it say?" Lucy said and she stood up.

With a sigh, Darla turned to acknowledge Lucy. The strange woman had deep, dark brown eyes with a tint of green along the edges and long, make-up-less lashes. "It's a document from a government-run laboratory. Some timeline information about experiments involving the virus."

"How did *you* get that?" Lucy asked. But Darla shot her a murderous look and Lucy lowered herself back down into her seat. "I was just asking," she tried to add, but no one seemed to hear her.

"It *says* that most victims die between twenty-four hours to thirty-six hours after exposure. Quickly. Instant death. Ninety-eight percent of all...human subjects...did not last beyond that timeframe. Then there is a second wave. The outliers. After exhibiting no symptoms, no reaction to exposure at all...after one-hundred-forty-four hours to one-hundred-sixty hours…another two percent."

"One-hundred percent death rate?" Lucy said and she looked up. She let that tidbit of truth wash over her. No one would survive this without that vaccine.

"Excellent math skills. Did our fine establishment help you with that ability?" Spencer shot a look upward and then back down at the camera. "So, what *Darla*," he said her name with a sneer, "is trying to say is that we just entered a time period where we are all at risk again. Is that right?"

Darla shrugged.

"And how opportune…I mean, what a great fortune for me that she has the perfect recipe to save my life." Spencer rolled his eyes. "I don't buy it."

"The way I see it," Darla answered without missing a beat, "is that I can win this thing two ways. One, you realize I'm right, and you let me buy Lucy with the vaccine. Or two, you think I'm wrong and you die of the virus. I walk out of here with Lucy either way."

"Then wait for me to die," Spencer invited with a toothy smile.

"Happily," Darla replied. "That was certainly *my* vote anyway. However, here is the problem." She frowned. "I need some things. Some big things and unfortunately, you're the only one I know who can get them for me."

Lucy's heart began beating ferociously. She didn't want to interrupt and ruin Darla's rehearsed dialogue, but she needed to know if *she* was in danger. She thought of Salem and Grant out there, outside, somewhere, not knowing that a second wave would soon hit them. Getting out of the school and finding them was key, even if she hoped that Darla's dog-and-pony show was an act.

"That is an interesting predicament," Spencer said, assuming his administrative tone, a cross between condescending and authoritative. "So many coincidences. I'm in danger *today*, but behold…*you* have just what I need."

"And if *you* don't give me what I need, then yes, you will die."

Spencer debated, his eyes flashed. "So, what do you need?" he asked.

"Antibiotics. And a doctor."

He laughed at her. "Those are no easy feats. What makes you even think I can do that?"

"Because if you don't agree to it…you'll die," Darla answered.

"Right, I see. Well, I don't have antibiotics right now," he told her unapologetically. "And you think I can just call up a doctor? How exactly do you suppose I go about making that happen for you?"

Darla leaned in closer. "I know how this works. You need specific things and you put different items in the window to call the looters. The traders. The Raiders, like I call them. Right?"

He didn't answer her.

"You do this for me and you live. The payment is handsome," she continued.

"Darla the Great, peddling her magical elixirs,

preying on fear and a sense of urgency. And of course you need the girl, but wait, if I don't give you the other things you need you'll let me die. A sham. I don't believe you, so I will call your bluff. No girl, no antibiotics, no doctor. Let's wait and see what happens. Do you need me to show you the door?"

"Are you done?" Darla asked, unmoving, and when Spencer failed to answer immediately, Darla nodded once. "Good." She grabbed the digital camera and turned it on, its tiny ding indicating it was ready. She passed it to Spencer, who regarded the first picture with confusion and then disgust.

Lucy stood up and walked over so she could see the screen. Quickly, Spencer clicked through pictures. At first it was just pictures of dead rats in various stages of decay. In front of the rats, someone had labeled them: Day1, hour 2. And then as the rats disintegrated into fur and bone, Day 5, hour 10. But at some point the subjects changed and what Lucy saw—despite the horror of the past six days—made her gasp. She clasped a hand over her mouth and her eyes began to water. She hated what she was seeing, but she couldn't look away.

Bodies. Real people. Dressed in paper-thin white robes. Men and women. Girls and boys. All ages, shapes, colors, nationalities. Dead. With signs. Day 2, hour 5. And on and on. Some subjects were shown alive. Day 1. Alive. Day 2. Alive. Some people held their signs in front of them without emotion, staring forward. Some of them had a hint of a smile on their lips. Lucy wondered if they knew what was happening to them; if they knew that they were going to die.

Sure enough, Darla's clear assessment of the paper's report rang true in pictures. Out of the people who lasted through the first phase, none of them survived Day 6.

Spencer finished the last photo, compelled to press the forward key until the first picture flashed back into view, and then he set the camera down at the table. His brusque manner had diminished and now he appeared pensive and, Lucy thought, afraid.

He opened his hand.

"Take the girl," he stated and open and closed his palm.

"Wise choice," Darla answered. "And—"

"I need two days for your other requirements."

"Everyone will be dead in two days," she replied.

"I understand," Spencer said between his teeth. "Two days and *all* those vaccines. If you expect me to deliver you a doctor, I'm going to need a way to keep him or her alive and the people who assist me."

"Deal. The vials are yours. Work *fast*. I'll be back."

Spencer turned his head to the side. "How do you know I won't just take the vaccines and run?"

Darla smiled. "Because I'm giving you a chance at life. Even when you get me what I ask for, you will *still* owe me. I'm trusting that has to count for something."

Then without waiting for a reply, she dropped the vials into Spencer's outstretched hand. And as they rolled from her hand to his, Lucy noticed they were marked with long strips of masking tape. Each one was clearly labeled with a name:

Galen, Malcolm, Monroe. And Harper.

CHAPTER SIXTEEN

The clean air hurt Lucy's lungs at first. She breathed it in too deeply, too quickly, and her chest ached. She gulped for another breath of air and then another and soon she felt light-headed. With a hand placed firmly against her lower back, Darla led Lucy to a red bench outside the school and sat her down.

"Put your head between your knees. You're hyperventilating."

"Don't…tell…me…what…I…am…doing…" Lucy replied between heavy breathing, her ribcage rising and falling.

"Fine," she replied, nonplussed. "We don't have long. It's not wise to stay out in the open like this. Come on, stand up. You're fine. "

"Give me a second." Then Lucy raised her head and examined the woman standing before her. In the sunlight, Lucy could see that her skin was flawless and she was tan. Not the orange glow of Oregonian girls, but the deep golden browns of someone who developed a bronzed body over time. After a deep breath, Lucy looked straight at Darla and steeled herself up to ask the question she needed to ask.

"Those vials in there…with vaccine."

"Let's be careful here, Lucy," Darla answered and she looked past her, into the parking lot, her eyes scanning the rows of cars with diligence.

"I need to know. Where did they come from? Why were my brothers' and sister's name on them…you have to tell me."

"Sorry," was the curt reply. "Those are questions you'll have to ask later. I don't have answers."

"Liar," Lucy muttered under her breath. She was seething. One night enduring Spencer's craziness, handcuffed to a table, and the woman didn't have the decency to give her a straight answer.

"Excuse me?"

"You *know*. You just told Spencer all of that stuff in there."

"Come on, Lucy Larkspur King." Darla said the name with a mix of kindness and amusement. "Let's get going." She put her hands on her hips. Then she took her thick black hair and tied it up into a spiky ponytail.

"Who are you?" Lucy asked. She tucked her hands up under her thighs and bounced her legs; the cement in the parking lot, still full of cars, was wet from the showers, but the clouds temporarily parted revealing blue sky surrounded by threatening, ominous dark gray rain clouds on the horizon.

"I already answered that. I'm Darla," she replied, annoyed.

"You *know* what I'm asking."

"Yes, I do. Well, a week ago I was a resident of Los Angeles, working as a wealth manager for a small capital management firm. But seeing as how all my clients are dead and there's no more stock market and I'm pretty sure currency is pretty much *invalid*, I found myself unemployed. So, now I'm a Raider. Among other things." Darla smirked. She wiped a stray hair out of her eyes and then put her hand back on her hips, standing with a wide stance above Lucy, her presence large and assuming, invading Lucy's personal space.

"I heard you use that word in the office. What's a Raider?"

"It's a term I made up."

"That's not what I asked." Lucy looked around.

"Professional looter. Raiding people's houses for items of perceived value to trade for other items of perceived value. In less than one week after the annihilation of mankind, it didn't take much longer than twelve hours to set up a pretty intricate web of black market trading. Although, I suppose it's not a black market if it's the only market. Principal Spencer here…he knew he had it made."

"Which is why he didn't want anyone near the school."

"You did the right thing by staying at the school. It's not pleasant out here," Darla added and she looked down on Lucy with mothering warmth, her affirmation the vocal equivalent of a pat on the back. "The first three days were the worst. Killing people who came on your property without so much as a pause to see if they were armed or hurting. Violence, disaster. You know the basics."

"My brother sent you?" Lucy asked.

"He did."

"He's alive." Lucy sighed and smiled.

"He is."

"Is he the one who needs a doctor?"

"I don't think I need to answer any more questions right now."

"Am I going to die?"

Darla paused and cocked her head to the side. She looked genuinely perplexed and then a wave of realization passed over her face. "You're fine sweetie. You're not in danger."

Lucy let out a small hum. "Yeah, people keep saying that to me. So far I'm not convinced."

"You aren't going to die."

She thought of the vials and the fact that her name was not among them. But what did any of it mean? The questions seemed too big and unanswerable, and Lucy kept breathing deeply, trying to calm the heaviness in her chest.

"That's all I know, so you'll just have to live with that." Darla reached into her messenger back and pulled out a pair of canvas slip-on shoes that Lucy immediately recognized as her own.

"I noticed you were without footwear yesterday. You own a surprising number of shoes…none of which are great for walking. So, what, the King family doesn't like to hike? Whatever, we'll make do."

Lucy mumbled a thank you as she slipped the shoes on her feet.

"Come on. Follow me."

Darla moved toward the bushes, pushing long branches with leaves out of the way and ducking under the greenery. A twig caught in Lucy's hair and as she moved forward it tugged on her scalp; she batted it away. Then something wispy and thin brushed her cheek and it felt like the remnants of a spider's web. She shivered and ran her hand over the tingling skin. She hadn't given much thought to the survival of all living creatures. Did spiders even still exist now or had they also been banished from the earth?

Lucy kept pace with her and matched her step for step. Their feet crunched along gravel. They passed some school storage buildings and one of the doors was wide open, the glass broken on the windows. Next they crawled through an open space in a fence and found themselves in the bus barn—fifteen buses parked for service in their usual spaces, bright and yellow. Darla put out her hand and stopped Lucy, then drew her gun up, flipping the safety off.

When Lucy opened her mouth to ask something, Darla snapped her fingers and motioned for Lucy to stay quiet.

With every step, Darla would pause.

Then even Lucy heard the crunch of gravel that continued after they had paused. Behind them were a set of secondary steps trying to match their own, but the attempt was imperfect. While Darla turned her head around one of the buses, her back flush against the exit door, Lucy felt someone grab her arm and she shrieked loudly. Darla spun back, aiming her weapon.

"Put down your gun!" Darla called. "I'm a better shot. I can already tell just by looking at you."

Lucy staggered forward and pulled out of the person's grasp. Then she turned to see Grant's sallow face as he stared down Darla. Grant stood there, holding Lucy's revolver in his hand and his whole arm was shaking.

"Let our friend go," he commanded, his voice breaking. The threat of using a weapon seemed to be making Grant physically ill. Sweat beads formed on his forehead. Lucy wanted to go over and hug him. Her heart was overjoyed at his act of bravery on her behalf, but she saw the glimmer of agitation on Darla's face and realized that Grant might be in real danger.

Lucy ran and stood between them with her arms outstretched. She spotted Salem hovering next to another one of the buses and she motioned for Lucy to run to her.

"Stop!" Lucy yelled. "Just stop! Both of you. Grant…it's okay…this is Darla. Ethan sent her. Darla, these are my friends. Don't shoot them."

"You know these kids?" Darla asked and she lifted her hands up in a show of faith and holstered her gun. "You have no idea how close I came to just shooting you. Maybe a warning next time."

Lucy dropped her hands and placed them on her knees, taking a moment. "How does a wealth manager know so much about guns?" she asked.

"Why *shouldn't* a wealth manager know so much about guns?" Darla replied.

"Spencer?" Grant asked, looking relieved to lower his gun too. And the moment the scene settled and everything seemed safe, Salem emerged and rushed over to Lucy, wrapping her arms around Lucy's shoulders and squeezing her tightly.

"He let me go," Lucy said, her breath constricted from Salem's monster embrace.

"We've been so worried," Salem said. "We spent all night trying to get back into the building."

"Fort Knox that place," Grant said.

Lucy wanted to believe it was true. She searched their faces and saw their exhaustion and worry and knew that they were being honest. Her rambling daydreams of Grant and Salem leaving her with Spencer so they could kiss unencumbered were unfounded. She let out a relieved sigh.

Darla cleared her throat. A noisy, exaggerated sound of frustration. She motioned for them to wrap up their hellos and hugs and then turned back to her original task at-hand, clearing the bus barn, taking glimpses of the undercarriage, peering into the windowed exit doors. The friends walked together after her and Salem grabbed Lucy's hand as they walked.

"I'm sorry we left you—"

With a small squeeze, Lucy smiled. "You didn't

have a choice. He would've shot you. I'm certain of it."

Salem noticed the raw cut in Lucy's right wrist and she brought it up to inspect it. "What did he do to you?"

They heard Darla's feet speeding toward them across the gravel and when Lucy looked up, she saw the dark haired woman bearing down on them, her face contorted with rage and fear. "Shut up," she seethed. "Seriously. The chummy reunion dialogue can wait until we're inside somewhere. Safe."

Grant stopped walking and tilted his head at Darla, blinking. "Why are you paranoid?"

"Where've *you* been the last week?" Darla asked. "That's right. Holed up in the school. With water, right? Food? Your basic needs were met that entire time. So whatever perceived hardship you think you might have experienced? No. You don't know what's going on out here."

Salem bristled at Darla's tone and let go of Lucy's hand. She took a small step forward and raised her shoulders. "We've been outside for twenty-four hours…and if you haven't noticed…there isn't ANYONE LEFT." Salem yelled, her voice echoing down the street and carrying into the abandoned houses and buildings that surrounded them.

No one moved for a long second and then Darla leaned in closer to Salem's face, she lowered her voice. "This corridor is used for people like me…making a beeline to that school to trade with your former principal. You're right. There's hardly anyone left. But those that decided to survive by shooting you, taking your little bag…with your last little bit of water…they'll be around here. You want to yell? Yell. But when they come, I'm not saving you from them. Not even if you beg me."

"Fine," Grant replied, not harshly. He looked at Darla and raised his hands in surrender. "So, you're the boss."

"I'm the boss?"

"You'll get us somewhere safe?"

Darla shook her head. "No. I have one task…to get Lucy back to her own house…back to Ethan. You two," she pointed to both Salem and then Grant, "have nothing to do with this. But if you're tagging along? Shut up."

The walk was serpentine. It might have taken an hour to walk straight from the high school to Lucy's house, but Darla kept them off the main streets. Without a word, they cut through yards and parks and crouched along abandoned cars in the strip mall. The shop windows were nonexistent, reduced to piles of broken glass and the furniture from the stores had been tossed outward into the parking lot. There were bodies everywhere: Against the steering wheels of cars, across the sidewalks, inside the stores. And everything was quiet. Their footsteps echoed down the covered corridor as they passed by a shoe store, a fabric store, and a clothing boutique. Darla nodded for them to head into a darkened drug store.

"No power," Darla warned. "From this grid and upward. Most of Oregon is out of power actually. Just a few zones left. I can't tell you why they're hanging on."

"Is there power at my house?" Lucy asked and Darla shook her head no.

"Power has been out there for a few days now."

The drug store was stripped clean. Shelves emptied of all essential and nonessential items. Even the rack of greeting cards was empty.

"Why would someone steal a congratulations on your bar mitzvah card?" Grant asked.

"To burn," was Darla's reply and Lucy's mind wandered to the book in her backpack. Then she cringed. She had left the backpack in Spencer's office. It seemed that leaving things at school was becoming a theme. This time, however, she would let it stay there.

They turned down an aisle and stepped over a man's decimated body. Lucy noticed that his hand was curled in a perfect circle around an imaginary object and she couldn't help but wonder if someone had actually pried a medicine bottle out of his cold dead hands. It was an expression she never imagined having a literal use and yet there was the evidence that nothing was sacred in the wreckage.

Darla, with the ease and speed of someone familiar with the landscape, pushed her way through two thick double-doors leading into a cavernous and nearly pitch black storage room. The back of the store was windowless and so they might have been blinded by the darkness, but the loading dock had been left open and the entire area was washed in natural light. They made their way down the cement stairs and found themselves on the back part of the strip mall.

Beyond the mall was an open field. A fence warned trespassers that the land was a nature preserve and violators would be prosecuted, but Darla held a flap of cut chain-link back and let the kids climb through one by one before following herself, shutting the small fence back into place with a loud clink. The field was muddy and wet and Lucy's canvas shoes kept getting stuck. She slurped her way forward, yanking one foot and then the other. When they reached the other end of the field, they were at a wooden fence leading to a soggy backyard.

Darla marched them over the wet grass and through a gently rocking swing set. Lucy let her hand linger on the chain of the swing and then let her fingers slide down. Grant and Salem were trudging along behind; Salem held her hands around her stomach and her eyes watered, Grant kept a hand poised to catch her if she fell. They were out of breath and weak, but they did not complain.

The next backyard was littered with rusting lawn furniture and several green plastic garbage cans filled with yard debris. The house sported an abandoned porch– a product of owners who had decided their home didn't need attention long before the world decided to crash down around them. In months, maybe years, the houses around this one would fall into the same sad state of disrepair. What had once been an eyesore to the manicured lawns and flower-basket neighbors was now just one more empty house.

Peering through the unwashed windows, Darla motioned for them to join her. Then she moved to the door, grabbed the handle and twisted it slowly.

"Probably empty," she said, as if she were a bloodhound, and she swung the door open wider and motioned for Grant, Lucy and Salem to follow. "Let's go. Inside," she instructed like they were half-cognizant toddlers.

"We're going inside? Why?" Lucy asked in a hushed voice as she stepped on the porch.

"To sit," Darla said. "To watch," she nodded toward the front of the house. "To wait."

"Watch and wait for what?" Grant asked.

"For what and for whom," she answered ambiguously, and then took three giants steps into the house, passing through a small mud room, filled from top to bottom with cardboard boxes, black sharpie labeling them—tax papers, kitchen utensils, Christmas décor—all in flowery, capital letters, script.

They entered after her and followed her into a kitchen. The blinds were drawn shut and the house was dim and stale. Lucy allowed her hand to travel over items dumped on to a wrinkled red and white gingham tablecloth. Among the debris, a dog collar. The tag read: Einstein. Lucy held the collar for a long time before setting it back down in the exact place it had been before. Each house was now a graveyard and its evidence of loss and grief was so clear and profound.

"Are they home?" Grant asked. He was standing near the counter. He reached for a coffee mug and picked it up, the coffee sloshed around—it had not been around long enough to mold.

Darla cracked her neck. "No one's ever home," she replied. "No one will *ever* be home." She opened the fridge and the front of the kitchen flooded with light spilled from the appliance. She tossed aside cardboard boxes filled with leftovers, mushy vegetables, and went straight to a can of soda, popping open the tab and sucking the whole thing down in gulps. Wiping her mouth with the back of her hand, she crushed the can and dropped it to the floor where it clattered and rocked; the echoes of tin on linoleum reverberated throughout the house.

Lucy waited until Darla had moved into the living room before she bent down and picked up the can. She set it on the table gently and looked around.

"This doesn't feel right," she said. "This was someone's home."

Salem nodded.

From the other room, Darla had found a piano and was plunking out a clunky melody; the strings were in dire need of retuning and the song pealed out its tinny tune through the whole house.

Grant moved past Lucy in the kitchen and made his way to the living room, where he sat down on the couch and picked up a discarded book, left open, mid-page, on the coffee table.

When Darla was finished with her piano playing, she wandered to the front window. She hooked her finger along the floral curtains and parted them and watched for a long moment, then let the curtain fall. The window looked out to the main street, and in front of that, a small corner market.

"We have to travel this way. But I know of a small group that's been hanging out across the way. Just a group of kids. Once I know the coast is clear, we'll just cross the street quickly and head up through the park. Lots of tree cover. Nothing to steal in the park," Darla said.

Above the mantel were pictures of an older couple surrounded by children. One framed photo stood out above all the others. It was a photo of a boy with a chocolate-smeared grin and missing teeth, his face smashed up against the wrinkled cheek of a chuckling loved one. Lucy walked over and took the frame in her hand and then flopped it facedown, the back-stand still sticking straight up in the air. She moved to the next picture, the people were so full of life and clueless about their future. They were smiling and hugging, cherishing moments together and Lucy pushed those downward also until the entire mantel was scrubbed cleaned of the memories of bright futures and happier times.

"Where'd you meet my brother?" Lucy asked, turning to look at Darla, then she sat down next to Grant and watched as he flipped the pages of the book mindlessly.

"The airport." But Darla shot Lucy a look that implied she wasn't in a chatty mood.

Threadbare nerves racked her and she wanted to shake Darla and demand all the answers. It had been a long time since she started following Darla's orders and still she had no idea who this woman was and how she knew Ethan. Lucy's eyes must have betrayed her agony, because Darla took note and exhaled. She leaned her head against the wall.

"Ethan was there, at the airport, looking for your family," Darla said. "They had grounded my plane to Seattle. There weren't any gates available, so they evacuated us out of the emergency exits. Those little slides aren't as fun as you would think," she paused, but then took a long look at Lucy and continued. "And when I was in the terminal, I saw Ethan trying to get *out* to the tarmac to look at the planes. He was convinced that one of the planes might have your family inside."

"My family made it to the airport?" Lucy asked. She didn't know what she wanted the answer to be. Was there a chance they made it out alive? Could it have been their plane submerged in the Columbia River? Was it possible the plane never left?

"They weren't at the airport. Either weren't there or they weren't able to be found," Darla continued without missing a beat. "Security was so diminished that it didn't take long for Ethan to find his way to the tarmac. He was running like a madman. Going from plane to plane. They had grounded flights by then. Whole planes of people just sitting there, with the infected, waiting to die."

"But Ethan *thought* my family was at the airport. So, they weren't at home?"

Darla waited and then she nodded.

"How many planes did he check? It's possible that they still *left*. Right?" Now she didn't know which version she wanted to be true. If her mom could have left her daughter and son behind or if somehow they had never made it to the airport, both versions seemed awful.

She gave a non-committal shrug. "Nothing was happening smoothly over there. It wasn't like he could just ask someone about a plane and they could point him in the right direction. But…Ethan believes the plane left. Took off. Escaped Portland."

She didn't know what that meant.

"So, you see this guy looking for his family and you decide to help him?" Grant asked.

"Not exactly," Darla replied. She swatted at an invisible fly, fully aware that she was being vague.

No one said anything. Salem shuffled her feet and stared mournfully at the ground. Grant reached into his bag and pulled out his water; he had only a sip left and he dripped the last few drops on to his tongue.

"Wait, was there a girl with him?" Lucy asked and she couldn't tell if she was hopeful for survivors or indifferent. Grant went back to reading and he flipped another page in the book.

"He was alone."

This was not surprising news, but Lucy took a

moment to process the implication that Anna was gone too. All those times she had encouraged her brother to end that dead-end relationship, her evil thoughts toward Anna's idiocy and her false friendship. And now, somewhere between leaving her standing outside the secret door and the airport, Anna and Ethan had been dealt a forced separation.

Lucy was sorry that Anna was dead. But she felt worse for Ethan and she selfishly hoped that he had been spared watching her die in the end. There were too many people to weep for; even if she felt a pang of compassion, she would not shed tears for Anna.

"Tell me about the vials," Lucy finally asked again. "Where did you get the information you shared with Spencer?"

"What vials?" Salem asked.

But before either of them could answer, Lucy heard the floorboards squeak. It was the familiar groan of a house bearing weight. They all heard it and paused, eyes, ears and heads pointed toward the ceiling. Their bodies shifted and they all went on high alert.

"What was that?" Grant asked and he stood straight up, crossing his arms over his chest. Darla stood up next to him, her gun slipping back into the palm of her hand.

"Nothing," Lucy said because she wanted that to be the right answer. "Don't houses just settle, make noises?"

But they heard the creak again, and then the shifting and shuffling and footsteps above them.

Unmistakable, distinct.

They had entered an occupied house.

"No way," Darla said and went to the window, moving the curtain back and peering out. She grumbled and nodded outward. "And there are the other Raiders. Fantastic."

Lucy darted to the window and stole a peek. A ragtag group of boys and one girl ambled up the street. There were four of them in a line. One held a semi-automatic weapon, another a baseball bat. They were dirty and weathered and none of them was over thirty. A boy on a motorized scooter with a wagon attached to the back was leading the crowd. They stopped in front of the storefront. The girl holding the baseball bat took a whack at one of the neon signs in the window and it cracked upon impact with the sound of breaking glass; she pulled it free, the cord trailing behind, and jumped on it for good measure. The group laughed, encouraging her. She batted at another sign and then took the bat to the hood of a car in the parking lot.

The steps above them had also paused. The movement ceased.

Two of the four people ducked into the store, shouting indecipherable messages to each other. It was just a lot of noise and consonants. Lucy made a move like she was going to back away from the window, but Darla put her hand out, commanding her to stay.

Grant, still standing between them, had no view of the outside, but he watched the ceiling with interest—his ears trained on the movement above.

Outside, with a swift motion, the girl raised her bat in mid-swing and then she stumbled forward. The steel slipped out of her hand and it hit the sidewalk with a clang. She clutched her stomach and slid to the ground. The boys watching guard rushed to her as she sank, then they recoiled. They called out and the looters rushed from the storefront.

Watching wide-eyed, Lucy covered her mouth with her hand as the boys dropped the goods in the wagon and took off. The boy on the scooter pulled ahead and the rest followed quickly on foot. There was a single boy who stayed and he held a gun in his hand. He spun wildly looking for something to shoot. Someone to dare cross his path in his moment of anger and surprise. He sat next to the girl, talking to her.

She doubled over in the street on her hands and knees and her body shook against the heavy burden of the virus. It was crippling her.

"Why?" Lucy croaked and took a tentative step back.

"Why what?" Salem whispered.

"The girl," she said, but she couldn't find the words to express her anguish. Lucy spun to Darla, "But I thought…" Lucy ran her fingers through her hair and kept her fingers tangled near her scalp. "You were just lying to Spencer. The stuff you said at the school." She couldn't even begin to formulate the words necessary to ask the questions on her mind.

"Day six," Darla answered as if it pained her too. "It's real, Lucy." And then her eyes shifted to Salem and Grant, who stood and sat respectively without comprehension.

Grant raised his hand up toward the ceiling. And then put a finger to his lips.

"On the move," he said.

The steps were heavy now and labored. A single thud and then another; Lucy's heart quickened, but her arms hung like lead weights at her sides.

There was no escape.

They could see two slippered feet appear at the top of the landing and they watched as the feet slid to the next step and the next step, with rigid and jerky movements.

"Zombie," Grant whispered. "It's finally the zombies." He yanked the gun out of his waistband and held it up at an angle toward the steps. Lucy noticed that his arm didn't wobble and he pointed the gun up the stairs with marked self-assuredness. It was as if Grant had never imagined he would have to shoot a person, but shooting a zombie came without effort.

"Don't you dare shoot me son," came a rough and steady voice, gravelly from sleep, but unafraid.

"*Not* zombies," Lucy said and pushed herself back toward the front door, her eyes trained on the emerging figure of a man in a salmon bath robe, bare, skinny legs, socks rolled down around his ankles and worn-white slippers. His hand gripped the railing and he took each step deliberately. When he had reached a spot where he could see all three of them, he paused and made eye contact with Darla and stared at her without blinking until she lowered her gun. Then he looked to Lucy, his blue eyes striking and bright despite the weathered, wrinkled face.

Outside, they could hear the boy cry out and the pop-pop-pop of rapid gunfire. Each of them ducked, expecting the bullets to rain in their direction. But the man stayed firm and upright, unmoving. As they rose, he cleared his throat.

"Houseguests," he mumbled. "If you'd have called beforehand, I could have put on pants."

Leland Pine's wife was still interned in their upstairs bedroom. After they had heard news that most of their children and grandchildren had perished, she retreated to the room where they had shared a bed for more than fifty years, finished off a bottle of pills, mixed with some clear alcohol from their freezer and drifted off to sleep.

He was planning on burying her in their garden, but arthritis and the constant threat of the Raiders across the street thwarted his attempts. He had given up hope that she would receive a burial and had taken to sleeping on the floor beside their bed for long hours. He'd been unable to take his own life in return and so he just waited for the illness to come claim him. Praying that he'd feel the unmistakable symptoms of the virus, he wished for death, but it never came.

Leland handed Darla a coffee mug with an illustration of an American Eskimo dog on the side filled with sweet tea that they had made with the all their remaining water and heated on Leland's old gas stove. She placed her lips on the rim then sucked up the hot liquid between her teeth, then raised mug in a cheers after swallowing, and smiled a thin smile, tight and still suspicious.

"I haven't seen many survivors beside the Raiders…the looters," Darla corrected. "Especially not anyone…"

"Older?" Leland finished for her.

"No offense," she shrugged.

"None taken," he replied. "Virus wiped out most the older population first. And the little ones too, I suppose. When you think about who was dying early on it makes it even more difficult to comprehend that someone could do this to us."

"Unfathomable," Darla agreed.

Lucy took a mug next; the sweet tea had an overpowering fruit smell and she gagged it down. She was thirsty, but fruity drinks always reminded her of the long road trips to her grandparents' house where her mother shoved juice boxes and packages of gummy bears at them to quiet the rivalry and announcements of boredom.

They all stood and sat around, drinking the sticky-sweet mixture out of an assortment of dime store coffee mugs and weighing their words. The clouds had rolled back over the area and everyone paused to listen to the sound of rain running down the gutters. Grant was the first to finish his drink and he set his mug down on the table and mumbled a sincere thank you. Leland raised his glass in reply.

"I never thought I'd have anyone in my kitchen again," Leland said. "Raiders, as you call them, would come by periodically and I'd watch them and it would just make me sad. Seems like such a shame. I've lived this long life, seen so many things. Served my country and raised my kids. And here I am, one of the last ones standing? A waste if you ask me."

No one said anything. Then Grant turned, "What branch of the military?"

"Navy," Leland replied, then he chuckled, wiping the corner of his mouth with his finger. "Cook. Oh boy, I was a mean navy cook. When I met my wife, she was this wispy little thing, all eager and excited to go on a date with me. Didn't take me long to fatten her up. Plump little gal she turned out to be after we got married. She blamed me and I knew it was true." His eyes were misty, but his smile was wide.

Lucy couldn't help but realize that maybe the Pines, in their old age, had pondered a life without each other. Mortality had to play an important role in their everyday thoughts; death was certain for everyone, but the closer you neared to the end of your life, you had to prepare your heart for imminent loss. Maybe Leland had hoped he'd go first and here he was, alone, without anyone.

"My dad wanted me to go into the military," Grant said and he slid his eyes to the table. He played with the edge of a paper napkin. "Threatened to send me to military school if I couldn't keep my grades up."

"Military isn't the same now," Leland said and he stretched his hands above his head. "Long ago, you didn't have a choice. You had to serve and you had to give up youth and plans. But now? Young people have all sorts of options. You have choices."

Leland's words were fresh in their ears when Darla laughed without missing a beat. It was loud and abrupt, but she cut it short when she saw their expressions. "I'm sorry," she then said, looking to each of them. "It's not funny."

Leland nodded. "I see my mistake. It's easy to forget."

"The opposite is true for me," added Salem from the back of the kitchen. "I can't forget. Not even for a second."

Grant looked at Leland with sympathy, bypassing Salem's comment. "But I guess we're in a war now though, right?" he asked.

"Oh really son?" Leland shook his head. "No, no. No war."

"There's nothing left to fight for," Lucy said. But Darla disagreed by sighing and shaking her head.

"We have plenty to fight *for*. It's just a matter of *how* to fight for it," Darla added. She turned to Leland. "You seem like a good man. Honest. And I'm sorry for your losses, I am. We can't take up too much of your time though. We really were just passing through."

Leland put his hands on the table. "Don't rush away on my account. The company is nice."

But Darla started to stand, taking one more sip of her drink before presumably announcing the group's departure. Lucy watched as Darla put the chipped mug to her lips. Then her eyes grew wide and her breath quickened. She was looking at something beyond Lucy, something that had caused her to freeze.

Without a word, Lucy turned and looked behind her, where Salem was standing. She had dropped her hand to her side, her fingers still gripped the porcelain of her I-Heart-Grandma mug, but her breathing was labored. Her face had gone an eerie shade of white. Her skin was milky and green and her eyes moved to each of them in turn, shifting, darting, afraid.

"Lucy?" Salem whispered. "Grant?" There was a tremor in her voice and it rose with panic.

"Salem!" Lucy jumped from her chair, knocking it to the ground, and started toward her friend.

She reached her just as Salem slumped forward, her mug hitting the kitchen floor with a crash and shattering into tiny pieces.

CHAPTER SEVENTEEN

In an instant Lucy knew exactly what was going to happen next. She knew because she had seen it many times before and she knew because Salem was not looking at her, but looking past her, like she was on the other side of a two-way mirror. She had never been so close to someone succumbing to the virus before and never watched someone she loved in the act of dying. Lucy wiped her hand across Salem's brow and her friend's skin was on fire, clumps of her dark hair stuck to her forehead. A small trickle of blood started dripping from Salem's left nostril and without thinking, without regard for her own safety, Lucy wiped the blood away with her bare hand; she only succeeded in smearing it down across Salem's cheek.

"Hey, Sal. Come on…please look at me. Sal?"

Salem was trying to talk and Lucy cradled her head, lifting her up into her nap, but Salem groaned and shook her head. Lucy set her head back down onto Leland's kitchen floor.

"Give it to me," Lucy cried over her shoulder. "Give me the vaccine." She was screaming, but her voice sounded foreign and strange.

For a second, she turned her head from Salem and looked around the room. Leland had pushed himself backward and he stood next to his refrigerator; he still clutched his tea with white knuckles. His wife had not died of the virus and Lucy realized that perhaps this was the first person he had seen succumb to it firsthand. She was sorry that Salem was in his house, sorry that he would never be able to look at this spot without remembering this moment.

Grant had taken a tentative step forward, but he looked lost and confused and he had started to cry. The look on his face made Lucy angry. She read resignation and futility in his eyes and she hated him for it.

Astounded by everyone's inaction, Lucy turned to Darla with tears dripping down on to her borrowed sweatshirt and she pleaded.

"She needs it now, Darla. I need it quick." But when she turned to Salem, her breathing had already started to slow. She fought for breath, her chest rattling with fluid with each attempt to draw air into her lungs.

"Please, please, please, please," Lucy begged. And then, with a voice that was nearly inhuman, she yelled with rage and fear. "Why won't you help me? Give me the rest of the vaccines!"

"Even if I had it, Lucy," Darla said, her voice calm and quiet, hovering at normal volume, "it wouldn't do her any good. It's too late."

"I don't...believe you," Lucy replied and she took a shaky breath and then screamed. She stopped when she felt Salem's hand wrap around her wrist and attempt a squeeze. "I don't believe you, I don't believe you!"

"It doesn't work like that," Darla continued. "She would've needed it hours ago. Before it reached this point. I'm sorry, Lucy." She slunk back to the rear of the kitchen next to Leland and rested her head against the side of the wall.

Lucy seethed and she watched as her tears dripped on to Salem's shirt creating a little pattern of slow-spreading circles. Then she looked straight at Darla, who didn't even try to break eye contact, and raised a shaky finger. "You wasted them."

"Lula, he…saved me," Salem mumbled, drawing Lucy's attention back down toward her friend. Turning back to Salem, she slipped her clammy hands into her own and held on to them tightly.

"I don't understand," Lucy sniffed. "I don't understand. What do you mean?"

"That summer. At the beach."

Then Lucy remembered. She knew what Salem was trying to say.

She remembered this story perfectly.

Her parents had always instilled a healthy fear of the ocean—the Oregon coast riptides were not trivial and insignificant. A King family friend lost his son to a sneaker wave the same summer Salem now remembered—it was a long Indian summer and they all loaded up the car for a day trip to the beach on Labor Day when the weather hit close to one-hundred degrees in Portland.

They were bodysurfing, pushing past the coldness of the water with the sun beating down on them; their bodies shivered, while their hair absorbed the heat from the sun. Her father yelled that they were going too far out, and Lucy dutifully obeyed his command by spinning around, treading water back until her feet could touch, and finding safety on the sand. It was Salem who pushed out further and ignored Lucy's and the King family's pleas to paddle back.

"He saved you," Lucy said now, finishing the story, even as her shoulders heaved. "You were drowning. And he saved you."

Salem had slipped below the surface and Lucy was terrified. Screams and shouting filled the beach and she remembered the alarm in her own voice, her fear of losing her friend. And Lucy's father had sprinted from the blanket, waded into the ocean fully dressed and pulled her up, paddling back to shore with a gasping Salem in his arms. He had lost one shoe in the sand; it was absorbed into the muck. Maybe it resurfaced later and was discovered by an early morning jogger. One lone shoe without a partner, bobbing in the surf, resting in the foam, or tangled with seaweed.

"I can't save you." Lucy dropped her head on to Salem's chest. Her forehead dug into the sharp edges of Salem's gold crucifix. "I've never been able to save you. I'm sorry, I'm so sorry. I'm sorry."

"But he saved me," Salem said again. "El me salvo."

And Lucy curled up beside her best friend, their bodies touching. She kept her hand placed squarely on her heart until the distressed breathing stopped and the rise and fall of her chest slowed to a stop.

Salem was gone.

The room didn't move.

Then Grant took a tentative step toward them and Lucy, sensing his approach, lifted her head. "No. Stay back."

"Lucy—"

"I said stay back," Lucy cried out.

A great and terrible fury passed through her. And in an instant she was on her feet, scrambling across the kitchen to Darla. Her foot slipped in blood that had seeped beneath Salem's body and she lost her balance, tripping into the table. Her body knocked around the plates and glasses as they clinked together. She ran her hand over the table and threw the items to the floor, where they shattered or bounced, and then gripping the sides she flung herself forward, pressing her weight against Darla's body and pushing her to the floor.

Darla darted out from under her and rolled to safety and then she lifted herself up and held her hands up in defense. She had the poise of someone who knew how to fight, but Lucy—who had only engaged in mock wrestling matches with her brothers—fought with blind rage. When she lifted a hand to scratch at Darla's tan face, she felt a firm grip around her wrist, digging into the same spot where she had been handcuffed. And Lucy crumpled to the floor, allowing Darla to stand up straight and catch her breath.

"She let her die," Lucy gasped. "She let her die! We had everything we needed to save them and you just let Spencer have it. How could you let me believe I was safe?"

"You are safe," Darla said again. "*You* are safe. Ethan told me—" she stopped, sighed. "I didn't know there were other people. I had *one* task."

"It's fine to be angry. It is normal for grief to look like anger," Leland's voice said near Lucy's ear. "But you should not fight with your friends in a time like this," he elucidated in a parental tone.

"She's not my friend," Lucy responded quickly and she yanked her hand away from his grasp. But she did not move from her place in the ground.

No one spoke. Grant wandered over to Salem's body and stood looking at her—a sliver of sun filtered through the window fell over Salem's legs. Then he turned back to the group, his skin red and blotchy and his eyes puffy. "What vaccine?" he asked.

Lucy stood by the window and looked out on the street. The boy had gone, run off somewhere, so the girl's body was alone on the wet concrete. The rain had not lifted and the water ran off her body like tiny streams.

Grant sat at the piano. He ran his fingers over the fake ivory keys, stretching them out, and then settled them into position. He hit a chord and another, running them together into a melody that Lucy had never heard before, even though it had the quality of something familiar, something memorable. Grant finished the song, sustaining the last note throughout the house until he lifted his foot off the pedal suddenly and he spun on the bench and stared at Lucy.

"A Grant Trotter original," he said in a half-whisper.

"You made that up?" Lucy asked, too tired and sad to even muster an impressed smile. "I didn't know you could play."

"I'm full of surprises."

"I should've said something." Lucy turned back to the window. "I should've put it all together and realized. I should've warned you both."

Grant stood up and stretched. "No," he said. "In some ways, it's better not to know. But I want it stated for the record. I was right. That first morning when I predicted that we were just taking longer to die? I don't know why I didn't take bets."

Lucy began to cry again.

He walked over and put a comforting arm around her shoulder. "I feel like *you* should be consoling *me* right now. I am the one that just learned I'm going to die sometime today."

Lucy leaned into his arm.

"I'm not afraid to die," Grant said.

Pulling back, Lucy looked at him and wiped her tears on her sleeve. "I don't understand. We've been fighting so hard to stay safe and alive…for almost a week…"

"You misunderstood." He took a step back and placed his hands on Lucy's shoulders. He was taller than her by almost a whole foot and he had to stoop his shoulders to look in her eyes. "I *want* to live. But I'm not afraid to die. This new world is much scarier than death, Lucy."

"It's not fair."

"Amen."

"We have to go back to the school and get one of the vials back from Spencer." Lucy mentioned this is in a rush of importance, begging him to agree. She had been thinking about the trip back and how they could pull it off. She had a plan. The vaccine in Spencer's possession was a travesty, especially since Grant was just playing a waiting game.

"No," was Grant's swift reply.

"Yes," Lucy replied. "Yes. We can do this. And if Darla won't help…I'll go alone."

"Lucy—" he shook his head. "I'm not letting you go. I'm not letting you or anyone else risk your life for me. There's no guarantee that it would work or that…in the time that it took…" he trailed off and she knew what he was going to say. She cringed.

"Please." She cried harder.

Grant shook his head and squeezed her shoulders tightly. "We're not talking about it. And you won't change my mind."

"What *do* you want to do then?" Lucy asked and

she tried to harden herself, stop the blubbering, and regain control.

Grant laughed. His genuine amusement shocked her and he put a thoughtful finger to his lips. "You mean…on your last day to live? What do you want to do?"

"No," Lucy stammered. Then, "Maybe."

Without missing a beat, he replied. "I want to bury Salem. Give her what no one else in our school or our lives got when they died. Something proper." He then looked at her with a sad smile. "Then I want to see *you* get home."

Abigail Pine's body had already started to decay. Not the rapid decomposition the virus caused, but the normal human rate of putrefaction. In an attempt to mask the smell, Leland had dumped two entire boxes of baking soda over her. Everywhere, except her face. And despite her whiteness and bloat, she still looked peaceful as she lay on top of their floral comforter.

With Leland watching, twisting his hand in his robe nervously, Darla wrapped her in a white flat sheet; her body was stiff, but still moveable. They rolled her onto the sheet in stages and then secured it at the ends. Grant grabbed her upper body, lifting her with a mixture of tenderness and sheer strength, while the girls congregated at her legs and feet. Then they shimmied and shifted, maneuvered and backed their way down the stairs, through the family room, out the kitchen, and into the garden—where Leland met them holding two shovels.

They dug two holes. The rain made them a muddy mess and the further down they got, the harder the earth was, slowing down their digging process. After fifty minutes, they had created large and deep enough holes to fit Leland's departed wife and Salem.

Grant bent down and picked Salem off the floor on his own and laid her to rest in the earth. Mud splattered on her cheeks and clothes and the sides of the grave started caving in almost immediately. Salem's golden crucifix peaked out of the earth and, spotting it, Lucy dropped to her knees. She reached down into the grave and she dug her hands under the mud until she was able unclasp the necklace from around Salem's neck. She held it tightly in her hands, the sharp edges of the cross digging into her palms.

Then Grant covered the bodies as quickly as he could. With Darla's help, they slung the thick sludge over the bodies until nothing on their bodies remained visible.

"I'll say some words for my wife," Leland said and gathered them together, where they huddled and listened to his praises, his prayers.

"My wife was a giving soul. And she had a spirit of fire and passion. And love. She loved. With everything she had. This is not how we imagined our end. But here we are. Here will she rest…with me by her side as long as I am able." Leland stopped. He turned to the group, "You go," he instructed and he pointed to Lucy.

Rain dripped on her head and she shivered, her teeth chattered. "Salem was my best friend. She…" Lucy stopped and took a second to compose herself, "gave everything she had to me. She was fun and loving. For many years, she was my sister…my only sister. I feel like I've lost my heart, my other half. I can't imagine a world without her."

Grant walked over to a rosebush and looked to Leland, "May I?" he asked and Leland nodded. He broke a single red rose off of the vine, between the thorns. It snapped easily in between his fingers. Tossing the rose on to Salem's grave, Grant cleared his throat, closed his eyes, and said, "God our Father, your power brings us to birth, your providence guides our lives, and by your command we return to dust. Lord, those who die still love in your presence, their lives change, but do not end. I pray in hope for my family and friends and for all the dead known to you alone. Wipe away all our tears. Unite us together. And all God's people said, amen."

Lucy stammered out a belated amen. And then she looked slowly over to Grant, her eyebrows questioning.

He shrugged. "Catholic."

"Full of surprises," she said.

CHAPTER EIGHTEEN

After they left Leland's house, it took one hour to reach Lucy's street.

Loaded down with bags of canned peaches, pickled green beans, baby corn, and strawberry jelly—something the old man insisted upon, despite their numerous objections—they wound their way through empty houses, a looted coffee house, a smoldering police station, until they reached Lucy's neighborhood. Passing by familiar cars and facades, they trekked down the road in the open, their heads panning from side-to-side in an effort to catch movement.

It didn't surprise anyone that the street was silent.

When Lucy's house came into view, she tossed her bag with Leland's food to Grant, who caught with a clumsy grasp. "Take this," she said and then bolted. She ran, full speed, down the street.

It pained her how much she needed to see Ethan and how much she needed to ask him. They had remained mostly silent as they made their way to the house. Lucy tried to pry details out of Darla, but she had remained focused during their journey, trading only barbs and not information.

Lucy ran past the front door and straight to the side-door to the left of the carport and crashed her way through into their laundry room, pushing off the washing machine, and then she took the steps into her house two at a time. She ran across the family room, past the stairs, calling his name loudly and without reservation.

"Ethan! Ethan!"

"Here Lucy! I'm in here!" came the reply and Lucy followed his call into the den. Ethan rested on their father's leather couch, the giant throw blanket from their mother's alma mater tucked up around his legs. He looked at her bleary-eyed and then broke into a giant smile and threw his arms up in response. Lucy rushed into the embrace, crouching down near the edge of the couch to get the best grip and Ethan held his hands tightly across her back and squeezed.

"I thought I'd never see you again," he said and Lucy was too overcome to respond, so she just tried to melt her body into his.

From the back part of the house, she could hear Darla and Grant enter from the carport and then slam the door. The house was alive with footsteps and muffled conversation.

"Who is with her?" Ethan asked and he dropped his arms, raised himself up on his elbows and craned his neck.

"Grant Trotter. A friend. But Ethan..." Lucy's chin trembled and she bit her lip.

Ethan interrupted, "Wait…there's someone else *alive*? Did you bring anyone *else*?"

Lucy shook her head. Tears rolled down her cheeks and she wiped them away. She wasn't ready to talk about Salem yet, the death was too recent, too fresh and too painful to mention.

Ethan blew air out his nose, muttered an expletive, and went back to lying down, crossing his hands over his chest and staring at the ceiling. "This is a mess." He reached a hand out and locked hands with his sister.

"Ethan—"

"We do have much to talk about little sister. So much." His tone implied disagreement, exhaustion and, Lucy thought, fear. But Darla swung into the room with Grant following behind. He slipped into the matching leather chair in the corner, and she walked right over to Ethan, ignoring Lucy's presence on the ground beneath him. Without a word, she reached behind his head and grabbed a prescription bottle of pills from a side table and shook the orange container, counting them audibly as they rolled around.

"There are extra. You haven't been taking them." She dropped the bottle on Ethan's chest and it started to roll, he caught it with his left hand and tossed it back up in the air. Swooping in, she caught it on its way back down. "I told you. No skipping."

"We will run out of the supply," Ethan groaned and sat up. He cracked his neck one way and then the other. "I'll make them last."

"No one likes a martyr," Darla sighed and opened

the bottle. She rattled it until two oblong white pills tumbled into her hand and she thrust them toward Ethan. He didn't take them at first and then she moved her hand in closer, her body an inch from Lucy's. He grabbed the pills, popped them in his mouth and swallowed them dry—opening his mouth and sticking out his tongue for effect, like a petulant teenager.

"Happy?" he asked.

"Let me see," Darla said and made a motion to tear the blankets off his legs, but Ethan ducked his body in front of her hand. Then she paused, looking between Ethan and Lucy, and back again. "You didn't tell her."

"She's been in this room for sixty-seconds!" Ethan replied, his tone angry and combative. "Come on Darla, give me a break."

"I'll ignore the opportunity for a joke," she replied and then she looked around the room. "Where is he?" she asked, softening. She unhooked the holster from her hip and gripped the gun, then placed it on a high bookshelf, standing on her tiptoes to store it out of reach.

Ethan pointed above him to the second floor. "In the twins' room. He discovered the Legos."

Darla ducked her head out of the den and called up the stairs, "Teddy? Mommy's home!"

Confused, Lucy looked between Ethan and Darla, and then she stood and wandered to the center of the room where she had a clear view of her family's staircase. Then she saw the little boy. Carrying her brother's tiger flashlight in one hand and a fireman hat in the other, the dark-haired child, with large eyes and a rash of freckles, bounded down the steps in a rush of energy and extremities. Arms flailing outward, feet stomping and jumping, the child didn't stop until he reached his mother as a barricade, moving Darla back a few inches as she absorbed the hug.

"You were good for Ethan while I was gone?" she asked and the boy nodded vigorously. "And did you eat?"

"Hamburger," Teddy answered.

Darla looked over her shoulder and saw Lucy staring. She put a protective arm on the boy and moved him into the light from the windows.

"Lucy, this is my son Theodore. Teddy, we call him."

"You have a son," Lucy stated and then immediately regretted not having anything else of value to say about it.

"I have a son." For the first time since she met her, Lucy saw emotion in Darla's eyes: A flicker of fragility underneath the comic-book persona. "He's five. He's sweet, and he loves to sing…and he's intuitive," Darla stopped and swallowed. "And he is alive because of your brother. *We* are alive because of your brother." She picked the boy up and he wrapped his legs around her middle and placed his head on her shoulder.

"Mama," Teddy whispered loudly. "What's the girl's name?"

"Lucy," she answered. "Her name is Lucy. She's Ethan's sister, sweetie. Go ahead, say hello."

"Hello," Teddy said and then he buried his head into his mother's shoulder, shielding his eyes. Then he lifted his head again and smiled, displaying a neat, straight row of perfect baby teeth, before burying his head again.

The child was around the same age as Harper. Lucy crossed her arms and smiled at the boy, her lip trembling. Then Lucy turned to Grant and she looked at him apologetically.

"I'm sorry, but can everyone just give me a moment with Ethan? Alone."

She waited until Grant had risen from his seat and wandered off with Darla before she turned her attention back to her brother. The discharged duo followed Teddy up the stairs, their footsteps echoing overhead. It amused Lucy that this was the quietest she had ever heard her house. She kept waiting for the rowdy shouting from her brothers, the crashing and tumbling, or Harper's whining that someone stole her toys.

"What's going on?" Lucy's voice was on edge. She took a giant step toward Ethan. "What the hell is going on here?"

"I don't know how any of this must appear to you…" Ethan started and then frowned.

"Let's start with this vaccine. With our siblings' names on them? Can we start with that, please?"

"Okay."

She gulped. "Okay, what? Just tell me what you know. Tell me everything."

"I can't. It won't work like that. I don't think you'd believe me."

"Then what am I supposed to do? Wait until you *feel* like filling me in?"

Upstairs, Teddy dumped out what sounded like a crate of blocks.

"I'm really glad you're home and that you're okay. You don't know how much I worried that I would lose you forever."

"Darla said that I was safe. Are we safe?"

"From the virus, yes. We were already vaccinated."

"When?"

"You don't remember being vaccinated lately?" Ethan asked with his eyebrows raised. When Lucy's stare remained blank, he sighed, and then added, "For our vacation. Our injections."

"The ones for the trip? But..." she lowered her eyes and her head began to hurt. Her father had been the one to supply them with their inoculations and, at the time, it seemed reasonable and normal—par for the course of living in their household. After a rant about lobbyists and health-care costs, their dad had convinced their mother that he could talk his co-workers into providing him with the vaccines on the cheap. Lucy was starting to gather the facts, but still there was a shadow over what those facts implied.

"The vials we gave Spencer were back-ups. A precaution. A safeguard."

"Where did *our* vials go then? The Ethan and Lucy vials?"

Ethan looked to the ceiling. Darla and Teddy's voices drifted downstairs.

"Oh."

"I couldn't—" he struggled with his words. "She helped me. And Teddy is so young."

"Of course." The decision seemed reasonable. There was no way Ethan could have predicted Salem and Grant surviving to Day Six. While she wanted to respect Ethan's compassion toward these strangers—especially a child—she fought the instinct to be angry with him for giving away the only way she could help her friends. It was too late for Salem, but she felt so impotent and lost with Grant, upstairs, just waiting to die. The power to stop that death was in Ethan's control and he squandered it.

"You should have kept some back," Lucy said.

"We had no way of knowing."

"That isn't the point!" She felt her cheeks blush. Arguing with Ethan always felt so personal.

"Spencer wasn't going to let you go. There were talks happening with Darla before he even got you to the front office. Don't you think we tried everything? You don't know what it would've taken to get you out of there. And besides…how was I supposed to know about the boy?"

"Grant."

"Grant. Right."

"He's going to die and we could have saved him."

"That isn't *my* fault," Ethan said to her, his voice rising.

Lucy threw her hands up in the air. "Then whose fault is it?"

Ethan shook his head. "Lucy. Just stop. It hasn't been a picnic for me either. Can we stop? Let's back-up." Whisking away the throw blanket from his legs, Ethan exposed the broken, beaten, and bloodied mess that lay beneath. His left leg dangled unmoving to the side; there was a swollen mass above the knee that seemed to float to the side, which defied Lucy's understanding of human anatomy. The skin was yellow and black like someone had attempted to paint him into an exotic animal.

Recoiling at first and then moving her body closer to inspect the injury, Lucy held out a tender hand and it hovered above the wreckage.

"This looks horrific," she said. "Ethan…what happened?"

He took a breath and then launched into his story. He had gone to the airport looking for their family and encountered Darla and Teddy there. It was the boy that Ethan encountered first; the child was calm, but rattled, and Ethan wanted to get him somewhere safe. Compelled, in the absence of his siblings and his mother, to do something good amidst the disaster, Ethan convinced Darla that he could offer them shelter.

"She wasn't convinced at first. But as soon as we got out of the airport and to a side street, this truck comes out of nowhere, barreling toward me. The driver…impaired by the virus…is—"

"Dying?" Lucy asked, interrupting, and the question drew Ethan out of his storytelling daze.

"Or dead already."

"He hit you."

"Pinned me to the side of another car."

Lucy gasped and looked down at his legs, imagining her brother stuck between two vehicles, scared and facing the realization that there was no one there who could help him. "You could have died."

"I should have. Darla...she had to pull the dead man out of the truck and put the car in reverse to get me out. But my legs were broken. Shattered, I suppose. Not like we could just call 911 and hightail it to the ER, right? And poor Teddy. Just standing there...so concerned. But so brave too. That's a brave little dude."

Lucy waited for him to continue.

"Good Samaritans brought me home eventually. Some couple in their forties, driving a minivan. Carting people around obstacles like some sort of taxi service. By that time, I think Darla figured she was stuck with me. She really did save my life though, by helping unpin me, flagging down the van. And then everything she did afterward to get me medicine. I was in shock. I should have died, but she just, I don't know, made it a priority to get me better and she didn't have to. She didn't know me."

"You owed her."

"Yes."

"And now she owes you?"

"Maybe she sees it like that, but I don't know. It

was…" Ethan paused, "it was awful out there…Lucy…everything about this. And I feel so…I felt like I couldn't help you…" Ethan began to cry. He collapsed forward and buried his head in his hands. She had never really seen Ethan cry before and it took her by surprise. "I just keep thanking God that you're alive," he said after he composed himself. "After everything…Mom's phone messages, the house…"

Lucy had put a hand on her brother's back and was patting him gently, but she paused.

"What phone messages?" Lucy blinked.

"I have a lot to tell you," Ethan said, his voice quieter and more alert.

Both heads turned in unison as Darla reappeared in the doorway. She had changed her clothes and she was now wearing a pair of sweatpants that belonged to Lucy's mother and a hooded sweatshirt that belonged to Galen; she stood barefoot clad from top to bottom in gray.

"Grant?" Lucy asked, attempting to make her question sound as casual as possible.

Darla shrugged. "He's playing with Teddy. He said if he starts to feel sick he'll leave the room. But Teddy knows what to look for. Teddy will tell us if anything changes."

"That's really sad." Lucy didn't mean it to sound harsh, but Darla bristled.

"The world changes and you change with it," she answered, clearly defensive. "A lot can happen in a week." She spun a lock of her hair between her fingers.

Lucy thought of poor Teddy, only a year younger than Harper. He seemed so oblivious, so fixated on his own needs, but also so aware that things had changed. Her heart ached for the children abandoned and orphaned, lost and confused. Those who, unlike Teddy, had no parents left to protect them. It was unfair.

"Ethan's been telling me about how you helped him," Lucy said. "Thank you."

"Yeah well. It worked out that way. And he's helped with Teddy and anyone who can be so nice to my kid, well, you know." She smiled, but it was reserved and lacking. It was difficult to get a read on her.

"Does Teddy understand any of this?" Lucy asked. And Darla took a step forward. She shoved her hands into the pouch of the hooded sweatshirt.

"Teddy? Sure. A little. He knows he's suffered a loss. He knows that our lives feel different."

"I'm glad he has his mom though," Lucy tried to smile. She meant it to be comforting, but Darla's face fell.

"He has only one Mom," she replied and she closed her eyes. "And I haven't come to terms yet with that…with the idea of doing this by myself. I never thought I'd have to."

"And you know? That—"

"That she's gone?" Darla nodded. "Yes. It happened at the airport. Right away after landing and before Ethan and I saw each other. She went so quickly. It was the three of us and it was chaos and then she slipped away and I couldn't stop to stay…I couldn't have Teddy see. Couldn't have him watch his mama die. Above all, he couldn't see that."

Ethan sniffed. "That's how we met," he said.

"I asked Teddy to stay by this trashcan to wait for me while I said goodbye." Darla looked straight at Lucy, her emotion was raw, but she didn't break. "And when I looked back, he was gone."

"I found him crying about thirty feet away. He was disoriented. Wandered a few feet, got pushed around, ended up down the terminal. I picked him up," Ethan added.

"Then I saw this guy holding my kid. I just lost my wife, I was a mess, and I thought someone was kidnapping my son. So, I took a swing at him."

Ethan smiled. "I'm glad you missed."

Darla returned the smile and then she closed her eyes. "Teddy was bawling for his mama. Over and over…just *mama, mama, mama*…and I couldn't help him. Ethan—it was Ethan. He said he had to find his sister, who was his age, and did Teddy want to help him on an adventure? It was the only way to distract him from the fact that we both just…left her there." She stopped, overcome with emotion and then she pulled her hand out and put it up as if to say, "*No more.*"

"I'm sorry for your loss," Lucy said and it felt so small and trivial.

"Me too." Then Darla let out a thoughtful hum. "You never think it'll be you who's left behind to pick up the pieces. And then all of sudden you realize it *is* you and you didn't get a choice. And maybe if you had the choice, maybe if someone had let you make the decision, you would have picked yourself to be the one to die. I mean, yes, I'm grateful to your brother." Darla nodded toward Ethan with a smile. "What I did is no repayment. If I hadn't decided to follow this kid around who was helping me with my son, we'd be dead. I may question how hard things are, but I can't imagine a world without Teddy."

Darla attempted to fill in some of the gaps of her and Ethan's story. Like Lucy's and Grant's, it was one of survival against the odds. Once they got back to the house, Darla had left Ethan, with Teddy as a guardian, shivering and feverish, aching and unable to move, to raid the local super store a mile from their house. Luckily for them, the looting was just beginning and Darla's tenacity and bullying got her right into the fray. During this Herculean task, she managed to locate heavy-duty painkillers and gauze. And she also happened to steal a wheelchair. She had marveled at the people still running out of the store with TVs and videogames, sporting equipment, clothes.

Food. Guns. Medicine. This was what people needed and those who knew what to steal were the dangerous ones. "Anyone using manpower to lug a fifty-inch plasma to his or her car was missing the point," Darla had said.

Lucy realized that, if the car had killed Ethan, it wouldn't have mattered if he had been vaccinated. From start to finish, the fact that they were alive was a testament to something larger than them. The thought reminded her of Salem's crucifix, shoved into her pocket. She took it out and held it in her hand, then put it on and clasped it around her neck.

With the sun setting, the house slipped into darkness. Darla started a fire in the den and then yelled upstairs for Grant so they could work together to get Ethan into his wheelchair for the first time—something Darla couldn't do on her own. He barely passed through the study door and into the living room, but out in the open he could move about freely. While Darla hunched over the fire burning brightly in the fireplace, Teddy ran matchbox cars over the hardwood floors. Between the fire and a collection of candlesticks, the room was lit in a flickering orange hue.

Everyone's features were cast in shadow.

Grant was quiet and staring at the wall. Occasionally he'd connect with a piece of conversation but, for the most part, he remained stoic and apprehensive. Lucy couldn't blame him. She wondered what she would be thinking about if she knew she had hours left to live. She hated that Grant was spending this time with the rest of them trying to carve out daily routines. They were catching up with each other and plotting to move forward. She got up and sat next to him and placed a hand on his knee.

Right as Lucy was about to ask him if he wanted to take a walk with her, sneak away to the darkened kitchen or the family room, Ethan cleared his throat.

"Darla," he said and she looked up at him. "Could

you get the video camera? I think it's time to show Lucy everything."

Following Ethan's orders, Darla rose and went over to the bookshelf and grabbed the video camera her parents used years ago to record first steps and school outings. Handing it to Ethan, he opened up the tiny screen and handed it to Lucy and instructed her to press play.

"What am I watching?" Lucy asked. Her hand shook and she wished that she could hold it steady.

"Mom left me a message. I didn't know if I would still be able to access my voicemail when the network went down, so I videotaped it."

She pressed play.

The camerawork was shaky and she could hear a news report broadcasting in the background. In the video, Ethan's phone was on the kitchen counter and he had put it on speakerphone. The Ethan holding the video camera leaned down and pressed a button to access his voicemail. Lucy deeply drew a breath as she waited anxiously to find out what she'd hear. The moment the message clicked through, she heard her mother's voice—it filled the kitchen on the video and as Lucy held the camera, her voice filled the den as well—the first syllable was immediately recognizable as her Mama Maxine. And Lucy bit back tears. For the first time she realized that she truly believed she'd never hear her mom say another word to her again, but there was her voice, captured for her to listen to again and again.

"Ethan. Ethan. There's no time. They took us. Dear God, they took us. Some guys, from an agency…I'm calling you from a car…a transport…I tried to get them to wait. But…" the voice was indecipherable for a moment. And then there was a click.

Lucy kept watching.

From the videotape, a woman's voice announced a second saved voicemail and said the date and time, mechanical and rote, like any other day. Like it was just any other message.

It was their mom's voice. Again.

"Ethan. Listen to me. Get to the airport. Get to the airport now. Get to the airport. That's where we're going…but I don't know yet…"

Another click.

Another announcement of a saved voicemail.

"No time. I'm sorry. You need this message." In the background, there was a rumble. It was the distinct and unmistakable rumbling of an airplane funneling down a runway. *"I called your dad. I…your dad says…"* there was a bump, a pop. Their mother was yelling and the phone was far from her mouth now, but her voice trailed after it, barely audible. She was yelling two words over and over again, screaming them, with vigor and intensity, until the line went dead and her voice disappeared.

The automated woman announced: *"That is the end of new messages…to replay this message press four…"* and Ethan in the video pressed four and listened to the last message again. Zooming in the camera to the front of his phone screen. Hearing it a second time didn't make her mother's panicked voice any less haunting.

Then Ethan turned the camera on himself.

"Lucy…I'm in a rush…I've got to get to the airport. But in case you get back…I need you to see this." He jostled the camera back toward the house and out of the kitchen and through the dining room to the entryway. At the time of the video, it was only a half hour or hour after Lucy had left that area. Ethan zoomed in on Lucy and Ethan's monogramed bags. The only bags left at the foot of the stairs. A lump formed in Lucy's throat when she saw those—their things had been left behind.

They had been totally and completely left behind.

Then the camera panned to the entryway. And when Lucy saw it on the camera, she opened her mouth in horror and turned to Ethan, who confirmed with a nod. There had clearly been a struggle. Lucy had watched enough cop dramas on TV to know the signs—the mirror was broken, a potted plant on the floor, the vase shattered, the roots exposed. The entry table was turned on its side.

Lucy hadn't gone through the front door when she came home, she had gone through the side door through the carport. Was this chaos still there?

Would it be a permanent reminder that something bad had happened at their house?

Not taking her eyes off of the camera, she spoke—shocked by the waver in it. "What was Mom saying?" she asked as video-Ethan opened the front door and panned to muddy tire marks in the grass which right led up to the door. A car had pulled up on their recently mowed lawn.

If what Lucy was seeing was true, then people got out and grabbed her family. In the midst of nuclear war, a deathly virus, and the end of the world and life on the planet, her family had also been kidnapped. It was mind-boggling.

"What was she saying?" Lucy asked again. The video had ended. She slammed the monitor shut and held the camera against her chest. "Do you know? Did you figure it out?"

Ethan nodded and glanced to Darla and Grant.

"Ethan?" Lucy asked again.

"Yeah," he finally answered, his voice small. He sniffed and looked at his sister and then tilted his head. "She was saying *fruit cellar*."

"Fruit cellar?" Lucy couldn't hide her incredulity. "Fruit cellar."

Their mom canned fruits and vegetables. As kids, she took them cherry picking and blueberry picking and made them go out and play on long canning days. Then she meticulously stored her goods in a dirt-walled fruit cellar in their basement. It was slightly raised off the basement ground and could be accessed by climbing up and over a two-foot wooden barrier. It was a fruit cellar—and their mother referred to it as such—but the children called it "the dungeon" and loathed stepping foot inside the tiny space. Monroe and Malcolm always chose to hide there during games of sardines or hide-and-seek; but they usually were left to discover on their own that no one was coming for them because none of the other kids wanted to open the giant wooden door to see if they were there or not. It was the only place in the house that elicited nightmares and phobias among each of the King kids. They hated the fruit cellar.

In her final message to her lost children, Maxine King had been shouting for them to go to the one place they dreaded more than anything.

"The dungeon." Lucy reworded. And then she shook her head. "Mom was sending us to the dungeon? No, I don't get it."

Ethan and Darla exchanged another look.

"Grab a flashlight," Ethan instructed. Then he turned to his sister, as the color drained from her face. "Lucy…Grant…there's something in the fruit cellar that you two need to see."

CHAPTER NINETEEN

The fruit cellar. It sat in the pitch blackness with the wooden door slightly ajar. It was cool and quiet and isolated. Every horror movie had a scene like this: Three shuffling people moving forward in a dank basement toward an eerie looking door—their flashlights only creating a small circle of concentrated light and leaving the rest of the space full of dreaded mysteries.

If Lucy had been afraid of her mother's dungeon before, she was petrified now. Without power, they had no secondary light to illuminate the way, and every box or broom or any other basement belonging seemed particularly foreboding and potentially murderous in the dark. Ethan had demanded Lucy just go explore for herself, like he had, without any warnings or hints about what she would find. Darla, who clearly already knew about the fruit cellar's contents, tagged along, but even she seemed turned off by the darkness of the basement combined with the growing momentum of fear and worry.

Unable to travel to the basement, Ethan stayed

upstairs with Teddy and waited for their return. Teddy seemed to adore Ethan; he was conscious of Ethan's pain and before they had opened the door to the basement, Teddy had climbed into Ethan's lap with a collection of books.

They approached the door to the fruit cellar and everyone slowed to a halt.

"You open it," Lucy said to Grant and gave him a small push toward the door. "This is massively frightening to me." Grant responded with a resounding no and, as the holder of the flashlight, turned the object onto Lucy and Darla, blinding them—their hands flew to their faces in protest. "Stop. Get that out of my eyes," Lucy complained.

"Make Darla open it," Grant said and when Darla sighed and consented, he lowered the light and lit her path to the door. Darla peeled back the door and it squawked at them.

"There," Darla announced and stepped out of the way. "Boys first." She motioned for Grant to crawl up and through, he hesitated and then took a step forward, sticking just his upper body into the cellar first and shining the light all around.

"It's a normal, boring fruit cellar," Grant called back to them, annoyed. He then climbed in all the way and shone the light on the door so Darla and Lucy could watch where they were stepping as they followed him inside.

All three of them shoved together in the confined space was suffocating—Lucy could move, but every time she did, she ran into another person. There were arms and legs and hands touching. Darla tried to scuttle away to the corner to give them space, but she stepped on Lucy's toe in the process. Grant tried to control the light, but viewing the fruit cellar through the lens of what Grant deemed important was making Lucy nauseous. She reached over and took the flashlight gently and then began to illuminate each area of the small space in turn.

The entire space was the size of a walk-in closet. Lucy noticed almost immediately that one of the shelves was empty. The cans their mother had carefully prepared over the summer had been moved to the floor. And the whole shelving unit was moved away from the dirt wall, giving just enough room for a body to slip behind it. Ignoring the tickling on the back of her neck, her warning beacon of intuition, she stepped over the grape jelly and peaches and asparagus spears and slid herself behind the wooden shelving unit. Up close, she realized that the wall was not dirt and earth, but wood. And there, sparkling brightly underneath the flashlight was a long, thin door handle.

"Oh my goodness," Lucy breathed out in a gush. "There's another room back here."

Darla's disembodied voice rose to her from the darkness, "Took Ethan ten minutes to find that door. Go ahead now," she instructed in a small, sad voice. Lucy paused. It bothered her that Darla knew her family's secrets before she did; she hated that Darla knew what was waiting for her in the next room and hadn't made an effort to tell her, warn her, keep her involved in the story. What did Darla gain from being secretive?

She closed her eyes, her hand wrapping around the handle. It was cold against her palm.

In the dark, Lucy could make out the sound of Grant's feet shuffling around, moving closer to the empty shelf.

"You okay, Grant?" she asked.

"I feel fine," he answered with a subtle hint of contrition—as if he was sorry that the unknown nature of his future caused a burden.

"Are you coming?"

He paused and cleared his throat before saying; "I just think…I feel like…you should do this by yourself."

She didn't feel like arguing with a dead man.

That whole day, Lucy wanted to know the answers. Who and what? Why? But as she stood on the precipice of discovery, Lucy was sure she didn't really want to know anything.

She was the child who went on massive searches around the house to discover Christmas presents, who always snooped out surprise parties. Her mind was finely tuned to disallow people from dropping startling revelations. She hated secrets and suspense. What lurked beyond the hidden door, in her mother's fruit cellar, seemed far too overwhelming.

"Darla?" Lucy called again. "I need to know…I can't go in…you have to tell me if it's awful. You have to prepare me for this. I'm begging you."

With a sigh, Darla spoke. "I suppose, in a way, it is awful," she said in a near-whisper. "It's petrifying. It's devastating. Because all secrets are." And then she paused, cleared her throat. "But then…it's time to know the truth. You're ready to hear it."

"You didn't actually answer anything," Lucy complained.

Darla's silence was her response.

Lucy turned the handle downward and door popped open. She adjusted her placement so that she could open the door wide enough to slide her body inside. Once inside, the door slammed closed and she spun; she had left Grant and Darla in the fruit cellar in total darkness. Unnerved and worried, she ran the light over everything, trying to make sense of this room, the space, the message it was sending her. A solitary cord attached to a single light bulb dangled from the ceiling of the room and Lucy tugged it out of habit. The light didn't engage, but the exposed bulb still swung gently, casting shadows as it moved back and forth. She scanned her flashlight over the room.

As she inhaled deeply, she instructed herself to calm down. The room was virtually empty except for a desk along one wall and a row of shelves along the other wall. Stored on the shelves were dozens of cardboard boxes. Lucy walked over and inspected a single box. On the outside in bright red lettering it read: Apack-Ready-Meals. She tugged one down to the floor and pulled open the top. Inside the box were more individual cardboard boxes marked with labels that read: *chicken and feta; lasagna in meat sauce; cherry turnover sandwich; pepper steak; pot roast.* And then in another box on the shelf, hundreds of pouches of purified water. Lucy held one under the light and gave it a squeeze; she could feel the liquid roll between her fingers.

She was standing in a doomsday shelter.

It was appropriately and secretly stocked with, what Lucy could gather, was at least a year's supply of food and water. She pocketed the water and turned to the desk. Her heart was racing as she approached.

The desk was small and it had been pushed up against the walls (which were nothing more than thin panels of sheetrock). On the desk was a single piece of paper; its edges were crinkled a bit. And above the desk was a map of the United States, taped with crude strips of masking tape to the wall. There were no marks, no circles, no arrows. No messages. One corner had been lifted free from the wall and the corner was bent. She lifted the map upward and it revealed a small cubby cut into the wall, which contained a shoebox

She started to reach inside, but then pulled her hand back and waited. Lucy recognized the box from a pair of shoes she had purchased a while ago—a pair of sequined flats that she begged her mom to get for her. Of course she had never missed the box, but here it was, inside a hidden cubbyhole in a secret room in the back of their fruit cellar. She closed her eyes. Everything inside the room seemed to be pointing Lucy toward the truth. Darla assumed that she was ready to hear it; Lucy doubted she would ever be ready.

She slid the box out of the wall and heard its contents roll and shift. She opened the lid and inside were two syringes and two empty vials. The masking tape labels across the tubing read: Ethan and Lucy. Here were the other two vaccines. Her thoughts went immediately to Darla outside the door and little Teddy upstairs. These were the vaccines that saved their lives. She held them up to the flashlight, searching for a fraction of leftover vaccine—a hope that there would be something for Grant, but they were light and dry.

Inside the box was also a note, typed, that read: **Attn: Box Contents. Lab results. Photographic evidence of data. Instructions for Administering upon the following circumstances**: *If we failed to complete your immunizations for our trip to the Seychelles. Take immediately.*

Lucy exhaled. None of that was new information and she braced herself for the next piece. She set her old shoebox down and shifted her attention to the paper on the desk.

She saw that it was a letter dated four months ago. Four months ago, when the biggest worries of her teenage life were winter formal and AP psychology tests, Salem's boy chasing and Ethan's clingy girlfriend issues. She almost laughed out loud at the ridiculousness of it all.

The note read:

My dearest family, if you are reading this note it means that our plans have not quite gone the way I hoped. If you are reading this note and it doesn't make sense to you, then perhaps the plan failed completely and totally. If that is the case, I can't even begin to imagine my fate. There is a chance you are reading this letter too soon, but I feel very secure that this room behind the fruit cellar will go unnoticed. I am sorry that this note is vague. It is best not to speak of things explicitly that are rooted so firmly in the future. I am sorry I cannot communicate to you fully. It is my greatest wish to explain how things came to be. You will likely have questions and I hope that I can someday answer them for you.

My heart is heavy with the knowledge that all that I have tried to do to protect you may not matter in the end. I suppose that is the greatest burden we carry as parents, no matter the situation. But there are two things you must rest in: Know that I love you all more than anything. And also: Know that I tried to shield you as best I could. It is not for lack of love that you may find yourself in a trying and difficult time. If, as you read this, and you understand the trials I am speaking of and you also find yourself without me, I am leaving you two things that will help you. The first thing is in this room: They are labeled for each of you, should you find that my initial protection efforts were not enough.

The second you will find if you follow my words. I cannot stress this more to you: Do whatever you can to reach this place. It is the only safe place. I hope to be there, waiting for you. Find this place and you will find me. I know that all of this will not be enough, but it is all I can give you for now.
With much love, Dad or, affectionately, Scott.

And on the bottom of the vague letter in her

father's distinct handwriting was a small quote that read: "When you are real you don't mind being hurt."

Lucy clutched the paper to her chest and spun around the room with the flashlight once more, making sure she hadn't missed anything. The food. The note. The vaccines. Food and water to sustain them should a virus wipe out a food and water supply. A note that pointed them to the vaccines. A note that seemed rooted in regret and apology.

A fire grew in her stomach and it seemed to want to burn her from the inside out. She didn't know if she should scream or throw up. With one last long look around, she took a deep breath and left the room behind, back out into the fruit cellar, where Grant and Darla waited. She trained the flashlight on both of them and they startled at the sudden light. Lucy didn't pause or hesitate; instead she shimmied out from behind the shelf and then walked straight to the wooden door, the light bobbing out in front.

"And? What did you find?" Grant asked, following on her heels. "Lucy, wait up! What was in there?"

Lucy didn't answer as she climbed out of the fruit cellar and on to the cement basement flooring, pausing only to light the way for Darla and Grant and, after they successfully navigated the small step, she kept moving.

"Lucy," Grant said, his voice turning breathless as he picked up his pace to catch up with her. "Lucy!"

She spun, still clutching her father's note to her body, "I need to talk to my brother," she answered as she reached the steps. Then she bounded up two at a time and left the others down in the darkness.

CHAPTER TWENTY

Ethan looked pale and his eyes were sunken and watery. He regarded Lucy with a thin wave and then he sunk lower into his wheelchair.

"Help me back to the couch?" he requested and Lucy pushed the chair back through the doorway and into the study, Teddy still along for the ride.

"Again!" Teddy instructed. "I like the wheelchair ride, uncle Ethan," the young boy said as Ethan tousled his hair. "My mommy took me to Disneyland when I turned four. They had rides there and I went on a fast one that went zoom-zoom-zoom. Do you know which one?"

"Lots of them go zoom-zoom, don't they? Disneyland is fun, huh?" Ethan replied. "I'm glad you got to go, Teddy. I'm glad. Hey buddy, you want to hop down real easy now?" He picked the child up under his armpits and lowered him to the floor. Then Lucy stepped in and snapped the side of the chair down and helped Ethan slide his body over to the couch. He winced the entire time, groaning in pain, but powering through the bumps and jolts.

"Why didn't you just tell me?" Lucy asked him once he was settled. She tossed him a pillow and he shoved it behind his back.

"Tell you? Like…hey…there's a secret room hidden next to the fruit cellar and Dad left us some cryptic note from around Thanksgiving that pretty much *predicted* the end of the world. Oh, and, right, like there's also a ridiculous pile of food and water there too. And some men in a van kidnapped Mom and everyone else and took them to the airport. Where they clearly took off in an airplane despite the fact that all the planes were grounded." He closed his eyes. "And I haven't heard from them. Or Dad. I've heard from no one. So."

"When you say it like *that*," Lucy replied and Ethan mustered up a small smile in return.

"You had to discover it like I did. You just had to."

Darla and Grant made their way back up to the main floor and worked their way into the room. Teddy whined about a snack and Darla whisked him off to the kitchen. Grant followed her, shooting Lucy a sympathetic look as he exited.

"Okay, but what does it *mean*?" Lucy asked. She had an idea, but she wanted or needed Ethan to say it first. She wanted him to be the one to admit it out loud, because for her to say those words felt like an immeasurable betrayal.

"It means our dad knew."

Her heart sank. Ethan did it. He said it and he validated the fear and uneasiness that she couldn't shake. She wished he could take it back, say that he was kidding, that he didn't know, but Ethan looked straight at her and kept going.

"He knew this was going to happen. And it means he didn't do anything to stop it," Ethan said. Lucy closed her eyes and felt the letter crinkle in her grasp. She resented how easy it was for him to speak those words to her, as if it weren't damning their father with one big swoop. But then he added, "And worse than that…"

"Please don't say it," Lucy said quickly, her anger rising. "I'm not ready yet."

He opened his mouth to speak, but she waved her hand in front of him and made a shushing sound.

"I'm begging you," she said and she blew air into her cheeks and then let it go slowly.

"Lucy, please, that's the whole thing. That's everything." Ethan looked sad, but she could tell he was going to take it further anyway and there was nothing she could say to stop him. "You have to connect the dots and understand why *we* are alive. Right? Why *our* family was taken."

"We have some pretty big blind spots. There's no way we have all the information. I can't make that jump with you. I can't!" Lucy's voice started to increase with intensity.

"That doesn't make me wrong."

"Just tell me the next part," Lucy said and held the paper out. "Tell me what he said. Where we're supposed to go."

Ethan looked confused. "There's no other message. I've told you everything I know."

Lucy cocked her head at him. "Dad said he was leaving something behind to help us and to do whatever we could to reach that place. Right? You honestly didn't find the next clue?"

"The next *clue*?" Ethan asked and shook his head. "I honestly thought he was just talking about the food."

Lucy took a deep breath. "He said, *find this place and you'll find me*, and you thought he was talking about chicken quesadillas? This is why you were such a bad student," she said, exasperated. Thrusting the paper out for Ethan to look at, she continued, "The message. On the bottom. It's a *clue*."

"I didn't catch that," Ethan said with a shrug.

She had known immediately because she had internalized that quote; it was as much a part of her childhood as playing with her American Girl dolls or watching How the Grinch Stole Christmas every year as a family on Christmas Eve. For a second, Lucy wondered if maybe the clue was just for her—a single nod to a shared memory. But then, she realized, that would've meant that her father expected *her* to be the one left behind and that he intended the note for her and her alone. That, she rationalized, was ridiculous.

"Wait here," Lucy said and she flicked her flashlight back on and scooted around the observers, heading back out into the main area, through the dining room, and up the stairs. At the top of the landing, she took in a deep breath and pushed the fear of the dark aside. She bypassed her own room and scooted into Harper's room and shined the flashlight over her sister's books. All of Harper's books had been inherited from her siblings, and they arrived to her already dog-eared and missing pages, falling apart at the bindings, and scribbled in with crayons. The stories were unmarred, but the books themselves had seen better days before traveling down to the youngest King.

And yet their soiled appearances had not stopped Harper from devouring them just like her brothers and sister before her.

Finally, after a prolonged search, Lucy saw the tan binding with purple lettering. She pulled it down gently as to not disturb any of the other books on the shelf. She held the hardback in her hand, trembling.

Without opening it, Lucy tucked the book under her arm and went back downstairs. Darla and Grant had returned and moved to the couch, they formed a semi-circle in her absence and were discussing something in low voices as the candles flickered around them. Teddy devoured a granola bar and a bag of fruit gummies. He asked if he could watch television and Darla said, "No power Theodore…you know that…let's just use our imaginations tonight."

With a full lower lip, Teddy huffed, "My imagination is too tired."

"Here," Lucy said and showed Ethan the book.

"*The Velveteen Rabbit*?"

"My mom used to read that to me," Grant said. "It's really sad."

Lucy turned and regarded Grant. His mom. It was the first time he had mentioned her the entire time they were at the school. His dad, whom he lived with, he mentioned in anger. His mom hadn't existed in conversation at all. She opened her mouth to ask about her, but Darla interrupted.

"But it's hopeful too," she added.

"Sad, but hopeful. Thanks Dad. Your stab at symbolism is bursting with heavy-handedness," Ethan muttered.

"I had a bunny," Teddy said.

"The quote at the bottom of Dad's note. It read…'*When you are real you don't mind being hurt.*' It's from this book."

"I had a bunny and it died," Teddy continued. Darla got up and sat down by her son and gave him a hug. She kissed his cheek.

"The rabbit in the book *had* to die, right? To become real? Or something like that." Grant remembered as he reached for the copy of *The Velveteen Rabbit* and Lucy passed it over to him.

"Did my bunny become real?" Teddy looked up at his mother.

Darla smiled, "Your bunny was *already* real, little man. Now shush."

"Dad didn't strike me as a children's book guy. Mom was always the one who read to us," Ethan said. He reached for the book next, but Grant shied away from his hand. "Come on, pass it over."

"Did you say there's supposed to be a message in

this book?" Grant asked, his voice tight.

"Help," Lucy stated. "He said he was leaving help."

"Like…maybe…coordinates?" Grant opened to an illustration of the rabbit enjoying a picnic outside. And written in marker over that idyllic image in her father's handwriting: *42°1'16"N by 102°5'19"W*.

"Oh my goodness," Lucy grabbed the book back and studied the numbers. "He left us *directions*."

"To where?"

Ethan laughed, a sardonic, quiet laugh. "Too bad we can't just Google it, right?"

"It's called an atlas, dumbass," Darla replied in jest and stood up, walked over to the myriad bookshelves and scanned the titles. Finally she found a spiral-bound atlas tucked away near the door. She tossed it to Ethan who looked at it and flipped it open.

"What am I supposed to do with this?"

"Seriously?" Darla asked. "Longitude. Latitude? Teachers don't teach you anything nowadays. High school graduate can't read an atlas?"

"Here," Grant reached up and pulled the atlas down off of Ethan's lap. "I got this. Shine the light."

Lucy directed the flashlight over to the open book, and Grant flipped to a page with a map of the United States. He marked an area with his finger and then looked at another area. "Nebraska," he announced with a triumphant grin.

"What?" Lucy leaned down.

"The coordinates…are…for," Grant looked around him for a pen and Darla tossed him one from the desk, "right here…in Nebraska."

"Do we know anyone in Nebraska?" Ethan asked.

"Who knows people in Nebraska?" Darla replied.

"Turn to Nebraska in the atlas," Lucy said and Grant turned, finding the state with ease, and he looked up the coordinates again. "This is in the middle of nowhere."

"Brixton, Nebraska," Grant read, squinting. "If the map is right…it's like a two-street city. But, hey, according to the key…at least there's a post-office. Good thing there are so many people left in the world to send letters to."

"What the hell?" Lucy growled. "Dad leaves us with a confusing letter and directions to *Nebraska*. Why not just tell us what to do? Or tell us what we're looking for?"

"Maybe he couldn't," Ethan posed. "Maybe he was afraid."

Lucy realized her brother had to be right. "I'm sure he had a reason. Do you think the people he was afraid of took Mom? Oh Ethan…I can't imagine…"

"Let's not go there yet, Lucy. Okay?"

"But this *is* real, Ethan. Right? This is where Dad is telling us to go. Brixton, Nebraska." As soon as the words slipped from her mouth, she realized they sounded like agreement, consent to go there.

"Nebras-ka," Teddy repeated.

Looking over at Grant, who was still holding the atlas, Lucy noticed his eyes were closed. He swayed and threatened to tip-over.

"Grant? Grant!" she cried and flung the atlas away, scrambling and shaking him.

He smiled a lazy smile and opened one eye and then the other. "I'm fine, Lucy. Just sleepy. Sal—" he stopped himself. "We didn't sleep last night. We waited for you," he pointed to Darla, "to come back for her."

No one spoke. But Lucy's face burned; she was grateful for the dark.

Then Grant rose and stretched, his lanky body reaching tall, casting shadows on the walls. "I—" he started. "I think maybe I should go lie down somewhere. I wish—" he stopped again and then sighed. "I feel like I should say something profound. But I'm not one for big speeches." He smiled. "So. Maybe I'll just say…I'll be upstairs." He ended the sentence softly, sadly.

"Grant—" Lucy whispered. "Stay."

"Here," said Ethan. "Lucy?"

She lifted her head to him and waited.

"Dad's Victrola?" Lucy smiled. She slipped up and walked to the corner, where their father had kept an old Victor Talking Machine phonograph from 1921. It had belonged to his great-grandmother and had been given to her as a wedding gift only a few years before his grandma was born. It was a wooden cabinet, equipped with a crank handle, and tucked inside the doors were shelves, where their dad kept all his records.

When Ethan and Lucy were little it was a treat to sit in the den and listen to the music. But they outgrew the pleasure. Only now did Lucy realize that this must have broken their father's heart. She couldn't even remember the last time her dad had played a record for her, letting her dance on his feet, swaying and swinging her this way and that.

She wiped away a layer of dust off the top of the phonograph and lifted the top. Leaning over to wind the machine, she placed the fiber needle on the record that was already in there. And when the music filled the den, Lucy's heart swelled with melancholy nostalgia. The melody was familiar. It was her father's favorite.

The song was Ethel Water's rendition of "Moonglow." It was a beautiful melodious love song, so pure and happy.

Unable to move from her spot by the Victrola, Lucy watched the record spin and spin, the scratchiness of the needle amplified through the internal speakers. She listened to the plucky trombones and the lazy drawl of the trumpet. When she turned back to the group, she had tears in her eyes.

Darla picked up Teddy and placed him in her lap, where the child's eyes began to close in increments as the song progressed. She stroked his hair and rocked him softly; her subtle swaying may have been instinct as she comforted her child or a response to the music, but it was clear that the song had transported her away from an Oregon living room, sitting with near-strangers.

The record stopped.

But the needle kept spinning.

Teddy's eyes remained closed and Darla shifted him to her shoulder and stood up. "The munchkin and I are heading to bed. Ethan," she said in a motherly tone, "pain killers in two hours." Then she disappeared upstairs.

"Where should I sleep?" Grant asked and at first no one answered him. "If you're concerned about—"

"Stop!" Lucy said quickly and firmly. "No. You'll sleep in my parent's room…if that's okay."

"It's perfect," he replied and he walked over to the doorway and turned around one last time. "Night. And…" he looked at Lucy, "I'll see you."

Lucy couldn't bear it and she rushed forward, wrapping her arms around him. "I'll stay up with you, if you want. A game of Monopoly? You haven't even had dinner…some of those meals downstairs didn't sound so bad." She knew how she sounded, but Lucy couldn't help it; the thought of losing him and Salem in the same day was too much. "I'll stay with you."

Grant kissed the top of Lucy's head in a brotherly way and smiled. "Let me be alone." He took a breath. "It's been a long time since I've had that much." And he turned and ascended the stairs, taking each one slowly and deliberately, looking down at his feet. Then Lucy watched as he disappeared down the hallway.

Ethan requested a peanut butter and jelly sandwich for dinner and Lucy couldn't help but gag as she spread the peanut butter on their mother's wheat and honey oat bread.

For the rest of the evening they danced around sensitive subjects and discussed their mutual horror stories. And Lucy even cried upon Ethan's retelling of Anna's death—although it happened as she hoped. He dropped Anna off at her house before heading back to their mom because he was too afraid to show up with Anna instead of Lucy and suffer the consequences. Anna's mother outlived her daughter and that was the heartbreaking moment: Ethan returning to take Anna with him as company to the airport and discovering her mother screaming in the street.

No one knew what was happening. It had only just started then.

Talking with Ethan felt natural, but every once in awhile he would wince, and Lucy was reminded of his pain.

"Is it bad?" Lucy asked.

He nodded. "The painkillers don't help. If we were dealing with a normal, everyday situation, I think I would lose my legs, but Lucy, I don't think I'll ever walk again."

"You don't know that."

"If Spencer can do what we asked of him, I'll have a doctor take a look at them soon."

Lucy was reminded of what those four vials

bought them—a chance to save Ethan's life.

"You think he can do it? Find someone?" Lucy asked and then as she watched Ethan's face fall, she immediately regretted it.

But he didn't respond. After a long moment, Ethan reached over and grabbed her hand.

"I love you," Ethan said. "Have I ever said that before?"

Lucy smiled. "Not recently."

"Well, I do."

"I love you too."

"Yes, I think he can do it. I have to believe that he can. And we're going to survive this. We're going to figure this whole thing out."

"Sure," Lucy said with a smile. "As soon as we figure out what *this* is."

Lucy wanted to sleep in her own bed. Ethan, sleepy and loopy from a cocktail of Vicodin and some of their father's scotch, passed out on the couch. For several minutes, she stood outside her parents' bedroom and pondered going inside to check on Grant, but the darkness and the distressing prospect of finding him already gone, kept her from fearlessly waltzing over with a flashlight. She opened the door and whispered, "Grant? Grant?" but he didn't answer. And with a heavy heart, Lucy retreated, prepared for the worst.

Lucy, who had navigated her bedroom and the

upstairs hallways during power outages and darkened lightless nights before, was not afraid of retreating to the shadows of her own room to sleep under her own sheets, under her own blanket. However, something about her house felt different than the other times she had been seeped in darkness.

She thought perhaps she could sleep and convince her brain that this night was just like any other night: Her parents downstairs, discussing the day in the absence of children with hushed voices. Harper asleep in her princess bed. Malcolm and Monroe tucked into their bunk-beds, trading fart jokes and brotherly quips. Galen reading contraband books by flashlight under the covers until someone caught him and forced him to bed. These were the rituals. This is what the house was supposed to feel like. Instead it felt like a tomb.

Their house was large and cozy, even if it had paper-thin walls and décor regulations through the HOA. Her parents paid for parks and atmosphere, the promise of safe streets and cozy cul-de-sacs. Whispering Waters, their little neighborhood was called. The name implied peaceful joy, happiness, and comfort.

If only her neighbors had known that the congenial scientist, quick with a smile and always available to offer a ladder, an hour of service, or a kind word, was starting a doomsday shelter in his fruit cellar. What would they have thought if they had known that somehow he had predicted the end of the world? That he was clandestinely spiriting away food and water and vaccines and pictures of top-secret experiments right under the noses of his unsuspecting family.

Unsuspecting. It was a true and frightening word.

Ethan had a theory that their mother was in the dark. Otherwise, he pondered, why would she have ever sent Lucy back to school for her homework in the first place? And while it wouldn't be the first time in history that a man kept secrets hidden from his wife, Maxine's potential blindness pained Lucy greatly. And it was this lack of knowledge cost her mother both of her eldest children. No doubt their mom assumed they were dead. And that was even operating under the assumption that her family was alive. It was a stretch and a myth; an idea born from panic and an inability to understand a world where just she and Ethan had survived Armageddon upon the human race.

All these things ran through her brain in a loop and it occupied every second of her time, keeping her alone with memories and flashbacks. She tossed, turned, flung her blankets off, then sought them out and covered herself again. Below, she could occasionally hear a muffled voice. Ethan. Moaning in his sleep. And she kept listening for Grant, a snore or a rustle of the bedsprings—but her parent's room was silent.

Lucy, back in the room she had dreamed of and wished for while trapped at the school, felt fully alone.

Careful to keep her voice small, Lucy prayed what she could remember from Grant's prayer at Salem's memorial and sobbed herself to sleep.

CHAPTER TWENTY-ONE
Seven days after The Release

Teddy's high, little voice roused Lucy from sleep.

"My mommy's making pancakes with syrup," he said and he poked her in the shoulder with a plastic sword from the King siblings' communal dress-up bin. "And I'm going to have an orange juice!"

"Oh?" Lucy wondered how this was possible, but she didn't question the child. She picked up her pillow and flipped it over to the cold side and then rested her head, closing her eyes again.

"I'm a pirate," Teddy continued.

Then Lucy's eyes snapped open and she swung her feet to the floor. Slipping past Teddy, who didn't seem too fazed by her quick departure, Lucy darted up the hallway to her parent's room and swung open the door. The quilt on their bed had a Grant-sized indent and a blanket that her mom usually kept at the foot of the bed for decoration was tossed to the floor. But Grant himself was nowhere to be seen. Lucy rushed back down the hall and got held up on the stairs as Teddy made his way down step by step. She grabbed him by the waist and then stomped down with him, Teddy protesting with, "Let me down. Pirates like to walk!"

Darla made pancakes over a refreshed fire. She held a skillet over the flame with both hands and then set it down on floor to flip them.

"Pancakes," she announced without enthusiasm.

"Where's Grant?" Lucy asked, setting Teddy down beside his mother.

Darla and Ethan exchanged glances.

"Did you take him outside without me noticing? You couldn't have. No. Tell me…where is he?"

Flipping a pancake, the thick batter sticking a bit in the pan, Darla nodded toward the back of the house. "He's outside," she answered, as if this news was mundane and expected.

"He's okay?" Lucy shrieked and she ran off without waiting for an explanation.

Lucy ran toward their kitchen and then out to their back porch. Grant sat by himself on the steps leading down to the backyard. The air was still damp, but it wasn't raining. He turned to her and then patted the step next to him. His hair was a mess of tangles and his scruffy chin was growing fuller, the whiskers more defined.

"I wasn't expecting to see you this morning," Lucy said, breathless.

"I wasn't expecting it either," he replied. "When I opened my eyes this morning I wondered why Heaven looked so much like your parent's bedroom."

She laughed and leaned into him. But she was overcome with worry—Grant's original theory, that they were taking longer to die, seemed to ring in her ears. Maybe he was just an anomaly, maybe it could still happen.

"What does this mean? Are you scared that—" Lucy stopped herself from asking the full question.

"Ethan and I talked this morning. The information your dad," Grant hesitated, "well, the information that *they* found was very definitive. No survivors. None. Not ever. In every single study."

"The virus was created with that endgame in mind, I imagine," Lucy said and she stared out into the sky.

"So, the fact that I'm still here. It means something. It's not an accident."

"Like I keep saying…"

Grant smiled. "Yeah, well, apparently I'm superhuman. *This* surprise replaces the piano playing I think."

"So…"

Grant nudged her with his elbow and he smiled. "I'm not going to die today Lucy *Larkspur* King. I think this means you're stuck with me."

"You promise?" Lucy asked.

"Pancake time!" came a cry from inside and then Teddy's little feet pitter-pattered over to the screen on the kitchen door and the little boy pressed his face against the netting. "Pancake time," he repeated. And they followed him inside.

"We have to go to Nebraska," Lucy said over breakfast. They crowded around the dining room table with Ethan in his wheelchair. "Dad told us to get there if anything happened and that's where we need to go."

"How?" Darla asked, cutting up Teddy's pancake pieces into smaller bites, even as he shoved her hand away. "The abandoned cars and all the wreckage? You can't get out of the city. On top of that it's…what…a month of walking? Two months?"

"Try three," Grant said as he shoved a pancake into his mouth.

"Ethan," Lucy turned to her brother. "We *have* to do this."

"You're out of your mind," Ethan replied, instantly angry, and the table fell quiet. "Really? You want us to go? How can I do that? I can't go. How can I go? How can I travel like this?" The timbre of his voice rose and fell, as if he were fighting back a wave of tears. "It's not like you can just put me in the back of a car and drive out of here. It's impossible. I can't do it."

"We can get you there—" Grant said after a long pause. "We can do it."

"I can't even take a dump by myself," Ethan said and Teddy asked what that meant, Darla whispered a reply in his ear and he snickered. "But you guys want to take me on a cross-country road trip? No, Lucy. I need a doctor. I need medicine…and we're working on that, but I can't go anywhere. Not for a long time."

The room grew silent.

"Besides," Ethan continued, "what's in Nebraska? Our family? If they're alive, why aren't they coming for *us*? Have you ever thought of that?"

"Dad went to the effort…"

"Writing some coordinates in a children's book."

"…to give us help on what to do if we got separated."

"From something *he* might have had caused?" Ethan's eyes flashed.

Darla drew in a sharp breath and then sucked her cheek against her teeth. "He has a point, Lucy," she interjected. "I think you're forgetting what you *know* to be true here. Nebraska could be dangerous."

Lucy looked down at her plate. "We don't know the truth. None of us know."

"Well, I'm beginning to think that the truth isn't going to help me," Ethan replied. He clattered his fork against his plate and reversed his chair away from the table and wheeled himself back into the den. They watched him go and then turned back to their breakfasts, each of them waiting for someone else to resume eating first.

Lowering her voice, Darla leaned in and narrowed her eyes. "You're just going to show up in this town in Nebraska and knock on some doors until you're reunited with your family? That's not a great plan."

"I don't have a plan," Lucy said in a small voice. "But I don't want to sit here at the house waiting for us to run out of the meals my dad left and not doing *anything* to try to find the people I love. I've already done that. I just stayed at that stupid school waiting for someone to come rescue me." She looked at everyone and put down her fork. "No more. This is something we *can* do. No more waiting around, I'm done with that."

The fire popped.

"You know you can't risk Ethan's life by asking him to go with you," Darla said with her mouth full. "Eat the pancake, Teddy." She looked at Lucy and raised her eyebrows in expectation of a reply.

"We can't just stay here. So, then what?" Lucy asked and she turned over her shoulder toward the den. She pushed her chair back away from the table and started to make her way to Ethan.

"Right," Grant answered. His voice was strong and confident. "Well, that makes it easy."

Lucy paused and turned to look at him. "What?"

"Lucy and I will go," he said to Darla.

The offer hung in the room, palpable and tense. Everyone collectively held his or her breath.

Then Darla looked thoughtfully toward the ceiling and then back toward Grant. Her eyes went between the two of them, assessing. Finally, she assented. "It's not the only way, but I suppose if you're hell-bent on going…it *is* the best way. You can drive once you get out of the city. Gas is an issue because you can't pump without power…but cars should be easy to come by."

"But you just said—" Lucy started, but Darla raised a fork at her.

"Look," she interrupted. "I'm not going to tell you not to take a risk. And I think you're crazy, but I'd be lying if I said that I didn't want some answers. I lost the love of my life and everyone on this planet I cared about with the exception of my son. You think you can do this? Then go."

"Is this happening?" Lucy asked and she took a step forward. "Everyone is okay with this?"

Shrugging, Darla looked over at Teddy. "I'm not *leaving* my son. And I'm not *taking* my son. Your brother can't travel. Neither of you should go alone. If Nebraska is in your future…then this has to be the way. I don't think it's safe and I am petrified about what's waiting for you there. But if you want to go, I'm not going to stand in your way."

Inside the den, Ethan flipped through records. Lucy entered and stood near the doorway, the sounds of the others clearing breakfast dishes in the background.

"You know what shocks me most of all?" he said with his back still turned to her. "Why would Dad just walk away from the life he built here? Why leave this heirloom? And his wedding pictures," he nodded toward an album on the edge of their father's work desk. "How could he risk losing us?"

Lucy sat down on the couch and leaned her head back—she stared at the white ceiling and the overhead fan above them—the blades decorated with some flowery design that had always looked like an abstract drawing of an owl's face. She turned to face Ethan.

"I'll ask him that. When I find him. He's got to be out there Ethan…I believe that. I think he *wants* us to find him."

"And you really want to do this?" Ethan asked.

Lucy exhaled out her nose. "This is our family. Our mom. And I *can* do this. Please trust me."

"I trust you. But it's scary…to let you go. What if you—" he couldn't finish his thought.

Teddy swooped into the room and made a leap to the couch. He jumped and jumped until Darla came in and swung him off the leather and planted his feet on the ground.

"Legos?" she suggested and he rushed away, shouting about building an all-blue spaceship. Grant came in and sat by Lucy and he gave her a reassuring smile.

Pushing her back against the bookshelf, Darla crossed her arms. "We heard before the communication ended that the bridge is down between here and Washington. Car backup along all major highways will be impossible to navigate. You could walk out…but Grant is a living testament that you might still run into Raiders…who knows what type of people are lurking at the major entrances and exits to the city."

"Sounds lovely," Grant said. "What if we head north?"

"Fine. But still I-84 is a traffic jam up the Gorge. You're walking out of here and *that* alone carries all sorts of risks," Darla explained as she rubbed her temples. "Too bad you can't just fly out over the wreckage. Land yourself beyond the miles of corpses and cars."

"What if we could?" Grant asked, alert and looking between everyone, his eyes flashing with excitement.

"Fly?" Darla laughed. "Oh yeah?"

"Well, more like float," Grant replied and he smiled.

From Up Above Tours was family owned and operated for thirty years. Grant's uncle was a commercial pilot frustrated by an aggravating schedule that kept him away from his wife and young children and Grant's aunt was a strong woman with an entrepreneurial spirit and unstoppable business acumen. For years they ran sunrise hot air balloon tours over the Willamette Valley, storing their massive equipment during the off-season in Grant's family's storage barn on their large lot with acreage. Abandoned and ready for flight, just miles from Lucy's home, were a collection of hot air balloons. Grant's aunt and uncle kept the balloons in trailers next to the stables, where Grant's horses grazed and slept.

"Horses? You have horses?" Lucy asked and she raised her eyebrows with a knowing look.

"Don't say it…just don't. I think the point's been made." Then he frowned as he remembered. "Had horses, though. We lost two the night before everything. Not all of them. But if it was just a precursor to everything else then I doubt I have any horses anymore."

"Wait, wait," Ethan turned to Grant. "So, you can fly these things?"

"Yes," Grant replied quickly. Then he shifted his eyes to Lucy and lowered his eyes. "I mean…I've helped fly them. I work every summer with the company. Setting up the balloons, assisting with flights. I can do it. I know how. I've done it a hundred times over the years."

"But you've never actually flown one solo?" Ethan wheeled closer and looked at Grant incredulously.

"I can do it," Grant said, his eyes lighting up, moving between each of them – eager to convince. "I'll need some extra hands, but I can fly us out over the wreckage. Right? That's all we need?"

"How far do they go?" Lucy asked, imagining a stress-free ride through the skies all the way to Nebraska.

"Depends on how much fuel we take, which balloon, which gondola. I think I can get us like fifty miles. But maybe more, I can push it to more."

"That's all?" Lucy crossed her arms over her chest.

"That's not even a start to the trip."

"Well, I don't want to walk fifty miles instead if those are our options," Grant replied.

"Where will you go?" Ethan asked.

"Well," Grant paused, "we don't have a choice. We go where the wind takes us. But from here? I'm hoping to catch the wind that travels south. Head toward Central Oregon…plenty of open landing space."

"This is brilliant, Grant," Ethan reached forward for a high-five, which Grant reciprocated. He turned to his sister with appraising eyes. She looked to Ethan, Grant, and then Darla who picked at the bed of her fingernails with the tip of a paperclip.

"I can't even believe we're talking about this as an actual *thing*," Darla muttered. She flicked the dirt and grime to the floor and bit off the top part of her fingernail on her right pointer finger.

"A freaking hot air balloon," Lucy added and Darla smirked—they shared a moment bonding over their skepticism.

"This can work, Lucy," Grant said, turning to her. "I am promising you." He lowered his voice. "I will get us to your family."

"Let's not get ahead of ourselves. We're following a cryptic letter. Nothing more." Ethan replied. "For now, we're following the hint of my family. That is what we're chasing. A hope. In a hot air balloon."

"A hint, a hope, a hot air balloon," Lucy mused out loud. She thought of Mrs. Johnston's alliteration poster and smiled to herself. Yes, fools, all of them, thinking that in the end knowledge of literary terms could ever be useful. "You'll need this for a successful future," some of the more idiotic educators pontificated. *What future?* Lucy thought. Apparently for her future she needed to know how to navigate a hot air balloon. And she shook her head, exhaled long and low, and then turned to the group. "When do we leave?"

CHAPTER TWENTY-TWO
Eight days after The Release

The day before the big trip, they planned and prepped and enjoyed their last full day together. Anxious to hear if Spencer would be able to uphold his end of the bargain, Darla had paced the length of the den while brainstorming a backup plan, while Ethan sat morose, dipping into their father's liquor cabinet again and self-medicating until he had passed out on the couch. Lucy could not blame him for wanting to check out. They could all see that Ethan's health was deteriorating and without antibiotics and someone to look at his legs, they all feared the worst.

Darla tucked him in and then asked them not to be too hard on him. "He wishes he could be the one to do this," she said. "He feels like he's failing you."

For the first time since they concocted the hot air balloon idea, Lucy felt guilty for her quick willingness to leave him behind. "If you think I should stay, please tell me," Lucy begged Darla.

"No, you should go," Darla replied. "Spencer's

network was intricate and vast. I would never have saved his pathetic life and offered him our most precious resource if I didn't believe he would help us save Ethan."

Lucy had to trust that she was right.

When sleep finally found her that evening, she crashed. There were no dreams. No midnight awakenings. And now, in this early morning, her body refused to budge and her mind kept shoving her back into the darkness. She could feel Grant's hand push on her shoulder, his voice call her name, but she refused to acknowledge his presence.

"Lucy? Lucy?" Grant said to her. "It's time. We have to go."

When she was able to pry her eyes open, Grant's shape was blurry in front of her as he knelt down by her bedside. Outside, it was still dark.

"Don't make me pour a bucket of water on you Lucy, please?" Grant pleaded and his words hovered in the place where sleep beckoned her, but where her mind was aware, but not awake.

"No—" she protested.

"Wake up, please. We have to go. I've checked the wind…heading south…at sunrise. It's a mile to my house, Lucy. We have to hurry. Who knows if the weather will be right tomorrow. It's Oregon after all. We have to catch the wind just right."

"I don't want to go—" she slurred. But she felt Grant reach a hand under her back, lift her forward.

"Okay, okay," she said when her body was upright.

"Pack a bag. Light. I'll be downstairs."

Lucy nodded, her eyes still closed.

She thought of the last time she had been awakened and then told to get her bags ready. She shivered at the comparison.

"Are you getting up?" Grant asked her in a parental tone as he stood in the doorway.

She nodded again, but felt her body slink back toward the warmth of her bed.

From outside she heard the sounds of heavy footsteps, her door banging backward, and Darla's exasperated sigh.

"Please Grant, this is not how you do it," Darla spat at him. "You're being too nice."

Lucy resisted and Darla grabbed her by her hands and pulled her to the floor, her chin hitting the carpeted floor with a thud. Then Darla sat her up and yanked all the remaining covers free.

"Five minutes. Go downstairs, Grant. I got this."

Grant mumbled a protest, but then retreated.

Alone with Darla, Lucy started to move.

"Not even nearly fast enough sweetheart," Darla said and pulled her to her feet. "Such a ridiculous life you lead. Bet your mommy got you up every morning with some soft rock and butterfly kisses, right?"

"Hardly," Lucy replied. Then her thoughts went to her mom.

Her mother was in Nebraska. She knew it, felt it,

like she knew that she was going to take another breath or blink. Her mommy was in Nebraska.

"I'm up," she said and walked to her closet. She knew she had been wearing the same clothes for the past few days and she could smell the stench as she shed them without a hint of self-consciousness. Then Lucy changed into a pair of cargo pants and a black hooded sweatshirt. She grabbed a change of clothes and shoved it into a backpack. The other night in the den, she found her father's copy of *Fahrenheit 451* and for comfort and reading material she packed that too.

Tying on Galen's hiking boots, which she was pleased to discover fit her quite comfortably, she was ready to leave, but Lucy still felt disoriented.

"You good?" Darla asked and then she retreated.

When she finally made it downstairs, she saw everyone waiting.

Now Lucy could see that Grant had changed too. He was wearing a combination of clothing items from Ethan and her dad, including a weather-resistant jacket with Ethan's college logo displayed across the back.

Off they marched into the middle of a war and they both just looked like co-eds heading to a rainy football game.

"I'm ready," Lucy announced.

Grant shimmied into a hiking pack. He nodded toward it as he lifted it up across his shoulders. "The ready-to-eat meals. Flashlight and a blanket." He leaned down and handed Lucy a pack of matches and a handful of glow-sticks. "These didn't fit in my pack."

She shoved them into the front packet, the crinkly packaging echoing loudly in the quiet front room.

"We'll be heading through unfamiliar neighborhoods," Darla said. "We stay close. We don't know who's alive out there. Grant has proved that much."

"And there definitely could be zombies," Grant whispered.

"No zombies." Lucy rolled her eyes.

"Grant, you'll have to lead the way," Darla continued.

Teddy sat on the steps, a found stuffed animal in his hand. He was sucking his thumb and his eyes were heavy with sleep. "Mom," he asked. "When are you coming back?"

"Later sweetheart. Stay good for Ethan."

"Mom?"

"Yes, baby boy."

"Can we go to the park to play when you get home?"

Darla looked at him and smiled softly. "I'll see. Let's just say maybe."

Grant and Darla started toward the side-door, but Lucy hesitated. "Go on, I'll be right out." They exited out into the carport and left the two of them alone. She turned to Ethan and walked over to him, kneeling, but careful not to touch his legs. "I don't know what I should say here," she mumbled.

"I thought I was the only one," he replied. "The lone survivor. When I realized there was a chance you were alive too, I've never been so happy."

"I always hoped. I never gave up hope," Lucy said.

He reached out and grabbed her hand. "I can't lose you."

"You won't. And I can't lose *you*."

"I have no immediate plans to die. Spencer will come through. I'm more worried about you. Be safe, Lucy. Please?"

"I'm doing this for us, Ethan. It feels like I'm abandoning you…but…I want to do this for us. See that and feel it. Believe it."

"I do."

"A hot air balloon," Lucy said and smiled.

"The great and powerful…" Ethan trailed off and then he looked up at her—his blue eyes searching hers. "But you are. You really are. So, it's fitting, I suppose."

"There really is no place like home," she said back, wanting to assure him she understood.

After a long pause, Ethan gave her hand a tight squeeze. "What home?" he asked. Then as she started to pull away he added, "Find them, Lucy. Find them."

"I will." She stood up and hugged her brother tightly, avoiding the dark thoughts of impending loss that flooded her and she hugged him until she couldn't anymore.

The others had generously offered her precious moments to say goodbye.

But now it was time to go.

The Trotter farm was a legitimate farm with a small grove of apple trees and a pasture for grazing horses. Just a mile away from sprawling housing developments, and only a few miles away from the buzzing metropolis of Portland, a more rural part of the city lived and thrived. The streets were empty and vacant, but everywhere they walked, they could not avoid the stench. It reminded them that once upon a time, people were alive. Rot and death wafted in from all angles and it blended with the early morning air, bowling them over.

Only their soft footsteps, sinking in mud or thudding along on the streets, made any sound at all. Occasionally one of them remarked at a sight—a person's body in the front yard, pajama clad, and left abandoned among the growing grass or a person in the middle of the street, or behind the wheel of a car.

All signs pointed to the fact that many people tried to go about their lives the day the virus claimed them, unwilling to let the disease stop them from going to work, watering their lawn, checking the mail. Everything happened so quickly. One minute they were walking to pick up a newspaper, the next, gone.

"Cut through here," Grant said and his voice broke up the silence.

They followed him, leaving the developments,

cutting through backyards, until they reached a long drive flanked by well-manicured grass.

Grant paused.

"This it?" Darla asked and started to walk forward.

He nodded.

"Let's go," she demanded. But Grant refused to step forward. Suddenly tender, Darla went back and took his hand. "We do what you say," she announced. "Okay?"

"Yeah, okay. Let's just, um, just go to the barn."

Darla nodded once. "You got it."

Lucy took in the sprawling estate with wide-eyed wonder.

Halfway up the drive, Grant walked straight through the yard and spotted a patch of yellow fur nestled among the green. He knelt down and hung his head, and then he stood up more purposeful than before.

"A pet?" Lucy asked.

Grant shook his head. "A stray," he replied. "But it doesn't matter. I'm just tired of all of this."

"Do you want to go inside?" Lucy asked and then immediately regretted it. "Never mind," she said, backtracking, realizing it was a ridiculous suggestion. "We'll just get the balloon up."

"I don't need to see my dad to know he's dead," Grant said with determined nonchalance. "Besides…we weren't close. And—"

"You don't have to talk about it now," Lucy saved

him. "We have a balloon ride ahead of us." Lucy hiked her backpack upward and her foot hit a mound of mush, her boots sinking, but she ignored it and kept following Grant and Darla up the yard toward a large brown building to the left and steering clear of the main house where the blinds and curtains were all shut tight.

When they reached the barn, Grant pulled the doors open one at a time, exposing a darkened stable on one side with empty stalls and on the other side a wall of harnesses, saddles, and riding helmets. Stored against the front wall were three small trailers, decorated with advertising from his uncle's company.

From Up Above Tours: Beautiful Adventures Daily.

Grant opened the first trailer and stood for a long time starting into the dark. Then he turned to the girls—his face determined, focused, transformed.

"It'll take all of us to get this thing in the air," he commanded. "I've never been in charge before."

"Now you tell us," Darla teased, but she clapped him on the back to give him courage.

Together they dragged a large blue tarp back out to the yard, smoothing it out across the grass and muddied land where piles of horse manure disturbed the landscape. They went back for the basket and Darla and Grant balanced it, dragging the bottom toward the tarp and then tilting it one way, then another. Grant looked up to the sky, pursed his lips, and then directed them again. They hooked in uprights, laid the basket flat, and while Grant tinkered with the burners, Darla and Lucy worked swiftly with the envelope containing the balloon and pulled it freely and outward onto the tarp.

The sun was now rising into the morning sky, turning the few clouds purple and pink.

An inflator fan hooked up to a generator blew cold air into the balloon and the nylon began to take shape. Only now could Lucy see a visible pattern on the outside—rainbow argyle. The loud hum was deafening and even more shocking since the world had gone quiet.

Grant watched the balloon start to rise over the landscape as he held a rope tightly in his hand, and then he beckoned to Lucy.

"Hold this," he instructed, handing the long white cord to her. He wrapped his hand around hers and pushed her hands tightly down around two handles attached to the rope. "Hold tight. If it sways, pull it back. This is the crown line," he told her in an educating tone. "Have you ever been waterskiing?"

Lucy shook her head.

"Well, it's like in the movies. Just hold it tight. Pull back."

Then Grant rushed forward, checking lines, pulling on the balloon, rolling it, inspecting it, and pushing gauges. Lucy watched him and realized that he was in his element and he was good at this.

After a few minutes, Grant called, "Switching to heat!" And with the fan off, the world seemed quiet once again and they could only hear the rustling of the fabric, swaying in wind. Grant directed Darla by the shoulders and positioned her to stand on some cables; then he switched the burners on and a large flame spewed upward.

The balloon began to rise.

Lucy kept a tight hold on her crown line as the balloon lifted off the ground, filling and rising, obscuring the entire yard with its size. Grant tied down the basket and when the balloon filled, he called to her. She rushed to him and they set the basket upright, where it lifted and bobbed, the balloon anxiously pulling itself toward the sky.

Lucy hoisted her bag into the basket—a woven undercarriage that looked like it was designed to fit six or more people—and Grant followed suit. He helped her climb in and Lucy oriented herself on the inside. She could feel the heat of the burners only feet away.

She was suddenly terrified.

"Grant—" she started and then stopped. What use would questioning do now?

He must have read her face. "We've already done the hard part," he said, allowing a smile. "My uncle let me fly before when we've been up alone. I've never put a balloon together before by myself. So, that was kinda cool," He ran his hand through his hair and broke into a proud grin.

Darla's eyes scanned the landscape and then she checked the watch on her wrist.

"No time for heartfelt goodbyes you two. Here,"

she reached into her waistband and pulled out one of the handguns. She reached up and handed it to Lucy. "And Grant's already got one of the guns packed. Be wise."

"For a world mostly empty…there sure are a lot of dangers," Lucy said.

"Curb the philosophizing for when you're flying," Darla suggested. "The world's no different than it's always been. Maybe you just never saw the danger before, but it was always there. Now go you two."

Grant climbed into the basket next.

Lucy looked at Darla, who started to work on releasing the lines. "Darla—"

"I got it kiddo," Darla answered. "I'll take care of him. I promise."

"Thank you," Lucy said to her and she put her hand over her heart.

Then Darla let the last line free and Grant blasted the burner. Up they rose, straight over the barn and the house and into the mild morning wind. Lucy had never been afraid of heights, so she peered over the edge, her hands gripping the basket and watched as Darla's shape shrank. The *phhhhssshhh* of the burner carried them upward and upward and Lucy's mind drifted to a particularly imbedded memory from her childhood: Losing a birthday balloon into the sky and begging her parents to follow it.

"We'll catch it when it lands," she had begged.

Her mother stroked her hair. "Baby girl…when it

lands, the balloon will be all out of helium. It won't be the balloon you want anymore. We'll get you another one." But she hadn't wanted another one, she wanted that one and she couldn't quite understand why that wasn't possible.

As the hot air balloon rose, Lucy had the feeling that they were staying still, rooted in one place and that the world pulling away from them. The revelation dizzied her and she pushed back a bit from the edge.

"You okay with flying?" Grant asked, not taking his eyes off of the gas tanks, watching their height.

"Uh-huh," she said and nodded. When she had regained her composure, she peered down again and let out a small gasp.

The world below was marked with the evidence of its destruction.

Fires still smoldered in the distance. The roads were littered with abandoned cars with open doors. Small lumps and shapes dotted the landscape and Lucy could only assume they were bodies. As they had walked along the roads and parks and backyards, she had seen the devastation, but to look down on it from the sky was different. Here were miles of bodies. Not just snapshots of a scene, but a full picture of an entire city laid waste.

"How high will we go?" she asked and Grant closed the burner lid, reached into his pack and pulled out a bottle of shaving cream. Leaning over the edge, he sprayed the cream and watched as it traveled in the wind. Then he surveyed the landmarks and he clicked his tongue.

"Southeast."

"That's the way the wind is blowing?"

"Yes."

"How far will we go?"

"Until I can't fly it any longer or until we run out of fuel. I'm determined to get us as far as I can." He paused. "You ask a lot of questions."

Lucy took another look out over her beloved city. The buildings of Portland were off in the distance. She could recognize their distinct, postcard-worthy shapes. The city itself was quiet, abandoned, but it was still there—a picturesque skyline, the west hills in the distance, the river bifurcating the east from the west. If Lucy wanted to, she could've tried to convince herself that her fellow Portland residents were slow to wake, that they were just bumbling along sleepy-eyed, half-awake, shuffling through another day. From above the ground, it was hard to notice the difference between a slumbering city and an annihilated one.

But then she gasped.

"All the bridges are gone," she whispered.

"Are you sure?" Grant asked and he walked over to her side.

"Yes. Look."

He boosted them up higher with a blast of propane to give them a clearer look.

"My God."

Wreckage jutted out of the lapping waves of the river. Submerged cars bounced and bobbed. Up and down the waterway were mounds of twisted metal and each and every bridge was gone—only remnants remained. Portland was a city known for its bridges and now there was nothing to look at but rubble.

"The bombs we heard. They were taking out the bridges. What does that mean?"

Grant stared at the debris, the absence of something they had taken for granted as they journeyed from one section of the city to the other. "To trap people, I suppose. Isolate the neighborhoods. Contain a virus that was uncontainable. Or maybe…just to destroy."

It was only then that Lucy noticed the full extent of their city's devastation. She could see the marina and capsized boats and the other vessels adrift on the Willamette River without a captain, unmoored and unanchored. Her eyes traveled to the tram—a bullet shaped vehicle that transported patients, doctors, and tourists to Oregon Health Sciences University. It was suspended above the trees, stopped midway up the track, and it swayed gently with the wind. Someone had written *HELP* in lipstick on the windows and a crack on one of the windows indicated someone had tried to break through the glass.

She looked away. With the horrors of the school still fresh in her memory, Lucy's hand shook with the understanding that her own personal terrors were only one small glimpse, one small moment.

The ethereal quality of their ride, combined the visual confirmation of the mass genocide was overwhelming.

"This is like floating…up here," Lucy whispered as they turned around 360-degrees, slowly, and her eyes surveyed the blue on the horizon and the glory of Mt. Hood in the distance. "All this beauty. Our world is so amazing…and yet…"

"I'm going to concentrate," Grant interrupted and brushed by her back to the center of the basket. But he only stood there, his eyes outward, his arms by his side, his right hand clutching the bottle of shaving cream.

Lucy watched him and she bit the inside of her lip. "Can you imagine? If you're a survivor and you look up in the sky today and see a hot air balloon floating past? It would be dreamlike, I suppose. Surreal."

Grant didn't answer.

"Grant?"

He didn't turn toward her, but he lowered his head. "Survivors?" he called back. "This was done to us so there wouldn't be any survivors. We aren't meant to be here." Then after a moment, he added. "No, well. Maybe *I'm* just not meant to be here."

"Don't say that," Lucy said.

"It's true, though," he replied. Then after a moment, "What do you think we'll find in Brixton, Nebraska?"

"Nothing, maybe." She waited, then added "or

everything."

The balloon spun and drifted and Grant boosted them higher up. They followed the path of the river and at this height, the tragedies beneath them were easier to ignore.

"Thank you," Lucy said after they had ridden in silence. He raised an eyebrow. "For coming with me."

Grant set the shaving cream on the floor of the basket and rubbed his eyes with both hands. Then he smiled, his single-dimple appearing for a brief second. He reached his hand out and Lucy grabbed it. It was an awkward, sideways grab, and she felt how cold and clammy his hand was and the small tremors from his fingers vibrated against her palm. She gave his hand a squeeze and he squeezed back, pinching her fingers down upon each other.

"Together," he said and his eyes scanned the horizon. "Whatever happens now...we're together. You're not alone. You need to know that, Lucy."

She nodded, biting back tears. "Together," she repeated. Then she closed her eyes and realized that she could not feel the wind or hear anything beside the hum of the balloon drifting effortlessly into the vast unknown. Lucy thought of her sister and her brothers and she saw their faces as she left them that fateful morning, poised and ready for adventure. Then she thought of her mother.

Strong. Resilient.

And waiting for her.

Lucy opened her eyes toward the horizon and intertwined her fingers with Grant's and held his hand until she could no longer tell where her hand started and his hand stopped. With her other hand, she grabbed the crucifix and held it inside her palm, pulling the chain tight against her neck.

"Together," she said again. "Wherever this takes us."

"Whatever happens."

"No matter what."

END OF BOOK ONE

ACKNOWLEDGMENTS

As a reader, I really love the acknowledgments page. It's like a writer's Academy Award speech, except no one can play you off with an orchestra and you are likely thanking people while you are still wearing pajamas instead of a fancy ball gown. And that's the thing about writing; I can just tell you that I'm writing this in a beautiful bright yellow Oscar de la Renta dress and you could believe me. But you shouldn't. I am clearly in sweat pants and a maple syrup stained t-shirt.

Here we go:

First of all, thank you Kevin. Thank you for hating every single book I tried to get you to read when you were in the 9th grade; thank you for your never-ending barrage of fourteen year-old opinions and your challenge disguised as an insult: "Ms. Wescott, I bet even *you* could write a better book than this." Challenge accepted. I hope I did okay. Sorry it took four years, but I'd like to think this is a pretty unique graduation gift. Plus, I feel like I've offered you a very cool pick-up line for college girls, "So, my freshman Reading teacher wrote a book for me. You wanna go out?" Now that I wrote that down, I realize that you can probably think of better pick-up lines, but that is why I wrote a book about people dying of a virus instead of a book about pick-up lines.

To every other student of mine at Centennial High School, past and present: I didn't become a teacher because I liked to hear myself talk about *The Great Gatsby*. I went into teaching because I think there is something special and amazing and powerful about teenagers. That little speech I give about being your teacher and your mother? It's true. Thank you for indulging me by letting me name characters after you and for stealing gossip from your own life and giving it to the people in my fictitious high school. Thank you for being early readers and being honest about what worked and what didn't work for you. Thank you for being excited about this and forcing me to finish when I was tired and didn't think I had it in me. I'm especially grateful to the creative writing students, who inspire me with their own talents, and to the *Talon* staff who believed in me first.

Book Club: You are more than a book club. You are my best friends, my confidants, my support, my lifeline. You are readers and thinkers and you are my biggest cheerleaders; you challenge me personally and professionally and have proven that there is nothing in this world better than amazing female friendships. Without hyperbole I can tell you: I don't know where I'd be without you all. I've decided that the best decision I can make in my life is protecting my time and my heart. Giving both of those willingly and without reservation or regret to you ladies is the best thing I've ever done. Thank you. Words are not enough. But from the bottom of my heart, thank you: Allison, Christy, Claudia, Lorrie, Melissa, Molly, Sunshine, Suzy, and Toni. (Special shout-out to Sunshine for forgoing sleep to give me honest feedback that forced me to admit my semi-colon problem.)

Nicole—we are the dynamic duo. Thank you for reading this first and championing publication. And thank you MOST for thinking of a title. Otherwise this would be called "Swimming Pool Full of Dead Teens" or "Trapped in a School with an Evil Principal" and no one would want to buy it ever. Your questions were the catalyst for major changes that made this book FAR BETTER than it was before and I am eternally grateful that I work with you and can call you a friend. Rana—your laughter and willingness to love me, despite knowing all my deepest and darkest secrets, is the best gift. Thanks for letting me put this book into your student's hands. Thank you for being honest. Thank you for making me laugh.

(Is this where the orchestra starts? Don't play me off! I have more!)

Mom and Dad: When I told you at age four that I wanted to be an "Arthur" and you thought that I meant I wanted to be an aardvark, but then you realized I meant "author", you have always told me to go for it. You let me wake you up at 3am to read you things I was excited about and you always pretended it was the best stuff ever, even though I'm pretty sure you were sleeping when I read it and only woke up when I asked, "What do you think?" Thank you for raising my brothers and me to be creative, musical, and passionate. Dad, thank you for the jazz music and the introduction to Science Fiction. Mom, thank you for reading everything I've ever written and thank you for reading other people's books and saying more times than I can count, "You could've done that so much better" even when it was very clearly not true. But that's what moms are for.   Also, thank you for never censoring my reading material, especially when I was in junior high and all I wanted to do was stay up really late and read Stephen King books.

I will be forever grateful to Samantha Lynn for saying, "Um, my mom wants the next chapter right now" and it kept me writing. Thank you to Sam's hotel bar at the Monarch for providing a mostly-quiet place to work without distraction. Thank you to all the screenwriters who write the amazing television shows and movies that get me excited to tell my own stories! Deborah Reed, thank you for offering me the encouragement I needed to try this publishing thing on my own. Thanks to Carin for your unbridled enthusiasm and I'm sorry I kept crashing your phone when I'd send you new chapters. And a huge thank you to everyone else—I have supportive and awesome friends. I don't deserve you, but I'm grateful you exist.

Lastly (as they push me off stage): To my little family. Matthew, Elliott and Isaac. In the event of a disaster, we will be together—fighting side-by-side. Actually, no, that's inaccurate. I will fight and Matt will be the comic relief. Elliott, you are my gifted storyteller. My heart bursts with love and admiration whenever I listen to you tell me a story you created. You are my inspiration. Isaac, you are so funny and your snuggles make all my hard days better. You don't understand why mommy is busy and doesn't want you hitting the keyboard. I'm sure your additions would've been spectacular, but readers usually get confused when sdf;lksdf is in the middle of a sentence. I love you all. I am loved. I am blessed.

About the Author:

Shelbi Wescott is a high school language arts, creative writing, and journalism teacher in Portland, Oregon. She loves board games, television, baseball, karaoke, and zombies. She lives with her husband (a local newspaper editor) and her two sons.

Visit her at: **www.shelbiwescott.com**

CPSIA information can be obtained at www.ICGtesting.com
Printed in the USA
LVOW13s1045290813

350196LV00001B/3/P